M000226812

THE
THROWAWAYS

USA TODAY BEST-SELLING AUTHOR OF
THE DROWNING GAME

THE
THROWAWAYS

LS HAWKER

Copyright © 2019 LS Hawker.

All rights reserved. No part of this publication may be reproduced,
distributed, or transmitted in any form or by any means, including
photocopying, recording, or other electronic or mechanical methods,
without the prior written permission of the publisher, except in the
case of brief quotations embodied in critical reviews and certain other
noncommercial uses permitted by copyright law. For permission requests,
write to the publisher, addressed "Attention: Permissions Coordinator," at
the address below.

ISBN: 978-1-890391-09-6 (Hardcover)
ISBN: 978-1-890391-10-2 (Paperback)
ISBN: 978-1-890391-11-9 (Paperback)
ISBN: 978-1-890391-12-6 (eBook)

Library of Congress Control Number: 2018910110

Any references to historical events, real people, or real places are used
fictitiously. Names, characters, and places are products of the author's
imagination.

Cover design & interior formatting: Mark Thomas / coverness.com

First edition 2019.

The Vanishing Point Press Ltd.
PO Box 620033
Littleton, CO 80162-0033

TheVanishingPointPress.com

For John Rasmussen

CHAPTER ONE

George Engle

Friday, May 23, 1986
Lawrence, Kansas
10:32 p.m.

One moment she was there, sitting in the front passenger seat with her back against the door, smiling at him. The next, she wasn't.

He blinked and she disappeared, like a dissident from an old Soviet photograph.

Gone, as if she'd never been there to begin with.

George Engle turned his head away from her empty seat, taking in the nighttime suburban street scene outside his window. He didn't recognize the neighborhood. Didn't remember how he'd got there, sitting in his car at the curb by a little park.

Didn't even know who the girl was. Why she'd been in his car.

He fixed his eyes on the small ranch house a hundred feet ahead, across the dimly lit street to his left, which generated an indistinct ping of memory.

And then the house blew up.

The fireburst rocked him sideways, seemed to bow his window inward. The flaming sphere mushroomed, shooting wreckage in all directions. As the appallingly loud concussion dissipated, smoldering debris hailed down on his Plymouth Cricket, accompanied by metallic *tings* and *clinks*.

The blast and noise stunned George into paralysis. Movement in the park to his right drew his attention. He turned to see three open-mouthed teenagers in jeans and flannel shirts walking zombie-like, lit up as if on stage, toward his car. Their eyes were fixed on the conflagration, the swings behind them abandoned so quickly they flapped and twisted. The kids' materialization broke George's stupor and he opened his door, activating the car's dome light. He stood and shouted to them.

"What happened?"

Their identical, mesmerized expressions showed no indication that they'd heard him or even noticed he and his car were between them and the burning house.

George slapped the roof of the Plymouth. "Hey! Did you see what happened?"

Two of the teenagers turned their gazes his way, and one of them shook his head. "The house exploded, man. It went bloof."

"Yeah, I know," George said. "I meant—"

One guy's face morphed from shock to fear as he yanked on his nearest friend's shirt tail and pointed at George's car. Then all three of them were gaping at the passenger-side back seat window.

George tilted to see what they were gawking at. Was the girl back there?

No. An open garbage bag was, full of items he couldn't quite make out.

He straightened to see the teenagers backing away, hands up.

One said, "We don't want any trouble, bud, we just…"

George took a step toward them, and they turned and ran.

He blinked at the retreating figures, then went around the car and opened the back passenger-side door to get a look at the trash bag. Spilling out of it was a bizarre collection of items: a large plastic bag of white powder. A hunting knife. A pistol. And on the floor, a gas can.

The knife gleamed red and wet.

Blood.

He reached forward and touched the pistol.

The slight warmth of it zapped him like an electric shock, and the scent of sulfur told him this gun had been fired recently. Wave upon wave of adrenaline hit his muscles, making him stagger backward as if shot himself. A howling wind in his mind blanked out everything except sheer animal survival as muffled blasts within what was left of the house clattered like a demonic drum solo. With each detonation, George's panic grew. What could *still* be exploding inside?

He slammed the back door then threw himself into the driver's seat and jerked the door shut. Fumbled for the starter while staring in the rearview mirror at the assortment of elements in the back seat, which had certainly not been there earlier, and which definitely did not belong to him.

But those teenagers didn't know that.

George wrenched the key and the engine blazed to life. He stomped the accelerator and tore out of the neighborhood, going as fast as a fifteen-year-old sedan could.

The headlight knob came off in his hand he yanked it so hard, and he nearly jumped the curb trying to gain control of the car. Houses lit up as he passed them.

He couldn't decipher the faded street signs in the dim illumination of his headlights. He had no idea where he was. Or how he'd gotten here.

But then cascades of memory washed over him.

The liquor store. The thunderstorm. The kiss.

The girl.

Stacia.

CHAPTER TWO

George

Ten hours earlier

George struggled to turn the key in the lock of his over-full mailbox. When the latch gave, paper burst from the opening and littered the sidewalk in a heap. Too late, he noticed three girls in bikinis dangling their feet in the apartment complex pool ten yards away.

The racket of the mailbox blowout drew their attention, and the heat from their stares and his embarrassment condensed on his glasses. He squatted both to hide and to make two stacks, one for junk and one for bills.

He sorted so quickly the envelope ended up with the junk. But the heavy texture of the paper, its pristine creamy whiteness made him snatch and flip it to check the return address: University of Kansas School of Law.

His vision shimmered as he tore the envelope open. With

exacting care, as if defusing a bomb, he removed the letter and unfolded it.

Dear George Engle: Congratulations!

He read no further and let out a whoop. He stepped around the mailbox bank and shouted to the girls, "I got into law school!"

They exchanged what looked like impressed glances. "That calls for a beer," said one. She turned and pulled a poison-green bottle of Löwenbräu from the cooler behind her and dangled it in his direction.

George came this close to asking for a rain check—he needed to make some phone calls—but his sudden elevation in status to Law Student propelled him to gather up his stacks of mail, walk through the pool gate, and pull up a chair.

"Did you just graduate?" the brunette asked.

"In eighty-two." Since he started college in 1976, he should have graduated in '80, but they didn't need that particular bit of information. "I wanted to take some time off, you know, save up some money, travel..."

"Wow," said the girl in yellow. The wet fabric of her swimsuit clung to her nipples and he forced himself to look away.

The girls asked George questions about his future plans while he drank his beer. When he finished, he stood to leave. "Gotta go to work, ladies," he said, like some disco-dancing, polyester shirt-wearing asshole. But he didn't care. Not today.

He tossed his empty, along with the junk mail, into the trash barrel by the candy machine. He placed the acceptance letter into the breast pocket of his button-down shirt and hand-carried the bills.

"G'bye," the girls chorused as he exited through the gate. Once he was out of their sight, he ran like an exuberant kindergartner to his first-floor apartment.

Inside, he lifted the kitchen phone receiver from the wall and called his ex-girlfriend Patty. It took some cajoling, but she agreed to meet him that night for a drink after his shift. He insisted on giving her the news in person, because four months ago, she'd delivered her own news over the phone: she was breaking up with him.

"I don't think you'll ever really *do* anything," she'd said, the TV blaring in the background.

"I'm practically a manager," George said.

"You've been doing that for five years now."

"I could buy a house if I wanted."

"But you haven't," she said. "Remember when we first got together? You talked about applying to law school, about how your Grandpop had defended that guy accused of murder or something—"

"Aggravated sexual assault, actually."

"And you went to the court house every day, and he got the guy off, and you felt like you were in *Twelve Angry Men*."

"*To Kill a Mockingbird*," he said, annoyed she'd dredged up this story that he'd confided in her, used it as a cudgel, and didn't even get the details right.

"You were so inspired, you said. You wanted to be like

him and help innocent people or whatever. But you never did anything about it."

"That's because I had to—"

"And then you carried that thirty-five-millimeter camera with you wherever we went," she continued as if he hadn't spoken. "You were going to be Annie Liebowitz, you said. You were going to roam the country photographing rock stars."

"That was a—"

She yawned right into the phone. "But the big goal was always law school. 'Someday,' you'd say. 'Someday I'm going to go to law school and be like Grandpop.' And every year…you don't *do* anything. And it's taken me this long to realize that you never will."

George swallowed his anger and embarrassment. "And what are you doing with *your* life?" he said. "You're volunteering at a—"

"I'm *interning* in my chosen field," she said, bristling. "That's what an internship is. You work for free, and they see how valuable you are and they—"

"I know how internships work."

She sighed. "I don't think *this* is going to work."

"After three years, you don't think we're going to work?" George said.

"I want someone who knows what he wants, who isn't just drifting. Who's a doer, not a talker."

Looking back, he'd been kind of relieved, because she was a symptom of his malaise and he didn't even realize it, part of his endless drift. Like so many other things in his life, he'd just fallen into his relationship with Patty, without intention or consideration. But that hadn't made her words hurt any less, didn't prevent him wanting to prove her wrong.

And then the same day, during a phone call with his parents, they'd both laughed when he told them he was again considering applying to law school. "I'll believe it when I see it," Dad had said.

After those two excruciating conversations, George dug through his desk drawers until he found the law school application that had been moldering in there for three years. That very day, he filled it out, hand-delivered it to Green Hall, and discovered the next LSAT was only five days away. He signed up, studied, and took the test. In March he'd been placed on the law school waiting list.

Until today. He was now formally a member of the class of 1989, and he wished he could tell his brothers, Chad and Vic. The twins would have given him the reaction he wanted. They'd been George's biggest cheerleaders before they died fifteen years ago.

Even though they were nine years older than George, they'd taken him everywhere with them until they went off to college when he was ten. They'd helped him with his math homework, taught him to ride a bike, took him fishing—all in between their jam-packed school sports and activities schedule. Vic played catch with him, and Chad brought him wild-west outlaw books from the library. They both taught him about rock music, and he'd inherited their huge vinyl collection when they died.

The twins would be proud of him, getting into law school, and George kept this at the front of his mind as he dialed his parents' number in Lake Havasu, Arizona.

After a few pleasantries, it took his dad a good forty-five seconds to coax his mother to get on the extension.

When she finally picked up the handset, breathlessly and without preamble, she said, "What is it? What's wrong?" Her words were mom code for *you only call when it's an emergency*.

He would not rise to the bait today. "I got an acceptance letter from KU law school today."

Silence.

"Did you hear what I said? Law school. I got in."

"When did you apply to law school?" Dad said.

"Could you say 'congratulations,' or 'way to go, son, we always believed you had it in you'?" George said. "Would it kill you to do that?"

"We *are* proud of you, honey," said his mother. "That's very exciting."

"Yes," George said, trying to keep the agitation out of his voice. "Very exciting. So very exciting."

"Congratulations," Dad said. "We were going to call you today anyway, because we've been talking about going on that new cruise to Alaska."

"Okay," George said, resigned. *Enough talk about me, evidently.*

"It's very expensive," Mom said, "and we wondered if you'd

mind terribly if we sold your brothers' car to pay for it. It's just sitting in your grandparents' garage in Niobe anyway, so—"

"That's because you won't let me take it!" A burst of outrage made George shout the words. They wanted to sell the last remaining object that connected him to his brothers: their 1971 Bridgehampton Blue Chevrolet Corvette Stingray LS5 convertible.

The way his parents deified the twins, he would have thought they'd want to bronze it.

"Don't you raise your voice to your mother," Dad said.

George forced himself to speak calmly. "That car is mine. You said the twins would have wanted me to have it. And now that I'm in law school, I think this is the time to let me take it."

Although his parents had promised the Corvette to him, they had also forbidden him from even touching the car until he had a "career" and a "permanent residence." The implication was clear: he wasn't adult enough, even now at twenty-eight years old, to be trusted with a valuable vehicle *that was supposed to belong to him*.

He remembered the first time he'd seen it after some rich tennis-player alumnus gave it to Chad and Vic as a thank-you gift for leading the KU men's tennis team. Vic brought it home to Niobe and took thirteen-year-old George for a ride down I-70, topping out the speedometer at 150 mph. It had been the most exhilarating moment of George's young life. The twins had died just weeks later.

Even as George tried to hold on to his indignation, he

realized he was rocking back and forth in his chair, his elbows tight to his sides. How could his parents not know how much this meant to him? His eyes stung with tears, which infuriated him even more. *The Corvette. Not the Corvette.*

Every inch of him felt limp with helplessness, with inevitability, as if he were melting away.

Then his dad said, "*That's* why you finally applied. So we'd give you the car."

A cyclone of fury rose up through him. "It's *my* car!" he shouted.

"I told you he wouldn't like the idea," Dad said.

George slammed down the phone, which gave him a childish thrill. The phone began ringing soon after. He let it ring and walked out the door, imagining what Chad and Vic would say about his good news, like *you'll make an amazing lawyer, great job, way to go, Grandpop would be proud.*

His brothers were KU seniors when they died. Their athleticism, charisma, and good looks drew more than six hundred mourners to their funeral. For months afterward, George walked around in a dream, stunned, thrown into another dimension, one full of frozen dinners and silent hallways and dark bedrooms, closed doors and muted sobbing. One without music or laughter. The earth's axis permanently shifted for him and he might have tumbled down the same dark abyss his mother did if it weren't for his best childhood friends, Curt, Bill, and Travis.

He needed to call them. It had been too long. But he'd see

them in August at their ten-year high school reunion. They could catch up then.

As he walked toward his car, he wondered if he should let his parents sell the Corvette, if only to prove he was a real adult.

George caught sight of the girls by the pool again. They waved at him, which lifted his spirits, and he waved back. And he reminded himself that, as of today, he was a law school student. He was going to be a lawyer, no matter what his folks thought.

And he would not let them sell the Stingray.

Nothing was going to ruin the best day of his life.

CHAPTER THREE

George

George put extra effort into his duties as a janitorial supervisor, thanks to the glittering future that loomed just beyond the horizon, and his shift flew by. Before he knew it, he was finishing up at his final stop, the bank building. With a flourish, he made one last checkmark on his supervisory checklist, even though Ron had done a crap job of mopping the main floor men's room and hadn't even touched the mirrors. George performed these chores and didn't write Ron up. Today, he could afford a little magnanimity.

When he stepped outside, the sky had changed dramatically. Thunderstorms were advancing from the west. Under dark, threatening springtime clouds like these, George always wondered, a decade and a half later: *Is this the kind of sky Chad and Vic saw?*

The anniversary of the twins' death had been the previous week. His traditional annual memorial involved drinking a toast to them and looking through photo albums of all the dead people in his life—the latest of whom was his Grandpop, who'd passed away two years before. Grandpop had been George's rock and confidant after the twins died, especially during the hardest days with his parents.

Chad and Vic were the first dead people in his life. On May 14, 1971, the day after a full night of heavy thunderstorms, his brothers left their rented house in Lawrence intending to drive the Corvette to campus for classes. Hail and falling branches had severed and downed a power line, which was submerged in a puddle of rainwater surrounding the Vette. The second Chad and Vic's feet made contact with the water, 4800 volts of electricity streaked through them. They died instantly.

George suffered vivid nightmares for years afterward. Although power lines no longer terrified him, he marked every approaching thunderstorm. He now eyed the dark clouds gathering above as he loaded his industrial cleaning supplies into the big, white company Econoline van. He hustled it to his boss's home office to clock out and pick up his own car, which he drove to his regular Friday night stop, Kansas Crown Discount Liquor. He ignored the lightning on the horizon and strode in like a man with a purpose.

Behind the counter stood Richie, talking the ear off a college-age customer. Richie was an aged-out frat-rat who'd never stopped living the campus life, hanging around his old fraternity, perpetually taking classes without ever graduating. A guy who permed his hair and still dressed in Polo shirts and topsider shoes as if he were about to board a yacht and talk mutual funds instead of clocking in at a minimum-wage job six nights a week.

"Guess how old I am?" Richie said to the kid, a lank, rawboned guy with a dark, skinny ponytail scraggling below his black t-shirt collar.

"Um. Twenty-nine?"

"Thirty-eight!"

"Wow." The kid gathered his six-pack and hot-footed it out of there.

Richie was always putting customers on the spot like that, and like the retreating student, people were typically gracious. But Richie's fake-and-bake tan, under-eye luggage, and curly graying temples gave him away.

"Hey, Ace." Richie turned his attention to George. "You ready to have your ass handed to you tomorrow?"

George's disc golf team was set to play against Richie's the following day.

"In your wettest of dreams, Rich," George said.

"Get real. You haven't beat us since September, when my finger was broken. What'll you have?"

"Let it be Löwenbräu, my good man, because tonight is kinda special." George withdrew the acceptance letter from his pocket and slapped it down on the counter. "Guess who's going to law school in the fall?"

Richie stared wide-eyed down at the lustrous white envelope and then at George. "Most triumphant."

This almost-forty-year-old's use of twenty-something slang never failed to crack George up.

He replaced the envelope in his shirt pocket. "Just got it in under the wire. My ten-year high school reunion's in August. Now I won't have to take artistic license when I'm asked the 'so what have you been doing with your life' question."

Richie laughed and walked back to the beer section.

"On second thought," George called to him over the well-stocked shelves, "let's stick with the usual. Bud. I just wanted to say the goofy slogan and mean it for once."

"Way ahead of you, bro." Richie returned with a flat of four Budweiser six-packs balanced on one arm. Then he grabbed a half magnum of André champagne and carried the whole shebang up to the counter. He aimed the bubbly bottle at George. "On me."

"Thanks, man."

Richie's fingers hovered over the keys on the register as he glanced out the window behind him at the wicked-looking black clouds advancing eastward toward them. The first large raindrops splattered the glass. Instead of completing the transaction, Richie sat on his stool. "I thought about going to law school for serious myself."

You'd have to finish undergrad first, George thought. Not that he himself had gotten around to using his own BA in history, beyond clawing his way up to middle management.

"When I told my dad, he wigged out, totally bagged on me. Said I needed to take over the brokerage firm when he retired.

But I told the old man—"

A sudden sweeping cataract of rain accompanied by lightning and thunder shouted down Richie's jackassery, so he had to yell. "—told him he'd have to decide the financial fate of the country on his own."

The bell above the door jingled and a remarkably pretty girl in tight Jordache jeans and purple Con high tops dashed in holding her purse over her head, her long blonde hair billowing out behind her. She ushered in the smell of wet concrete on a blast of wind.

George pulled out his wallet so he had something to do with his hands.

"Can I use your phone?" the girl asked Richie after bestowing a dazzling smile upon them both. "My car won't start."

Richie stretched the extra-long cord and offered her the receiver.

"Can you dial the number for me?"

"All day," Richie said.

The girl recited a string of digits, and he punched in the numbers. She held the handset to her ear and listened, then consulted the red watch on her wrist.

George sized the girl up out of the corner of his eye. Her eyes were sapphire blue, sparkling and mischievous. She couldn't have been more than five feet tall, and he guessed her age at about twenty-four. He could practically feel the electric energy radiating off her as she moved constantly, observing everything around her.

"Damn it," she said and handed the receiver back to Richie. "Guess I need to call a taxi." Her eyes tracked to George, bringing heat to his face.

He swallowed, turned toward the door, and studied his wallet.

"Hey, cowboy."

He detected a bit of an accent, Southernish. Then he sensed a light touch on his back.

"Love me tonight."

His heart twanged and he locked up. But then he remembered he was wearing the button-down with the Head East logo on the back. She wasn't asking him to take her home. She was naming a Head East song. One of his favorites, as a matter of fact.

She stepped in front of him. "I love that band."

"Seen them in concert twice," he said. "Once in Wichita and once in—"

She snapped her fingers. "Kansas City?"

"Kansas City. At Municipal Auditorium."

She stabbed her index finger into his sternum excitedly. "I was there."

George studied her face more closely and thought she might look familiar. "Maybe that's where I know you from."

She smiled up at him. "I think we live in the same apartment complex. Highpoint. Right?'

"Yeah," he said, picturing her in the community room or the parking lot there. "Maybe."

"Think maybe I've seen you in here from time to time too."

"Every Friday night for the last six years," Richie chimed in.

George had forgotten all about Richie, who gave George an encouraging and, at the same time, creepily suggestive smile.

George turned back to the girl. She really was very good-looking. "What's your name?"

"Stacia."

"Sascha?" he said.

"No. Stacia. With a T."

"Nice to meet you, Stacia."

"Nice to be met," she said.

"I'm Richie," Richie said, hand to his heart. "And that's George. Also known as Ace around the Lawrence City Disc Golf League."

"What's disc golf?" Stacia said.

"Frisbee golf." George mimed throwing a disc.

To Richie, she said, "Why do you call him Ace?"

"The only reason is because he's made more aces than me," Richie said. "But not for long."

That was ridiculous, because George had close to twice as many aces as Richie.

"Aces?" Stacia said.

"It's like a hole in one in regular golf," Richie said. "George is the Secretariat of the league."

"What are you, his pimp?" Stacia said to Richie, softening her barb with a wink.

George was actually thinking the same thing. Why was

Richie talking him up like this? Was it some sort of psych-out tactic to rattle him before tomorrow's big match?

"My man don't need no pimp," Richie said.

Stacia turned her intense gaze back on George, appraising him. "Is that true?"

George resisted the urge to swallow. "You mean about the record? Or the pimp?"

She laughed.

"Maybe you should come and watch the game tomorrow," Richie said.

George tried to keep from rolling his eyes. Why in the world would Stacia want to do that?

"Where is it?" she said.

"Riverfront," Richie said. "Ten a.m."

She turned back to George and stuck out her hand. He shook it. She didn't let go. "I'll be there."

The way she said it, George almost believed her, even though it was just meaningless flirting. He'd take it. Everything about this day had a golden glow.

She was still holding on to his hand and started swinging it before raising it up and twirling under it. She stumbled—on purpose, it seemed to George—and he caught her, her back against him, pressing his arm around her collar bones, and he could smell her shampoo. She smiled up at him over her shoulder.

What a contrast to his reserved ex, Patty, who would never touch a guy she didn't know, much less execute a dance move in public.

George kind of liked this girl.

"Hey," she said, squeezing his arm before disentangling herself from it. "Any chance you could give me a ride?"

George glanced at his watch. He had forty minutes before his date—or appointment, or whatever it was—with Patty, which now held less appeal than it had a half hour ago. "Where you headed?"

"Across town, but it's like ten minutes from here. I've got a sorority thing I need to get to."

George shrugged, nonchalant. "Okay."

"That would be amazing," Stacia said. "I'll pay for your stuff."

"Oh, you don't need to do that."

"You can pay for his beer," Richie told her. "The champagne's on me."

She produced a multi-colored wallet from the massive purse, plucked a twenty from it, and extended the bill to Richie, who winked again at George. Richie rang up the beer and gave her change. George hoisted the flat of Bud cans from the counter, and the girl slid the champagne under her arm and held open the door for him.

They paused under the awning. The storm was of the late Kansas-spring drencher variety, as if God himself were standing right overhead emptying a stadium-sized bucket. The torrential rain was deafening, so he bent toward her and said, "I'll put all this in the back, and then you can get in."

He ran out into the downpour and arranged the case of beer

on the back seat before getting behind the wheel. He beckoned to Stacia, who raced to the car, again using her purse as an umbrella with one hand and clutching the champagne with the other. She got in and stowed the bottle then shook the rainwater off her purse and swiped it off the arms of her jean jacket.

George started the car and wiped his face with his sleeve. "Where to?"

She flipped down the visor and, finding no mirror, turned the rearview toward her. She ran her fingers through her long blonde hair then licked her pinky and removed a mascara smudge beneath her right eye. She twisted the rearview back into its proper position and sat back. "Turn right then go south on Tennessee."

Every shape outside the car was gray and blurry. He blinked to center his contact lenses before backing out of the space and creeping toward the parking lot exit. He eased out onto Sixth Street.

"You said you've got a sorority thing," George said. "You still in school?"

"No," she said. "I'm kind of in an advisory role now."

Her presence filled the car like incense, suffusing everything. She never stopped moving—crossing her legs, jiggling her foot, looking from window to window and back to his face.

"Can I have one of your beers?" she said, laying a hand on his forearm. Before he could reply, she reached into the back seat and retrieved two cans. She popped one open and tipped it to his lips, and he took a drink. The intimacy of this action, her hand and face near to his, her eyes on his mouth and breath on his cheek, brought everything into sharp focus. He took hold of the can and she sat back.

"Thanks," he said.

She sipped at the foam rising from her own Bud. "What's the champagne for? You celebrating something?"

"Well," he said, glad she'd asked, "I got an acceptance letter from KU Law this morning."

"Straight up?"

"Straight up."

"That's amazing! Congratulations!" She squeezed his arm again.

The steely clouds blotted out the sunset; night was almost on them. Bolts of lightning ricocheted from cloud to ground as the rain poured down unabated.

George punched in the dashboard lighter, pulled a Merit filter out of the pack in the console, and then regretted it. What if Stacia was anti like Patty?

Instead she grinned and reached forward. "Oh, can I have one?"

Relieved, George slipped another cigarette out of the pack. When the lighter popped, he lit them both and handed one to her. She took a long drag, exhaled a stream of smoke upwards, and sighed. She turned up the radio, which was playing "What I Am" by Edie Brickell and the New Bohemians and sang along.

George resisted the urge to join in singing with her. He didn't know her well enough for that. Even though they'd danced together. Or she had danced with him. But he wanted to know her better.

"Go left up there," she said.

They were in an older part of town now, one George hadn't been in before. Stacia must be lost, because this was not exactly Greek central.

"Turn right," she said. "Now slow down."

She abruptly poked the power button on the stereo, silencing the music. "Pull over before the curve up there." She pointed and he obeyed. "Cut the lights. I want to scare 'em."

"Scare them?" George said. This was odd. Why would she want to do that? "Are you serious?"

"Yeah," Stacia said, straightening her jacket and squaring her shoulders, as if she were getting ready to walk into a board meeting. "No, I know it sounds weird, but we do this to each other all the time."

"Okay," George said.

He stopped next to a neighborhood park with an old metal swing set and a lone bench beneath several large oak trees. Across the road to the west squatted two little ranch-style houses, and to the south and east were fields. The only light came from the intermittent lightning flashes and a dim street lamp a hundred feet to the north.

Both houses were dark. "Looks like nobody's home," George said.

"Like I told you—we do this to each other all the time. They're probably trying to scare me too." She leaned toward him, her face inches from his. "So, law school, huh?"

"Yeah." He hardly dared to breathe. It had been three long months since he'd been this close to a girl.

Her voice dropped lower. "Once I'm done, you want to go out to Clinton Lake and drink more of that beer? Celebrate?"

As she smiled at him, meeting up with Patty seemed even less important.

"Clinton Lake is my favorite place," George said. "Let's do that. Yeah."

"Wait here. Won't be more than fifteen, twenty minutes. Then we'll party."

Without warning, Stacia pressed herself against him. She fastened her open mouth to his in a deep, wet, lingering kiss that lit his nerves on fire. She pulled away, looked into his eyes, and let her fingers whisper along his cheek.

"Yeah?" she said.

He nodded again, unable to trust his voice.

"I've got something special to get the party started."

For a split-second George imagined her face sinking into his lap but banished the thought from his head.

"What's that?"

She maintained intense eye contact then said, "You ever heard of absinthe? It's illegal here, so—" She held her finger to her lips in a *Sssshhhh* gesture. "I was going to share it with my friends in there, but since you helped me out, I want you to have some."

She dug through her giant bag. "It's made with wormwood.

It'll give you visions. You ever had visions?"

He was having visions now, but he didn't say so.

She smiled and held up an oversized flask. "Okay, here's the deal. It smells super-nasty. But it's worth it. First, take a big drink of beer and then down just a couple swallows of the absinthe. You have to shoot it. So it's kind of like a regular shot in reverse. Got it?"

"Yup."

She handed him the container.

He cracked it open and couldn't resist taking a sniff. She was right—an almost medicinal smell jump-started a long-buried memory he couldn't quite catch hold of.

He chugged the rest of his Budweiser, then tossed back a mouthful of absinthe. The liqueur burned like liquid flame going down. He let out a series of epic, smoldering belches. Then floods of warmth infused his entire body.

He'd sampled a good variety of controlled substances in his time but never one that kicked in this fast. Every object around him glowed. He turned to Stacia, who kissed him hard on the mouth then faded back against the passenger-side door. In the darkness, Stacia's grinning face expanded, and soon all he could see were flashes of her gleaming white teeth, which morphed into birthday party balloons that grew and grew and grew, threatening to crowd everything else out of the car.

This was the best damn day of his life.

He blinked, and Stacia disappeared.

And then the house across the street blew up.

CHAPTER FOUR

George

10:48 p.m.

George stopped at the red light at Twenty-third Street next to a jacked-up pickup truck. He reached into the back seat and maneuvered the plastic of the open trash bag to cover the weapons and baggie of what must've been cocaine. Sirens wailed from the east, probably the Harper Street fire station, five minutes away.

Maybe he should go to Patty's. Or the police station. But how would he explain this to either? How would he justify leaving the scene? How would he rationalize the collection of incriminating items in the back seat, not to mention his fingerprints on that gun and knife?

When the house exploded, was Stacia inside? Did she set the fire? Nausea and dizziness rolled through him as the light turned green, and he punched the accelerator. The car lurched forward, almost rear-ending the Datsun in front of him, and he made himself ease off. He needed to dump this car or hide it.

When he returned to Kansas Crown Discount Liquor, he parked on Arkansas Street. He had to use the flat of his key ring to turn off the headlights since he'd yanked the knob off in his panic back at the burning house. If he'd only said no to Stacia, he'd be at the Sanctuary right now, basking in Patty's admiration.

Should he throw the weapons and drugs into the dumpster back there? Too risky, he decided. The Lawrence PD had George's fingerprints on file from a DWI five years ago, and this was his neighborhood. He'd need to find a more permanent way to dispose of the stuff far from here.

The half-block walk around to the liquor store steadied him. He tried to make sense of what had happened. Who was Stacia really? Was that even her real name? It sounded made-up now that he thought about it. Had she led him to that house to frame him for the arson she was about to commit? Had she burglarized the house of drugs and weapons? Cut herself accidentally? Had to go back for some reason and blew herself up? No matter how he rearranged the details, nothing added up.

When he entered the liquor store, Richie's head bobbed up and he dropped his book on the floor with a bang. "What…are you…?" He bowed to pick it up and peered over the counter.

George scanned the aisles and hurried toward the rear door to be sure the shop was empty. Back at the register, he said, "Is there anyone else in here besides the two of us?" His voice was a couple of octaves higher than normal.

"Nope."

"Before today, had you ever seen that girl I gave a ride to?"

"The blonde?" Richie said. "Not sure. Why? Didn't she say she'd seen you in here?"

"Never mind. Forget it."

Concerned, Richie said, "Dag. You're hardcore out the door."

George's stomach started to rise, and there would be no stopping it. "I think I'm going to throw up."

"Not on my tile!"

George skipped back to the restroom. By the time he got the lights on, the nausea had subsided. He turned on the water, and in the brownish light of the filthy fixture over the sink, his hands looked like they were covered in axle grease or something. He soaped them up, and the sink backed up with red-tinged water. He glanced up at his reflection and—what the hell? The lower half of his face was covered in the rusty red shape of a handprint.

Whose handprint? His own? Stacia's? Looking down, there were blood stains all over him. He checked for injuries, broken skin anywhere, but found nothing. Then all he could think was *My Head East shirt is ruined!* Which infuriated him, his shallowness. Because blood that wasn't his on the shirt meant...

Everything went into overdrive. George scoured his face in a frenzy and spat until he gagged. He ripped a wad of paper towels off the holder, held it under the steaming hot water until soaked, and scrubbed his shirt. But the more he scrubbed, the more vivid and vibrant red the stain became. He was the very picture of an axe murderer.

He recalled how Richie had dropped his book when he came in. He'd seen the blood. *Shit.*

Was it possible? Could he have wandered into that house while blacked out and done the unthinkable?

He catapulted himself out of the bathroom and covered the distance to the front door in seconds. The phone was ringing as he raced past Richie, flung the door open, and dashed outside.

As he ran around the building toward his car, Richie called to him. "Ace! Come back here! I've got a—"

George got in the Cricket and flipped a U-turn, almost side-swiping a station wagon in the process. He took the back way home on Seventh Street and parked, but not in his assigned space, just in case.

Scanning the grounds for police, George only saw residents meandering in the direction of the clubhouse. He walked as fast as he could to his ground-floor apartment, got the door unlocked at last, and stumbled inside. He had to take this bloody shirt off. He fumbled at the buttons as he careened into the bathroom.

Removing his shirt proved an almost impossible task, as if he'd lost the operating instructions to his hands. He yanked at the neckline, popping off two buttons, and peeled the sticky, sweaty, bloody shirt off over his head and tossed it in the tub. He caught sight of his acceptance letter, still in the pocket, now wrinkled, stained, and ruined.

Law school. How was he going to—

No time to think that far in the future. He had to think about right now, and what he needed to do right now was ditch his car because the teenagers in the park across from the burning house had gotten a good look at it. And at him and his bloody face and shirt. But once he did that, what was he going to do?

A thought popped up in his head like toast.

The Corvette. The idea sent George's hopes soaring and just as quickly dashed them on the rocks when he thought of the distance to the old beauty: a hundred and twenty miles to the west in Niobe, his hometown. The car was stored at his Grandpop and Grandgum's house. His Uncle Howard, who lived in Wichita, now owned the house since both grandparents had passed. He maintained the house as his own personal retreat during pheasant hunting season. His rule: no visits without permission.

But if ever there was a time to defy Uncle Howard and his folks, this was it.

One step at a time. Snag the car then figure out what to do. He wet a washcloth and washed off all the blood smears he could see, then dumped the rag in the tub on top of the other bloody items and dragged the shower curtain closed. Then he spotted a dirty t-shirt crumpled in the corner of the bathroom, which he put on.

He had to steady himself on the sink, try to get more oxygen. This feeling was familiar. It was the same dread and despair he'd felt upon learning what benign, arbitrary evil had taken his brothers' lives. He looked in the mirror and knew the difference between this feeling and that one: the evil that had barged into his life tonight was undeniably arbitrary, but it was anything but benign.

George forced himself into action, fighting the urge to curl up in a ball and rock. He took out his contacts and slid on his huge tortoise-shell framed glasses. Now, time for a haircut. Using scissors, he cut his hair almost to the scalp, and as he snipped, he tried to imagine stabbing another human being. He closed the scissor blades and placed them in his fist slasher-style and immediately dropped them into the sink, his hands seized by violent shaking. He grabbed the sink again.

He had to think logically, or he would be swept away by panic. Wouldn't his arm muscles be sore from the unnatural movement? Wasn't it likely his own hand would be sliced up from plunging a bloody knife into a body? More than likely.

He gathered up the wiry, curly remains of his hair from the sink, and flushed them down the toilet.

There. Now he didn't look like George Engle anymore.

And maybe he wasn't George Engle. Because George Engle would never stab or shoot anyone.

CHAPTER FIVE

George

11:36 p.m.

He soaked a wad of paper towels under the tap and carried it out of the apartment with him, his brain on high alert for suspicious-looking characters or cops. But it was the usual college kids going out or coming home. He got in his car and wiped the blood off the steering wheel as best he could, then stowed the paper towels beneath his seat.

Before backing out, he glanced at the fuel gauge. The indicator pointed below E. *Shit.* He needed to buy gas on his way out of town, at least five dollars' worth. He conducted a quick mental search: There was a locally owned self-serve station near the grain elevator by the railroad tracks.

He headed that way, going the speed limit, signaling for lane changes, keeping his eye out for cop cars, feeling like his bones were going to snap from the tightness in his muscles.

No matter how he tried, he couldn't call up any details from the time he was blacked out. He'd never even been in a fist fight, much less stabbed someone. But he didn't know anything about absinthe or what it could do. One of his friends had done angel dust once and jumped through a plate glass window and nearly bled to death.

The gas station was deserted but open. One of the overhead lights had burned out, which only slightly lessened his anxiety. He got out of the car and slid a five-dollar bill to the cashier, who sat half-asleep behind Plexiglas.

George stalked back to the car and removed the gas cap then lifted the nozzle and shoved it in. He pressed the lever and locked it in position.

Tiny hairs from his impromptu haircut tickled his neck and even his nose, and he scratched at the itchiest areas while he watched the numbers on the meter display roll with insane slowness. The pump seemed to be dispensing a penny's worth of gas at a time, which it had to think about before giving up.

Seconds stretched to minutes as George scratched and waited, shifting from foot to foot, dread wrapping its cold fingers around his guts. A VW bug pulled up to the pump opposite him. George turned his back and ducked his head, eyes still on the meter, his heart rate doubling again.

A tap on the shoulder made George pogo into the air and spin around. The pump clicked off with a loud *thunk*.

"Didn't mean to scare you," a bummy looking guy with greasy hair and a stained shirt said. "Do you think you could give me a lift to—"

"Hell, no!" George shouted, and the guy jumped back, his face screwed up in fear. George jerked the nozzle out of his tank, dripping gas everywhere, and replaced it on the hook. He opened his car door and tumbled inside, reeking of fumes. He started the car and traveled west.

George's eyes kept flicking to the rearview mirror as he steered toward the Kansas River. He traversed the Second Street Bridge before he remembered the road construction on the railroad overpass just beyond Locust Street.

Damn it.

He turned right on Locust and spotted a van behind him in the rearview, in all likelihood a patron leaving Johnny's Tavern there on the corner. George signaled left to take Third. Behind him, the van's left blinker flashed.

Going straight would lead him to a dead end, so he had to take the turn. The old Farmers' Cooperative grain silo loomed to his right.

A single siren whoop iced George's heart. His eyes once again darted to the rearview mirror which reflected a revolving dashboard cherry light.

Oh, fuck. Oh, no. No. The van was an unmarked police vehicle.

Crazy thoughts sparked through George's mind.

I'll pretend I don't think the siren's for me and keep driving.

No. I'll stop, but then open the door and run like hell. George stopped twenty yards before the railroad crossing, put the car in neutral, and pulled the parking brake because of the slight incline up to the tracks themselves.

Maybe he'd been speeding. Maybe he had a tail light out.

His craziest thought of all: *I'll pull the gun from the trash bag and shoot the cop.*

Instead, George fumbled with shaking hands for his license, and his eyes went to his side view mirror. The van idled forty feet behind his car. The red glow of his taillights illuminated a tall man, the cop, exiting the van, walking toward the Plymouth.

But why had he stopped so far back instead of right behind George?

Did cops even use vans as unmarked vehicles?

The sharp, loud *clang* of the railroad signal drew George's attention to the descending crossing arm in front of him. *CLANG! CLANG! CLANG!*

He turned to the side mirror again as the man grew larger in the frame.

The blinking signal light intermittently stained the world red as George glanced frantically from the side mirror to the windshield, the man drawing nearer.

CLANG! CLANG! CLANG!

His heart buffeted his rib cage, pounding out a fight-or-flight rhythm.

The man wore no hat, no uniform.

In his hand…

Was that a gun?

Not a cop. Couldn't be.

No choice. Had to.

The silo blocked George's view. He couldn't see the train. How far away it was.

CLANG! CLANG! CLANG!

George eased in the clutch and simultaneously floored the accelerator, the engine over-revving to a high-pitched whine as his car slowly rolled backward down the incline.

The car hiccupped as it clipped something, and his eyes tracked to the side mirror in time to see the man fall to the ground. Oh. Shit.

No time to think.

He shoved the stick into first and released the clutch. His mind went blank as the car screeched forward, Indy-car fast, faster than he'd expected. The car crashed into the crossing arm, which grated across the hood toward him, crumpling steel. George ducked. The arm smashed into the windshield's passenger side, cracking but not breaking the glass, and took the wiper with it. Metal screeched as it scraped over the roof.

He looked to his right. A train was rising, growing, rushing at him.

The accelerator was to the floor. RPMs pegged out. More speed impossible.

He shut his eyes and braced for impact in blazing forward motion, flattened against his seat with the Gs. His bones shuddered, the train's horn blared so loud. The pressure and vibration flexed and ballooned George's eardrums.

The bellowing was right on top of him. Inside him.

And then the deafening pandemonium curved and descended in pitch.

The freight crossed behind George's back bumper and glided on down the tracks.

The Cricket continued blasting through the little neighborhood between him and the city limits. Houses flashed by as he slowed, listening for any engine noise that indicated damage and hearing none.

He released the lungful of air he'd been holding for roughly a minute and headed for the interstate.

For two hours, George chain-smoked and replayed his worst best day again and again. He hunched over the wheel like a gargoyle, neck stiff and head pounding, feeling as if his skin would burst off him. The only time he stopped was to throw up, when the lights of Lawrence faded behind him and the adrenaline subsided.

Just before one a.m., he turned onto a two-lane that led to Niobe through fifteen miles of grazing land. An almost painful attack of nostalgia walloped him: there stood the stone fencepost that resembled the chiseled face of an Indian chief. How long since he'd seen it? This was the landmark where he and his best friends Curt, Bill, and Travis would meet up on childhood summertime days to ride horseback. They liked to pretend they were cowboys, taming the wild west.

He was a stone's throw from Curt's place right this moment. He hadn't spoken to him or the other two in about a year and a half, but nothing ever changed around here. Time had gone by, and he hadn't even noticed, and like everything else in his life, he'd just let his friends fall away.

The full moon illuminated the prairie around him, creating eerie, disorienting shadows as he crested the hill above the little valley in which Niobe sat. The two-block line of street lights along Main pointed the way home.

But as he turned on to State Highway 16 and headed toward town, the earlier surge of elation returned. He'd outrun a motherfucking *train*. He was alive, without a phony cop's bullet in his head.

And then a chilling string of thoughts paraded through his mind:

What if it actually *was* a cop, and he'd radioed in George's plate number?

What if George had only imagined a gun in his hand?

And what if—his stomach heaved at this thought—what if George had not just clipped him but killed him?

CHAPTER SIX

Curt Dekker

Saturday, May 24, 1986
Niobe, Kansas
12:48 a.m.

Curt Dekker pulled Gracie Bauer tight against him and she shivered as their hips met. He kissed her, hands in her back pockets, listening to the *clunk!* of pool balls colliding on the table at his back. As "Slow and Easy" by Whitesnake blared from the jukebox, the kissing began to take on a more urgent quality.

Bill Altenbach emerged from behind Gracie and waved his arms. "Dekker," he said. "Your shot. Hello? Anybody home?" He leaned on his cue stick, sipping at a flask of Jack Daniel's whenever Mac the bar owner turned his back.

Curt kissed Gracie one last time and twisted away from her, but she wouldn't let go, her arms around his neck, her breasts pressed into his back. He eyed the green felt of the better of the two pool tables in McWhiskey's Tavern. Couldn't make a shot with her hanging on him like an overcoat. He turned his face into her beer breath and said, "You're working with Bill, aren't you? You get me all hot and bothered and he wins. Right?"

She gave him a lascivious smile and backed away. He lined up the cue ball with the eight and shot. Missed anyway.

"Guess we're on the backside of the drunkenness-versus-competence parabolic curve," Bill said.

With Gracie's arms around his waist from behind, Curt bent forward and knocked the eight ball into the pocket with his knuckles.

Indignant, Bill said, "That was my shot!"

A whoop went up from the small crowd sitting on stools at the bar top, watching the Royals-White Sox game. It looked like they were playing in an epic blizzard thanks to the static on the shitty little black-and-white TV bracketed to the wall.

Gracie twisted her lips. "You getting any better TV reception with that new cable receiver station across from your house?"

"It's not really a receiving station," Curt said.

"'Cause I'm not. You probably should talk to those people about it."

"Is that what they put on the land you sold to...who was it?" Bill said.

"Sorazin-Hesper-Atkins. Everybody calls it S.H.A., though. Which I think really stands for Secret Heavy Anti-Nuclear-Weapon Agency."

Bill laughed. "I'll drink to that."

Gracie slid her hands up Curt's arms and around his neck and whispered, "Maybe I should come to your place and check out your reception for myself." She kissed him and got the reaction she must have been looking for. He met her eyes and understood it was time to cash in the chip she'd dangled in front of him for weeks.

He raised his eyebrows at Bill. "I need to see you in the office for a moment."

"Sir yes sir!" Bill said.

"Gracie, babe." Curt said, kissing her and removing her arms from his neck. "Gotta consult with my colleague for a minute. Be right back."

"You better be."

Curt led Bill out the door into the misty night. The street lights illuminated a smooth, low-hanging layer of cloud the color of dryer lint.

The temperature was sixty-nine degrees according to the giant electronic digital clock on the Farmers National Bank on the corner, but it felt chillier and their breath came out as steam.

"I take it I'll be sleeping at Mom's tonight, huh?" Bill said with a smirk.

"That's about the size of it. Think of how happy you'll make old Marge."

A few cars cruised slowly down Main Street in front of McWhiskey's, competing music spilling out the open windows. The usual suspects—Starvin' Marvin in his candy-apple red pickup jacked up to heaven, chassis peeking out like a slip showing under a skirt. Hot Rod Wentz's green Pontiac Le Mans. Mean Dean's primer-gray Chevy Nova. Dirty Dick Winslow with his station wagon-load of ankle biters, faces pressed against the fogged-up windows.

Curt's nose wrinkled in disgust. Who went out cruising at midnight with kids under five?

"Yo, G-Ho!" Bill yelled, waving his hands overhead like a desert-island castaway. Curt turned as Travis Mussberger's '77 Gremlin passed by on the opposite side of the street. But he hadn't heard, and moved on.

George Engle had dubbed Travis Gung-Ho—eventually shortened to G-Ho—in junior high because of his life goals: become a Marine after high school and a police officer after that. He was mister law-and-order, a real rule follower, which was hilarious since the other three were decidedly not those things. But their childhood bond stayed strong because Travis prized loyalty above all.

He'd nailed the Marine goal, but the police officer dream was still just a dream.

"You hear what he did a couple weeks ago?" Curt said.

"Who, G-Ho?" Bill said. "Where would I have heard?"

Curt shook his head. "He was out patrolling," he said, "and a call came over his police scanner about a car wreck, and he went out there to help, setting out flares and whatnot like he does, and some guy at the scene said, 'What is this? A security guard uniform? You ain't no real cop!' You know, razzing him, and G-Ho tells him to back off. The guy Captain Kirks out and draws down on him and—get this—G-Ho disarms the asshole."

"Oh, bullshit," Bill said.

"Shit you not. The sheriff told me, straight to my face."

"Old Junior," Bill said.

"Yup," Curt said. "Guess he chewed G-Ho's ass up one side and down the other, like it was his fault the guy pulled his piece. He's all, 'We let you patrol because it saves the county money, and you keep the drag racers off the street and the skinny dippers out of the pool, but if you ever pull that kind of cowboy crap again, I will see to it you never work as a police officer.' I asked Junior what G-Ho was supposed to do—stand there and take a bullet? And Junior says, 'The guy wouldn't have shot, but the gun could have gone off when Travis grabbed it.'"

"G-Ho's gone get hisself kilt," Bill said, real country.

"Yeah. That's what Junior's afraid of. But there ain't much chance of him ever becoming a real cop anyhow, right? He's taken the academy exam, like, three times and he can't pass it."

Bill shook his head again. "Poor old G-Ho. He's either the bravest guy I know or the dumbest."

"For sure."

"On my way into town," Bill said, "I saw that Minnie's was all boarded up."

"Yeah, man—she died. Finally."

"What was she, like a hundred and ten?" Bill said, shoving his hands in his pockets. "She's been around since Moses was a pup."

Minnie's liquor store had been an institution in Niobe ever since Curt could remember. When they were in eighth grade, Curt, Bill, and George used to visit Minnie's pop machine, which stood sentry beside the front door of her store. One of them would take a handful of change and drop it on the ground so Minnie would come outside to help pick it up, while the other two snuck in the back door to grab whatever bottles were closest—peppermint schnapps, apricot brandy, anything sweet and alcoholic. Travis never joined them on these missions because he refused to break the law.

One night when Curt was out front, Minnie was particularly quick gathering the change. He had to fake a coughing fit to stall her so Bill and George could escape out the back before they were caught.

"It's the end of an era," Bill said.

The door to McWhiskey's opened, strains of the Power Station's rendition of "Bang a Gong" issuing from the jukebox inside. Curt and Bill turned toward the sound as a billow of cigarette exhaust fumes escaped the open door.

Gracie leaned out. "Curt?"

"Yeah?"

"You coming back in?"

"Gimme a minute."

"Don't take too long." She blew him a kiss and backed into the bar. The door clicked shut, cutting off the music and smoke.

Curt turned back to the street in time to see the ass end of a blue Plymouth Cricket heading west down Main.

"Hey," he said. "Is that—"

"George fucking Engle." Bill sounded as surprised as Curt.

A thrill zipped up Curt's spine. He couldn't remember the last time the four of them were together outside of George's grandpop's funeral two years ago, and he hadn't even talked to George in a couple of years. Curt was overwhelmed with a sentimental urge to round everyone up. But first, they would make George pay for the extended radio silence.

"Oh, no," Bill said. "I know that look. Poor Gracie."

"I'll send her out to my place to wait for me," Curt said, rubbing his hands together. "Better go in and settle up."

Bill gave him an evil grin. "And then saddle up."

CHAPTER SEVEN

George

1:40 a.m.

George turned off Main Street into the alley behind Grandpop's little lavender house. He opened the glove box, pulled out the keyring with the house and garage padlock keys on it, and left the car idling.

Once he removed the lock from the detached-garage doors, he flung them open like the gates to the Emerald City and took in the sight of his salvation, the Corvette, inside. Again, his eyes pricked with tears, but as he gazed at it, the itch of defiance spurred him forward. Not only would he touch this old beauty, he was going to drive it. George was confident the car would start because Dad had tasked Uncle Howard with driving it every time he was in town to keep it in fighting trim.

He swung open the driver's side door, slid into the low seat, and found the key in the visor. With trepidation, he slipped it into the ignition and turned it. He barely tapped the gas and savored the rumble of that 454 big-block V-8 engine sparking to life, and it was like nothing he had ever even hoped to experience.

The Stingray growled and purred as he backed it out of the garage and into the alley. He resisted the strong impulse to just drive away to parts unknown because he couldn't go off half-cocked. He needed to make plans to navigate all the shit that was surely coming his way.

He stationed the Vette next to the garage then guided his mangled Cricket inside. He cut the engine then got into the back seat to hide the trash bag under the front. The case of Bud with two cans missing was right where he left it, but his soft-side cassette carrier was not. It was on the back seat floor, wide open, all his cassettes scattered around it.

He remembered moving the carrier aside to make room for the Budweiser before letting Stacia in his car. Had it been unzipped at that time? He couldn't remember. Maybe the carrier had fallen and spilled during his game of chicken with the train.

George removed the baggie of coke from the trash bag and placed it carefully under the passenger seat to prevent the knife from piercing the plastic and diffusing the white powder all over everything. Then he twisted the trash bag closed with the knife and gun inside it, careful not to stab himself, and pushed the package under the driver's side seat. He left the gas can. Plenty of people carried gas cans in their cars.

After locking up the garage, he walked toward the dark house, across the crumbling cement patio, thinking about where he was going to go, what he was going to do. No way would he go down to Havasu. His parents could not know about this. Maybe he'd go to Denver for a while. He had a college friend who lived there. He unlocked the side door and stepped inside, where he was pulled from his thoughts by a cloud of homesickness.

How could the house still smell like Grandpop two years after he'd passed? Did the caretaker walk through the rooms spraying Right Guard deodorant, Aqua Velva aftershave, and Vitalis hair tonic? George was whacked with an all but incapacitating longing for his favorite grandfather.

Even though Uncle Howard now owned this house, George secretly thought of it as his. Growing up, he'd ride his bike the two blocks from his own home to escape on the days his mother barricaded herself in her bedroom with a photo album of his dead brothers—their birthday, the anniversary of the day they'd been killed, the anniversary of their high school graduation, Easter, Mother's Day.

For the first year after the twins' death, he spent those days and nights with his grandparents, going to Grandpop's tiny law office and the magnificent old limestone Niobe County Courthouse with him in the summers, doing jigsaw puzzles and making caramel corn on weekends with Grandgum in the winters.

On each of the five occasions his mother tried to kill herself throughout the years that followed, George found refuge in this house.

He did this until he was old enough to hang out with his friends during Mom's dark days.

George deflated onto his grandpop's threadbare red easy chair. The February 11, 1984 issue of *TV Guide* sat on the end table next to him. Kate Jackson and Bruce Boxleitner of *Scarecrow and Mrs. King* smiled up at him.

He could almost pretend Grandpop had stepped out to buy a box of White Owl cigars and a six-pack of Bubble-Up.

He was too keyed up to sleep but too exhausted to do anything but sit here staring at the red and gold flocked wallpaper behind the console television.

When he could resist no more, he plodded into the den to face up to what he always thought of as The Altar, an entire wall dedicated to photos and keepsakes of the handsome blond twins, Chad and Vic. His mother had put it up after Grandpop died, because Grandpop hadn't let her when he was alive. His parents had a much larger Altar in their Lake Havasu condo.

He examined the sports action photos, some of which George had taken himself after Grandpop had given him his old Brownie camera.

"They were good at everything they did," his mom would say. Photos of the golden Engle twins holding trophies for high school football, baseball, basketball, and track. Photos with identical crowns as joint Homecoming and Prom Kings. Photos of them winning the science fair, the history fair, 4-H, as the leading men in Niobe High School plays. Playing tennis and rugby at KU. Mugging with their fraternity brothers. Posing like movie stars next to their cherished Vette. As student body president and vice president.

Their death came at an awkward age for George, just hitting puberty. He'd been his parents' middle-age "oops" baby and had managed to live comfortably in the shadow of the superstar twins his whole life. After they died, he found himself under the microscope of his folks' attention. All their hopes and dreams they now pinned to George with his average academic performance, his average sports talent, his average looks. Their disappointment was like a physical presence, an elderly, hypercritical aunt scowling from every corner of the house.

George Engle was the pale imitation of the wanted children, the back-up son whose photos now might have a chance of making the Altar wall—once he was put in prison.

He shuffled into his grandparents' room and kicked off his shoes, confident that this was the best place in the world to hide from the authorities and whoever's cocaine it was in his back seat. Surely they'd come looking for it. But no one would find him here. He'd stay until he could figure out what to do.

He lay down on the bed and stared at the ceiling tiles and the water spot that resembled the state of Illinois. His eyelids grew heavy and he dozed.

A hammering sounded at the front door.

"Open up in the name of the law," came a shout. "Police."

He shot upright. It *had* been a cop, and he'd radioed in the

Plymouth's license plate before he died, and they'd tracked him here.

He cowered, clutching a pillow, his blood congealing in his veins.

"Open the fuck up!"

CHAPTER EIGHT

Bill Altenbach

2:13 a.m.

Curt and Bill were laughing so hard they could barely stand, rubbery with booze and their spectacular prank. The porch light snapped on.

Then in the door's window loomed a waxy, sunken face with bulging eyes and hair that looked like it had been cut with garden shears, and Bill gasped in surprise. It took a moment to realize the face belonged to George.

Curt likewise went silent. They glanced at each other. George looked terrified. Not just terrified. Panic-stricken.

Bill's mouth dried up.

George's face went quaggy with relief and recognition, and now more resembled the friend Bill had known all his life. George unlocked the door, opened it, and stood aside while Bill and Curt trooped in, soberer than they'd been seconds ago.

George went back to the door and peered out, his breathing shallow and jagged.

Curt frowned at Bill.

George slammed the door, his back against it, his lungs heaving. He clutched at his own shirt front as if trying to either keep his heart from shooting out of his body or to free it.

"George," Curt said quietly, reaching out a hand.

"Don't," George said, twisting away. "Can't breathe. I can't breathe. I—"

He dashed through a doorway toward the bathroom at the back of the house, and Bill heard retching sounds.

"What…the…*fuck*," he said.

"Yeah, I don't know," Curt said, scratching his head.

Bill had a sudden urge to laugh and hated himself for it. He was too wasted for whatever this was.

The toilet flushed, and George surfaced in the living room, chuffing and wheezing like a cat trying to cough up a hairball. He collapsed on the divan and stooped forward, his face in his hands.

Bill needed to go to the bathroom, but this was not the time. Weakness snaked around his ankles and surged upward, the silence intensifying it with every passing second.

"You gonna tell us what's going on, or what?" Curt burst out.

George's shoulders began to shake, and with horror, Bill realized he was crying. Hard. Bill hadn't seen George cry since he'd broken his arm in grade school.

He sure as hell didn't want to see it now. He escaped to the bathroom. *This* was the time.

Bill took longer than necessary washing his hands and snooping through the medicine cabinet when he was finished, hoping George had wound up his outburst. But when Bill returned to the living room, George was crying even harder. Curt sat next to him on the divan, patting his back and asking over and over *what's going on?*

Bill stood by the console TV, antsy, his hands moving almost of their own accord, looking for something to do. He heard the back door swing open.

George jumped up from the divan, his tears cut off like a sluice gate closing. Bill's heart beat so hard he could feel it in his fingertips.

Travis surfaced in the doorway dressed in his security-guard uniform.

"G-Ho," Curt said. "What are you doing here?"

George hurled himself into the corner, cowering. His wide eyes stared at Travis as if beholding a demon.

Bill felt an inappropriate tickle of laughter at the back of his throat, which required a super-human act of will to suppress.

Travis hadn't noticed. "Saw Bill's wife's car out front and wondered if you two yahoos…"

Now he noticed.

"George?" he said, concern on his face.

"C-cop," George stuttered. "Cop! G-Ho's a—"

"No, George," Curt said, holding his hands out. "Security guard. Not a cop."

"Yet," Travis added, straightening.

Curt led George back to the couch. "Take it easy, man," he said. "Seriously. What the hell? Are you on acid or something?"

Bill watched George struggle to get his breathing under control.

"How did you get in here?" George finally asked Travis.

"Hide-a-key in the garden." Travis shrugged as if the answer was obvious.

And Bill wanted to laugh again, so he walked around touching things—the blue glass candlesticks atop the console TV, the lampshades, the little Asian figurines. But then he decided maybe laughing was just the thing to do right now. He stopped and tapped the plaque on the wall emblazoned with the Kansas State motto: *Ad astra per aspera*. "I've come up with a new one," he said. "*Nihil est enim mali*. 'Kansas: There Ain't Nothin' Wrong With It.' "

His joke was greeted with silence and blank stares, which sparked an irrational and disproportionately violent desire to smash something.

Travis cleared his throat and looked around at everyone. "Did they tell you my big news?" he said to George, who lit a cigarette and inhaled.

"G-Ho," Curt said, "George was about to tell us—"

"I'm getting married, and I want the three of you to be groomsmen." Travis focused on George with a wide smile. His face and ears turned several shades of red beneath his white-blond brush cut same as they always had when Travis was embarrassed, wound up, or whenever anyone made an off-color remark, a trait that provided his friends with endless entertainment.

George blinked at Travis, whose smile faded as he looked from one face to another.

"George is happy for you, buddy," Curt said, as if interpreting at the UN. "And we will totally be your groomsmen, but he's got something to tell us." He nodded at George. "Something… really bad, I think."

Travis seemed to shake off his disappointment and lapse into fix-it mode. He removed his security guard uniform jacket, rolled up his long sleeves and sat in the chair opposite George, elbows on knees. When George didn't speak, Travis held his hands out. "Well?"

George sighed, but it came out a shudder. "I can't tell you."

"What the hell?" Bill said. "Why not?" His urge to laugh and the need to contain it resulted in an emotional concussion, amping his irritation by a factor of ten.

George blew out another long stream of smoke. "I can't tell you because you won't believe me." He tapped ashes into his grandpop's huge marble cigar ashtray on the end table.

Bill had to concede this point. Back in elementary school, George had been a chronic liar. He'd talk about the adventures he didn't have since his parents virtually ignored him, shining all their light on the golden twins. Like the time George told his friends he'd written to early '70s teen idol Bobby Sherman—Bobby Sherman!—and persuaded him to perform a concert at

Niobe City Park. Or the time he told them he'd been invited to training camp with the Chiefs. And each time, he'd have to come up with another lie to cover up why those things never happened.

He'd never quite lived the reputation down.

"I guess you'll just have to live with that, George," Bill said. "Tell us or don't tell us, but if you don't, then you need to cut out the dramatics."

Curt glared at him, and Bill felt it all the way to the back of his skull. Why was he glowering at Bill? Why wasn't he as pissed as Bill that George had all but disappeared from their lives eighteen months ago? *He should be.*

Curt turned away from Bill and said to George, "I can tell something huge happened to you today, George, so I feel like we're going to believe pretty much anything you say." He nodded reassuringly. Travis fixed his laser stare on George, a look of almost comical concentration on his face.

Then George told this fantastic tale, and Bill found himself caught up in it in spite of himself.

All through the telling, Curt and Travis's expressions of shock and horror matched Bill's.

"And then, as I was leaving town," George was saying, "a van with a dashboard cherry light pulled me over. A guy got out and I'm pretty sure he had a gun in his hand. So I—a train was coming, and the crossing arm was down, so I had to…bust through it and outrun the train."

Bill traded glances with Travis and Curt, and as if in wordless agreement, the three of them busted up laughing. What a sweet relief it was.

"Wow," Curt said. "You had us going there."

The laughter grew to hysteria.

"Outran a *train*!" Bill hooted.

George rose, his fists clenched, a look of fierce determination on his face. "Tell you what. Let's go take a look at my car, shall we?" He stalked to the back door and nabbed his keys off the hook. He turned back. But his audience hadn't budged. "Come on. Don't you want the opportunity to prove me wrong, Bill? Prove I'm still winding everybody up?"

Bill would take that challenge, but he had a sinking feeling that George was telling the truth.

Travis was the first to follow, then Curt, and last of all Bill, trailing George into the dark back yard.

CHAPTER NINE

George

Resentment supplanted George's terror, clearing his mind and energizing his body. Travis, Curt, and Bill tramped behind him in silence out to the back yard. At least they'd stopped laughing. As George stuck the key in the padlock on the door, the others circled the Stingray.

Curt trailed his fingers over the fiberglass. "Oh, wow, I forgot about this thing. Your folks finally going to let you have it?"

George didn't respond, instead leading the way inside the garage where he pulled the cord on the naked ceiling bulb, illuminating the ruined front end of the Cricket.

Curt's face lost its drunken grin.

George grabbed a large flashlight and trained its beam on the car's hood—the crumpled metal, scratches, and dents, the missing wiper, the spiderweb-shaped cracks marring half of the windshield.

He beckoned them closer, then unlocked the driver's side

door and opened it. Bill and Curt lingered by the garage door, Bill constantly on the move, jittering all over the place, but Travis took the flashlight from George. He shone the beam on the back seat, then the front passenger seat. He examined the steering wheel and gear shift then looked under the seats. Like a good cop wannabe, he didn't touch anything. He straightened, gave a low whistle, and returned the flashlight to George.

"Glad you're okay, pard," Travis said and stood guard by the garage door.

"Thanks, G-Ho," George said, grateful for the validation, and walked the flashlight over to Bill with growing confidence and held it out to him.

Bill didn't take it but stared, deadpan, at George, whose arm began to shake holding out the heavy flashlight. Curt looked from Bill to George then snagged it and thrust it into Bill's midsection. "What's wrong with you, man? Go look. Just go look, will you?"

Having the truth on his side emboldened George to say what he truly meant for once. "He doesn't want to. Because maybe everything happened exactly the way I said. Maybe he's *wrong*. And we can't have that."

George locked eyes with Bill, who held the gaze for a beat before snatching the flashlight from Curt and folding all six-foot-five-inches of himself into the front seat. The beam flitted about, illuminating parts of Bill's face, until he bent forward and the light was only a muted glow, casting weird shadows on the walls.

Of course Bill would be looking for some flaw in George's story.

Curt stood on tiptoe, trying to see in, nervous, bouncing from one foot to the other.

"You can look too, if you want," George said.

Curt wagged his head back and forth. "I believe you, man. I don't need to look. But Bill does."

Bill backed out of the car, closed the door, and opened the back seat door and squatted to investigate under the seats. Then he called out, "Can I borrow these tapes?"

George and Curt exchanged a baffled glance.

Bill backed out again and stood, his long arms draped over the door. "My car got broken into, and they stole all my music. Can I borrow these and dub them?"

"*That's* your reaction?" George said. "'Can I borrow your tapes?'"

"I acknowledge," Bill said, "that something horrible happened. You were right. I was wrong. Now can I borrow the fucking cassettes?"

"I guess," George said, his face flaring. How did Bill do that? How was he able to make an admission of error sound like an insult?

"Thanks." Bill dove inside again and the sound of tapes clacking together came from the back seat. Finally, Bill exited the car, George's cassette carrier under his arm, and closed the door.

They left the garage, the smell of loam and spring rising in the cool air. The earlier fog had gathered in the greening grass, which soaked George's socks as he secured the door padlock. Bill walked the cassette carrier to the Subaru parked out front as the other three trooped inside and huddled around the kitchen table, grim and silent.

"What's taking Bill so long?" Travis said. "Did he leave?"

Curt rose and looked out the kitchen window. "Nope. He's still out there."

"What the hell is he doing?"

Curt shrugged, looking annoyed, and sat back down.

A few minutes later, Bill came in through the front door and joined them in the kitchen.

"Hope we're not keeping you up or anything," Travis said to Bill, who smiled around at everyone as if he'd completely forgotten what was going on.

"Not at all," Bill said and waved his arm. "Please. Continue."

"We were waiting for *you*." Travis propped his elbows on the table and looked up at Bill, who lost his smile.

"Here's what I'm afraid of," George said. "What if I—I don't know if this absinthe made me...if I...set that fire. Or...did something to Stacia."

Silence saturated the room as it seemed to shrink. His friends regarded him with an intensity that nearabout strangled him, as if he lay on a metal table and they were dissecting him.

"You couldn't have," Curt said, shaking his head. "No way. You didn't hurt anyone."

"You're not a violent person," Travis said. "We all know that."

"And let's face it," Bill said, his face breaking into a nasty grin, "he's just not that ambitious."

Travis laughed.

"Bag your face, G-Ho," Curt said. Travis went straight-faced.

Now that everything was out on the table, George was able to crawl out of his own head. He sat looking at Bill, who he'd always thought was kind of funny-looking—with oversized everything, from his too-close-together hazel eyes to his gigantic loose-lipped mouth—and currently appeared to be winding up a month-long bender. He now resembled a middle-aged Depression-era hobo, his eyes glazy and smudged underneath with dark half-moons. George wasn't sure if he'd have recognized Bill on the street.

Travis hadn't changed a bit, on the other hand, and Curt, though largely the same, had grown his dark blond hair almost to his shoulders. At five-ten, Curt was the shortest of the four of them, with an athletic build and intense, bright blue eyes.

"The only logical conclusion," Bill said, "is this Stacia girl drugged you on purpose, to set you up for burning that house down."

This explanation would ease George's conscience, but he still wasn't convinced he hadn't done something horrible.

"Even if I didn't do anything to her, Stacia may have been inside that house when it blew up for all we know. And whose blood was all over me? It wasn't mine."

"We need to find out," Curt said. "Maybe the chick wanted to collect on insurance or something from the house. You say it was a dump, so maybe she couldn't sell it."

"But then why leave a shit-ton of coke in my car?" George threw his hands up.

"Maybe she dropped it by accident when she was planting evidence," Travis said.

Bill stood. "What's the name of the radio station there in Lawrence?"

George just stared, but Bill snapped his fingers. "Radio station?"

"KLZR," George said. Bill lifted the handset from the wall. He put it to his ear and dialed 411.

"What are you doing?" George asked, standing and going to Bill, who held up a hand.

"Relax," Bill snapped with such authority that George obeyed. As much as he was able at this point, anyway. Into the receiver Bill said, "Lawrence, Kansas, please." Silence. "KLZR."

Panic made George reach for the phone, but Bill turned away and covered the mouthpiece with his hand. "I'm not going to give them your name, nimrod," he said. He uncovered the mouthpiece and said into it, "Could you connect me, please? Thanks."

George went over to Curt. "What's he doing?"

"I don't know." Curt's expression was tense.

"Hi, there," Bill said into the phone, pitching his voice higher. "This is Carl Bender and I'm an intern with the *St. Louis Dispatch*. I got a tip about a house fire in Lawrence that happened a few hours ago."

Silence.

"Carl Bender?" Travis's eyebrows knit together. "Where'd you come up with that name?"

Bill placed his hand over the mouthpiece. "Quantum physicist," he said. He removed his hand and said, "It would help me a lot if—like I said, I'm an intern, and—any details you can share?"

More silence, and George's breathing quickened. He had to sit down.

Bill nodded, his eyebrows drawing together. His eyes shifted to Curt's and they took on a grave cast. "Really." His eyes turned toward George. "They give a description?"

George's heart played pinball in his chest. He plucked the Canadian Lord Calvert Blended Whiskey from the liquor cabinet, steadied himself against the counter, uncapped the bottle, and drank straight from it. He shouldn't have let Bill and Curt in the house. He cursed himself for allowing his very recognizable car to be seen on Main Street. But of course he knew why he had. He'd yearned to see the comforting, unchanging storefronts, the signs, the town's one blinking stoplight at the east end of downtown.

"Thanks for the information." Bill hung up the phone and sat back in his chair. He ran his hand through his hair.

George's vision went filmy.

Bill expelled a puff of breath. "No word on whether there were people in the house, but the neighbors said a white male, on the tall side, clean-shaven, no glasses, wavy hair—"

"*That's* why your hair is butched." Travis scrutinized him. "And why you're wearing your glasses."

"—was driving a blue or green '70s four-door sedan," Bill said. "Didn't catch the license plate. Said he had a gun and a gas can in his car."

"Why didn't he mention the coke or the knife?" Curt said.

"Law enforcement always holds back some evidence from the press," Travis said. "Helps them weed out false leads." He scrubbed his hand over the top of his crew cut. "There's only one thing to do."

"Right," George said. "Stay away from Lawrence."

"Go to the cops," Travis said simultaneously.

"What?" George said.

"You have to report this. You have information about a crime. This Stacia is involved, and you have to help them find her."

"You can't be serious." Curt tilted his head back. "So George, matching the exact description the witnesses gave, walks into the cop shop and says, 'It wasn't me. A mega-foxy magical sorority chick gave me sleeping potion and then within sixty minutes was able to plant a ton of evidence.' And I'm guessing every bit of it is covered in George's fingerprints."

"And if she's dead inside that house," Bill said, "they'll track her down soon enough."

Curt reached for the Lord Calvert and took a swallow. "And what if Stacia's alive and did all this on purpose like you said, Bill? And she put George's fingerprints on other evidence while he was passed out and planted it *out around* the car?"

Travis said, "What George needs to do is—"

"What George needs," Curt said, "is positive vibes."

Bill stood. "Be right back."

"Again?" Curt said. "You got the runs or what?"

CHAPTER TEN

Bill

In the bathroom, Bill dried his hands and looked at himself in the mirror. He was almost grateful to George because suddenly his own problems in contrast shrank to a manageable size.

When he returned to the kitchen, Curt was saying to Travis, "Give the man a break. He's been through a dramatic experience."

"*Trau*matic." Bill was more heckled than usual at Curt's malapropisms.

"Whatever. I think he needs to just *be* for a while, you know?"

Bill didn't want to hear any more non-sequitur Zen koans from this guy. He loved Curt, but why couldn't he shut the fuck up and let the adults sort this out?

"But the sooner George goes to the authorities," Travis said, "the better. Because even if they can't collar him for murder and arson, they can get him for aiding and abetting, obstruction of justice, destruction of evidence, leaving the scene of a crime, failure to report a crime—"

"Shut up, G-Ho," George snapped.

Travis's light blue eyes clouded. He withered a little then shored up his resolve. "Maybe you ought to consider what the *right* thing to do would be."

"Nobody wants to hear one of your Howdy-Doody American Way speeches." George's new nasty, sarcastic tone reminded Bill of…Bill.

"Hey," Bill said sharply. "G-Ho is trying to help you."

George's face took on an incredulous cast in response to Bill's disingenuous defense of Travis. Bill was usually the first to make fun of Travis's straight-arrow nature, but Travis eagerly jumped on the bandwagon.

"Yeah, George," he said. "When the cops track you down— and it is *when*, not if—you're going to be in a heap of trouble. You need to go *now*."

"I'll definitely take that into consideration," George said.

"Right." Bill crossed his arms tight. "I'm sure you will. Definitely."

The befuddlement on George's face was supremely satisfying, in a petty, childish way.

Bill cast his eyes to the ceiling. "And then again," he said, "you may blame the whole thing on me."

Curt shook his head in exasperation at Bill.

George's jaw got tight as a banjo string. Then he slammed his hands down on the table. "You've got to be fucking kidding me."

"That was thirteen years ago!" Curt said. "How many times does he have to apologize?"

Travis's head pivoted from face to face, evidently not remembering what Bill was referring to. Curt leaned toward him and said, "When George's folks busted him for pot, he said he was holding for Bill, remember? But he's apologized. Like forty-thousand times."

Bill waved his hand dismissively. "Nothing's changed."

"How would you know?" George said. "You don't know *anything* about me anymore."

Bill experienced a thrill of vindication. "Exactly. We don't know anything about you, and you don't know anything about us. Because you pop in and out of our lives whenever it's convenient. We're only your friends when you need something. Otherwise, we don't even exist for you."

George sputtered as he looked to the other two for support, but both Travis and Curt averted their eyes from him, to Bill's satisfaction.

"You'll always be my best friends," George said. "Always."

Bill opened his palms in mock surprise and let the hostility flow through his veins without resisting it. "So *that's* why you were a no-show at my wedding. Because I'm your best friend."

Curt snapped his fingers at Bill as though reprimanding a dog. "Stop."

Bill ignored Curt's repeated attempts to rein him in. Curt would not prevent him from saying what was on his mind. Not tonight.

George was flabbergasted. "I told you I was sick!"

"You weren't sick," Bill said. "You flaked. Like you always do. I had to eat the eighty bucks for your tuxedo!"

To be fair, Bill had never mentioned this to George before, but Bill was no longer interested in being fair, or even civil. Not anymore. He let his face display every ugly thought he was having.

Somewhere in his consciousness, the piece of him that stood apart and helplessly observed the insane things that Bill more and more frequently did, was impressed at George's self-control, speaking in measured tones. "I'll write you a check, okay?"

"Okay," Bill said, crossing his arms again.

"What the fuck, Bill?" Curt said. "You're going to make him write an eighty-dollar check for—"

"It's the principle," Bill said. "And I prefer cash."

George's face colored. Bill noted George's embarrassment, reveled in it, bathed in it, which adequately mitigated the horrified expressions of the other two.

"Now?" Travis said. "When George is in this pickle? You're going to make him pay *now*?"

"Not like my life is on the line or anything," George said. "Bill's eighty dollars is much more important than my fucking life."

"It's about integrity!" Bill said.

"Integrity?" Curt said. "We're talking about friendship here, we're talking about—"

"Face it, George," Bill said. "We're only with you now because we happened to see you driving down the street. You don't give a *shit* about us. I want my money."

The room was silent as George pulled out his wallet and removed four twenties, which he laid on the table.

Bill plucked the bills up, folded them, and put them in his pocket.

Curt stared at Bill, looking disconcerted and even a little frightened. He had to be wondering who this angry, resentful person who'd taken over Bill's body was. This angry person hadn't made an appearance at McWhiskey's earlier in the evening. It was George's fault. George brought out the worst in him, but Bill couldn't think too deeply about why.

Now that Bill had revved himself to full frenzy mode, the monster was loose and no way to call it back. The pent-up rage toward every person in his life, living and dead—toward his whole fucked-up life—overflowed and threatened to drown them all.

Curt rose and approached him, his hands out in supplication. "You need to calm down, man. What is up with you?"

Bill's fury blasted outward with hurricane force. "Back the fuck off!" he shouted and shoved Curt, pushed him hard enough that he fell on his ass and smacked his head against the cabinet doors. Curt didn't get up, just sat back against them. Bill stared at the palms of his hands, disbelieving, and then at the faces of George and Travis, both slack-jawed.

But he couldn't stop his mouth. It wasn't controlled by him

anymore. "None of this matters, George," he said. "Because this is the last time we'll see you for years, maybe ever. But I swear to God, if you take us down with you, I want to let it be known that—"

George shouted over him. "Why is everything you say a proclamation, as if every word that drips from your mouth is the most important thing anyone will ever hear? This isn't commencement and you're not valedictorian anymore, so cut the speeches!"

"Don't try to make this about me! You're the one who—" Bill flung his hands up. "You know what? You were right. I *don't* know you anymore. I don't even *want* to know you anymore." He headed toward the door.

"Bill. You guys have been friends for twenty-five years. That has to mean something to you." Curt's imploring tone tweaked Bill's conscience. But what little remained of it had no more power over him.

Bill stared at the other three, who stared back, accusing, as if they knew all about the trouble he was in, as if they knew all about his catastrophic choices. Could they see it, like a blazing red neon sign above his head? Bill had to leave now. Soon, everything would be fine.

"It has to mean something," Curt repeated.

He could feel it now, the tingle in the back of his gullet, and all else melted away. Bill turned, marched out of the kitchen, and through the front door.

Nobody tried to stop him.

CHAPTER ELEVEN

George

Saturday, May 24, 1986
Niobe, Kansas
8:42 a.m.

He was surrounded by flames. An irresistible, invisible power forced him to stab and stab, the force jarring his bones.

Blood everywhere, and it came to life and crawled up his arms to his neck, covering his face and rolling down his throat.

George woke up gasping and choking, sweat-covered, shuddering, the sheets damp, twisted, and flecked with blood. Half a minute passed before he understood the blood was his own. The dream had been so vivid, George had clawed at his arms and chest.

A dream? Or a memory? He slid on his glasses and glanced at the bedside digital clock, which read 8:42. Travis and Curt had left only four and a half hours ago. He lay back on the sweat-stained pillow, willing his heart to slow.

In the midst of the slide show of the previous twenty-four hours playing on an endless loop in his mind, George puzzled over Bill's blatant animosity toward him. It wasn't like Bill had gone out of his way to keep in touch with George, and he'd never expressed any anger over the eighty bucks. Why now? He couldn't help but worry that Bill would carry that animosity to the extreme by calling the Lawrence cops and turning him in.

If he kept thinking about all these things, he was going to lose his mind, so he got out of bed and used the toilet. Then he called his answering machine at his apartment in Lawrence. Luckily, for Christmas his folks had given him one of the newfangled ones you could call from another phone. He'd never actually used this function before, and at the time he thought it was a little over the top. But now he saw the wisdom in it, because he could listen to any messages left and return them as if he were still living his regular life.

He dialed the machine's number, entered the code, and heard the beep. He had two messages, both from a very angry Patty. Since George wouldn't be going to law school after all, no point in returning her calls.

He went back to the bathroom and got ready to shower. As he reached to turn on the water, he heard a key in the lock of the side door.

"Damn it, G-Ho," George called, turning the water off and wrapping a towel around himself. "I told you to knock."

"Hello?" It was a man's voice, but not Travis's.

George couldn't make himself answer.

"Who's in there?"

He stuck his head out of the bathroom door.

"Am I in the right house?" the voice said.

"It's me, Freddie," George said.

His cousin Freddie Baumann strutted into view, wearing a red JC Penney Le Tigre Polo-shirt knockoff, khakis, and Keds, his fluffy brown hair blow-dried to perfection. His baby face hadn't changed since toddlerhood, still round and soft and jawless. He'd been adorable then, but adorable was not a good look on a grown man, with his button nose sprinkled with freckles. He was eight years younger than George and a junior at Washburn University in Topeka.

Freddie's smile was huge. "George! What are you doing here? Haven't seen you since, what? Grandpop's funeral?"

"That's right," George said. He tried to think if there was anything in the house here that Freddie shouldn't see, but all the incriminating objects were locked out in the garage. He feared that somehow Freddie would figure out something was not right. He could not be here now, not during this crisis.

"How'd you get in?" Freddie said. He hung a garment bag from the top of the door jamb into the guest room.

"I have a key." George tucked his towel tighter around his hips and exhaled, trying to sound casual. "What brings you to the big city of Niobe?"

"I decided spending the summer in this podunk shithole

was better than having Mom breathing down my neck for three months."

A flush covered George like a bodysuit, his blood pressure rising.

Freddie knew just how to rile George up, disdainfully referring to him as his country cousin. He now looked George up and down. "Yeah, Dad got me a job at his friend's company in Salina."

Oh, hell. "Seriously?" George said. "You're staying here? At the house and driving to Salina every day? It's forty-five minutes away."

"Yeah, but I'll have the house to myself." Freddie focused on George again. "Dad didn't tell me you'd be here."

"It was a spur-of-the-moment thing." George pushed up his glasses, which were fogging up. "Yeah, I forgot to call your dad, but I'd rather my folks didn't know I was here. Or your dad, for that matter. You understand. I needed some time away—"

"Time away from what?" Freddie said. "Not like you're in school or anything, right? Last I knew you were a trash collector or something like that."

Freddie had idolized George as a grade-school kid visiting from Wichita in the summers. Back then he didn't know enough to be contemptuous of his small-town kin. And George had taken advantage of the hero worship, sending him on errands, but also taking him to the movies and the county fair. Freddie seemed to have forgotten the good things George had done but would never forget the other stuff.

"I'm not a trash collector. I'm a supervisor for a janitorial company."

"Same diff," Freddie said. "Anyway. I'll just give Dad a quick call."

George's adrenaline spiked so hard he was afraid it would knock the towel off him. "I'd consider it a favor if you didn't," George said, trying for an offhand tone. "He'll tell my mom. You know how they are."

Freddie's eyes narrowed, and his lips curved in a devious smile. "Remember when I was a kid and you were always making me wash your car and go downtown and buy you pop and stuff like that?"

"But I also took you horseback riding and to the pool, as I recall."

"I'll make you a deal," Freddie said. "I'll let you stay here, and I won't tell Dad if you do a couple of things for me."

Good God. George didn't have time for this. He forced a smile. "Sure, cousin. I'm happy to help."

"Could you get the rest of my gear out of my car?" Freddie dug in his pocket and pulled out his keyring, held it up, then tossed it.

George reflexively caught it, and gawked at the keys then at Freddie, who stood grinning at him.

"And after that, if you could clean the trash out of the front seat, that would be the jam."

If he protested, Freddie would call his dad, and Uncle Howard would tell George's folks. The more people who knew where he was hiding, the more likely the word would spread, and he'd be discovered.

"Will you at least let me put on some pants first?"

"Sure, cuz," Freddie said, beneficent. "No hurry."

After George got dressed, he found Freddie sitting in Grandpop's chair, his feet up, flipping through the TV channels. "Car's out front," he called.

George went out the door and there sat a black 1986 Camaro IROC-Z, brand new, no doubt bought and paid for by Uncle Howard.

George lugged in Freddie's suitcases and golf bag.

"You can move your stuff to the spare room."

George did and then went back to the bathroom, sweaty and even more ready for a shower.

He ran the tub water and switched on the radio which was tuned to KSAL in Salina. He was in college before he understood how uniquely Elvis this bathroom was. Equipped with a radio, a clock, and a wall phone with notepad and pencil attached to the side of it, he imagined they would have put a TV in there if they'd had room.

"I Wanna Be a Cowboy" by Boys Don't Cry issued from the tinny speaker and cross-faded into a commercial. Cheesy, perky music, much louder than the novelty song, blasted forth as he undressed.

"Have you always dreamed of traveling the US? Do you have a flair for the creative? Are you adventurous and flexible? Would you like to earn up to one thousand dollars a week?"

81

That last question focused George's attention.

A thousand dollars a week? That was twice what he made as a janitorial supervisor. He turned off the water. K-Mart was holding interviews in Salina the next weekend for traveling portrait photographers.

George took hold of the handy pencil attached to the paper pad and scribbled down the number the announcer repeated twice.

He experienced a shiver of excitement and coincidence. He remembered Patty's mention of his failed aspiration to be Annie Liebowitz. How he never followed through with anything.

He would follow through right-the-fuck now.

He called and set an interview for 2:30 the following Saturday afternoon. This was a sign. His interest in photography would become more than a passive pursuit. He'd always wanted to travel, and the company rep said the territory he'd cover included the Dakotas, Nebraska, Kansas, Oklahoma, and east Texas. He'd be on the move all the time, driving from little town to little town, snapping portraits in K-Marts with a portable studio.

He could do this until things chilled out, until the authorities caught Stacia or whoever the real perps behind the house fire were. Then he could go to law school if he still felt like it.

But he might not feel like it.

And best of all, the people in Lawrence who'd set him up wouldn't know where he was.

After he showered and dressed, he went into the living

room where Freddie was still lounging on the easy chair and watching TV. As George sat on the divan, Freddie said, "I made you a list." He held it out. "I need you to pick up some things from the IGA for me."

George stared at the notebook paper in Freddie's hand.

Freddie waved it. "Here you go."

George snatched it out of his hand and stalked out of the house to the back yard and got in the Corvette. Just starting the car up made him feel better, feeling the power beneath him, and he drove the two blocks carefully to the IGA. He parked and got out, and spied Travis across the street, holding the hand of a sturdy little tow-headed boy.

George got out of the Vette and walked toward them.

Travis's face lit up. "George! This is AJ. My fiancée's son."

The boy clutched Travis's pant leg, his lips curled over his teeth in bashfulness, never taking his eyes from the Corvette. This was as rare a sight in Niobe as the Concorde.

"AJ, this is George, one of my best friends in the whole world. Now, remember how I taught you."

The boy looked away from the car and timidly held out his right hand. "It's nice to meet you, Mr. George."

"Just George." He shook the small, chubby hand. "Nice to meet you, too. How old are you?"

"Five," AJ said, holding up his hand, looking at the fingers as if counting them to make sure he was right.

"AJ's named after his dad. Andy Junior. He was K-I-L-L-E-D in a C-A-R W-R-E-C-K."

"Wow," George said. "That sucks."

Travis looked George up and down. "You look rode hard and put away wet, pard. How you doing today?"

"Had nightmares."

"Guess what?" AJ piped suddenly. "Travis is going to be my new daddy." Matter-of-factly, eyes back on the Corvette.

"Is that right? How do you feel about that?"

"It's good. After they have their married, we're going to Disneyland."

George looked at Travis, who smiled and shrugged.

"When's the big day?"

"August tenth," Travis said. "The weekend of our class reunion. Can't believe it's been ten years. Figured it would be easier to get everyone together that way."

"Good thinking," George said, but then he deflated. He had no idea where he'd be when the wedding took place. Dead? In prison? If he got the photographer job, he'd be somewhere out on the road. Though Travis had made no mention of the fact that George hadn't showed up to Bill's wedding, he would probably end up doing the same thing to Travis. He'd just have a legitimate reason this time.

The little boy squatted down to watch hose water run down the gutter from up the street. Travis straightened. "I gotta take this kid home then head to work, so I'll check you later, okay?"

"Sounds good," George said and watched Travis show AJ how to look both ways before crossing the street.

When George was done shopping, he piled the bags into the

Corvette's tiny trunk. He didn't want to go back to the house just yet, so he decided he might as well make the pilgrimage.

He drove to the west end of town and through the gates of the Niobe cemetery.

The day after tomorrow was Memorial Day, and this place would be packed with respect-payers, the American Legion, and the VFW guys putting on their annual parade. But today, he was the only visitor. He walked over the hill to the Baumann plots where Grandpop and Grandgum were buried. Then he hiked a little way farther to the north-east edge.

As a high school junior, he'd got drunk one spring night at a Far Roadside party and wandered away. According to Bill and Curt, they searched for him for the better part of an hour. They'd found him here, shouting incoherently and trying to push the twins' headstones over. George didn't remember any of this. Curt only told him after George asked repeatedly over the next week why his hands were scraped up. But they'd never given him any grief over it.

Now he contemplated the twin stones, side by side, four feet tall, chiseled marble, nearly identical, like the brothers buried beneath them.

Victor James Engle and Chad Alexander Engle. Both were carved with *1949-1971. Son, brother, friend* beneath their names.

He sat down on the grass and told them everything.

CHAPTER TWELVE

Curt

Sunday, May 25, 1986
Saw Pole, Kansas
10:30 a.m.

Curt opened his eyes to a tapping at the front door and the sight of the back of Gracie's tousled blonde head on the pillow next to him. He slipped out of bed so as not to awaken her and quietly shut the bedroom door. Curt stepped over the dog, who was snoring softly in a square of sunlight on the carpet, then peered out the shade that covered the window in the door. Blake Emerson, one of the engineers who worked on the project across the road for Sorazin-Hesper-Atkins, stood there talking to…a chick. Long, dark curly hair. Raybans. Button-down shirt. Who was this?

He almost opened the door before realizing he was nude. Fortunately, last night's clothes were piled in the living room.

He pulled on his jeans, socks, and boots before opening the door.

"Hey! Blake! What's the latest? And...who's this?"

Emerson grinned. "Curt, this is my colleague Rita Pavlakis." He shook Curt's hand then turned to the girl and said, "This is Curt Dekker."

"Hi," she said to Curt. "I was beginning to think you didn't exist."

Curt's forehead knotted up. "What?"

"Yeah, I've been hearing about you for a year and a half around the office in Topeka, and you started to sound like Big Foot or the Loch Ness Monster or Michael Jackson or something."

"Michael Jackson?" Curt echoed.

"You never see Michael and LaToya together, do you? One of them is a myth."

"What?"

"Can we come in?" Emerson said.

"The place is kind of a mess." Curt looked over his shoulder then pointed to the picnic table. "Why don't we talk out in the yard?" He did not want Gracie wandering out of the bedroom in nothing but her altogether while he had guests.

Emerson and Rita descended the stoop stairs. They congregated at the picnic table in the shade of the largest oak tree on what was left of Curt's property. Emerson and Rita seated themselves opposite each other, and Curt sat next to Rita. Normally he'd sit way too close, but she'd knocked him off his game with that weird comment about Michael Jackson and questioning Curt's existence and all. Who talked like that? No one he knew.

"Just wanted to let you know we're breaking ground on the next phase of the project across the way there," Emerson said, "and Rita will be here all week for it. I told her if she has any questions about the area or needs a friendly word, you're the guy to see."

Curt was surprised at this. He wasn't sure anyone had ever recommended him as a guide before. "I'll give you more than a friendly word," Curt said.

"We're also running some night tests between ten p.m. and one a.m. on the other side of the facility, about a half mile back."

"Right," Curt said. "The part you won't let me see."

"It's not that we won't let you see it," Emerson said. "There's nothing to see."

"Right." Curt drew the word out. "What kind of tests?"

"It's pretty technical, nothing to worry about. You probably won't even notice. Maybe some lights, some vibration, what have you. Totally safe. We'll be conducting most of them when you're asleep most likely."

"I stay up pretty late," Curt said.

"Curt?" Gracie stood at the window covering her nakedness with a t-shirt clutched in front of her. "What's going on out there?"

Curt sighed and rolled his eyes at Emerson. He made a megaphone of his hands. "I've got some visitors. Don't worry about it."

She disappeared from view.

Rita smirked.

"Didn't know you had company." Emerson grinned and stood. "We'll get out of your hair."

Rita rose from the table. "Nice to meet you. Sorry for... interrupting."

"You didn't interrupt anything." Curt kept a straight face.

Her smile was impish. "Come on, Blake. We've got work to do." To Curt, she said, "See you."

"Have a good," Curt said and raised a hand.

Emerson stopped. "A good what?"

"Your choice." Curt climbed the steps and opened the front door. "There you go, dog."

The tired old Basset hound gave a mournful sigh and slowly ticked down the stairs, surveying the ground as if deciding whether to dirty his paws.

Rita and Emerson made it to the edge of the lawn before stopping and Curt overheard Rita animatedly telling a story.

Curt went inside and left the door open for the dog.

Rita's voice drifted in from the open door and windows. "... Got a call from the chapter president of my sorority..."

Curt opened the fridge, eying the Tupperware containers inside. Ever since the fight with his dad, his five sisters traded off bringing him meals once a week.

Gracie came down the hall and paused in the doorway. She'd put on Curt's Jerry Doucette concert t-shirt and, he guessed, nothing else. She stood there, smoking a cigarette.

"What's your dog's name?"

"I don't know." He shut the fridge. He didn't want to delay Gracie's departure any longer than necessary. He was itching to split to the barn and start painting. "You remember John Blackwell? When he left town, he asked me to look after the dog for the next two-to-five."

Gracie laughed.

"He told me the dog's name, but I forgot it," Curt went on. "It's a Grateful Dead tune title."

"...Car accident?" came Emerson's voice from the edge of the yard.

Curt put his hands in his pockets and trained his eyes on his boots. "I gotta go into town, so, you know, later days."

"You gotta go, like, right now?" Gracie tossed her cigarette into the sink, slunk over to him, and placed her hand on his belt buckle.

"Murdered." Rita's voice wafted in from the yard.

Gracie kissed Curt's neck as her hands wandered southward.

"Inside the sorority house?" Emerson said.

Gracie began unbuckling Curt's belt as she kissed him. Blood rushed to his groin.

"No," Rita said. "...off campus..."

Gracie unzipped his fly.

"...must have turned on the gas before setting the fire, because the water heater blew the whole house up."

Blew the house up? Curt's head jerked toward the door,

knocking against Gracie's.

"Hey," she said sharply, pulling his chin toward her. "Am I boring you?"

"Shut up, will you?"

"'Shut up'?" Gracie said. "You don't tell me to shut up, you—"

"Listen," Curt said, pushing her hands away and buckling his belt. "They're talking about a murder out there."

She placed both her hands on his buckle again. "And I'm trying to—"

Curt batted her hands away and zipped up his jeans, then ran out the front door, down the steps, and straight up to Rita.

"Where did this happen?" he said.

Rita and Emerson both startled at his sudden appearance.

Emerson said, "Where did what—"

"I'm talking to *you*," Curt said to Rita. "Where did this house blow up?"

She smiled and her eyebrows rose above her sunglasses. "Were you listening in on—"

"Curt!" Gracie's voice sailed across the yard from the front door. "What the hell are you—"

Curt shouted over his shoulder, "Will you give me one fucking minute?" He turned back to Rita. "Please," he said, "tell me where this happened. What you were talking about. The house that blew up. Where did this happen?"

"If you don't come back in this trailer this second, I'm going to—"

Curt whirled around. "Gracie. Go home." He turned back to

Rita, who drew back, lips tightened in the face of Curt's intensity.

"I'm so stupid," Gracie said, slamming the door. Curt listened to her run into his room and loudly gather up her things.

Curt grabbed Rita's shoulders. "Tell me! Where did this happen?"

Emerson took a step toward Curt, who released his grip on Rita. He realized he'd been squeezing too hard. Emerson backed off again but kept a concerned eye on him.

"It was in Lawrence," Rita stammered. "A couple of miles from the KU campus."

Curt's heart constricted. He took a breath, trying to calm down. "You said someone was murdered. Who was murdered?"

"Three of my sorority sisters."

"Three girls?" Curt said. "Are you sure?"

"Yes."

"When?"

"Friday night," Rita said. "It happened Friday night."

Curt raked his hands through his hair, chilled down to his socks. "Do you know their names?" He heard the sharpness of his voice, saw the effect it had on Emerson and Rita, but he had to know. Three dead girls. In Lawrence. Friday night.

Murdered.

When Rita didn't answer, Curt said, "Was one of them Stacia?"

Her face changed. "Stacia? Stacia Visser?"

The emotion that overcame Curt was unnamable, jumbled, confused. Rita knew this girl who ruined George's life.

And what did that mean?

"I don't know her last name, but…"

They stared at each other.

"How do you know her?" Rita said, frowning at him from behind her sunglasses.

"Is she one of the girls who was murdered?" Curt said.

Why was Rita looking at Curt like that?

Gracie burst through the front door and down the steps.

Everyone turned toward her. She stood quivering and red-eyed. "You…are such…an asshole!" she shouted, then got into her car. Her tires kicked up dust as she pulled out onto the county road.

Emerson grimaced and Rita gaped as they watched the Toyota speed away.

"Yeah, well," Curt said. He addressed Rita again. "Thank you for telling me. Sorry I was so—and sorry for all the—"

"Wait," Rita said. "You need to explain—"

"I gotta go."

He trotted to the Jeep, swung up into the seat, started it, and peeled out of there.

The image he'd been carrying in his mind of the burning house in Lawrence filled in like a paint-by-number.

It now included three murdered sorority girls.

Murdered while George sat passed out in his car across the street.

Curt couldn't shake the feeling that Rita had been talking about the murders loud enough for him to hear…on purpose.

And when he mentioned Stacia's name, the look on Rita's face reminded him of something.

What was it?

And then it came to him. It was that moment in the mystery movie when the suspect blurts out something that he wouldn't know if he wasn't involved in the crime.

Which means I know something I'm not supposed to know, and I told it to someone who shouldn't know that I know what I know.

But Rita wasn't a cop. Couldn't be. There'd be no reason for her to go undercover. They had plenty of evidence to just swoop in and arrest George.

And that could only mean one thing. Whoever was behind all this sent Rita down here to smoke George out.

Or assassinate him.

CHAPTER THIRTEEN

Bill

Sunday, May 25, 1986
Hays, Kansas
11:25 a.m.

Bill maneuvered Liz's Subaru into a parking space in his apartment complex lot in Hays.

He'd come home a day early because a miracle had happened. A solution to his problems had presented itself. It was a dirty solution, but you couldn't pick and choose. Now he could move all the money back to its proper account first thing Tuesday morning, and Liz would be none the wiser.

He sat in the Subaru psyching himself up to go into the apartment. He got out of the car and slung his backpack over his shoulder but left the cassette carrier in the car. After Liz went to bed tonight, he'd sneak back down and collect it.

He climbed the stairs to the second floor, unlocked the door, and went inside, where he found Liz sitting on the couch, arms and legs crossed. Waiting for him.

He'd hoped she wouldn't be home. But where would she be, since he had her car?

Bill swallowed. Couldn't take it any longer and averted his eyes. Or tried to. They landed instead on three suitcases lined up opposite the sofa.

"Did you really think I wouldn't find out?"

"About what?" Bill stalked into the kitchen to avoid making eye contact.

"I went to the bank on Friday—"

This curdled Bill's blood.

"—and what do you suppose I discovered?"

"What?" But of course, he knew.

"*Four thousand dollars* missing. They told me this was the third time you'd cashed out one of the municipal bonds my parents gave us as a wedding gift."

He stood gazing at the curling snapshots on the refrigerator of him and Liz in happier days. How could he finesse this? "It was going to be a surprise. I was going to—"

"Where did it go, Bill?"

"I was telling you—"

"The question was rhetorical. I'm very aware of where it went." She sniffed dramatically.

He couldn't respond, but he also couldn't stand in the kitchen all day. He came out and sat on the recliner, trying to compose his expression into the picture of innocence and good intentions.

And then like manna from heaven an explanation fell from the sky and into his brain.

"George is having some legal difficulties, and he needed the money for a lawyer." He studied her face. Would she buy it?

"He's going to pay us back," Bill went on, warming to the fiction, "in the next couple of weeks. I'm sorry I didn't mention it, but I didn't want to worry you with the—"

"That sounds plausible, but I can't believe a word you say anymore."

Bill snatched up the phone receiver and thrust it out. "Call him. He'll tell you. He'll want to thank you, I'm sure."

He prayed she wouldn't take the phone from him, and now he saw that his hand was shaking as he held it out.

Liz waved him off, and he gratefully replaced the handset in its cradle.

"It's not just the money," she said. "I told you I'd leave you the next time you brought drugs into this apartment. And you promised—you swore on your father's grave, as I recall—you'd never do it again. Remember? I made you write it down." She brandished a scrap of paper covered with his own mathematician's scrawl.

The neurotic file-clerk hamster in his brain chittered and clawed through his mind, searching for the incident she was referring to. "But I didn't bring—"

She held up a silencing hand. "Just—don't, okay?" She sighed, a long-suffering sound that raked fingernails down the chalkboard of his frayed psyche. "Before you left for Niobe. I saw you standing in front of our apartment building scoring from a guy in a *Rabbit* in broad daylight, children going by on bicycles—"

"That was one of my students and he was—"

Liz raised her voice and talked over him. "Turning in a paper. Right."

Oh. He'd used that one already. Balls.

"I've frozen our accounts."

"Frozen…our accounts?" *What fresh hell is this?*

"Not one more dollar will go to your dealer. Not one more cent. I'm done with all that, pretending I don't know why you withdraw a hundred dollars at a time."

"That's *my* money," Bill said. "Yours and mine, I mean. Our money, and I need—"

"I'm not going to contribute toward your gradual suicide. No more. I'll give you an allowance for food and gas, but you will have no access to *our* money until you get help."

"Baby," Bill said. "The pressure's off. Semester's over. I swear to you that—"

"How do you manage to lure me into the same circular conversation every time we need to discuss anything important?" Liz's face became a torment of suppressed tears, anger, hurt, and even bewilderment that she was now in this situation, a place she'd no doubt never imagined she'd end up. "There's no point in talking to you. That poison you jam up your nose has liquefied your brain. You can't hear me anymore. It's like you're in a glass jar, and I'm outside with my hair on fire, yelling 'Help!' and you're going, 'What? What?'"

Thank you, Sylvia Plath. Sarcasm would not serve him here, so he swallowed the retort. "I hear what you're saying. I've been preoccupied with publishing and you've taken the brunt of—"

"You've got two choices. Either you go into rehab, and I mean today, or I'm gone."

Bill couldn't respond. Rehab was out of the question. The word itself felt like an oversized lead sinker in his gut.

He studied her face and tried to remember what had brought them together in the first place. A vague, faraway vision of two people, a couple, emerged. One of them was trapped inside a bell jar, but he wasn't sure which one.

"So you're leaving me," he said.

"That all depends on you. I won't wait forever."

He inhaled. Exhaled. "I don't have a drug problem."

She held up a hand. "Your drug *addiction* is only a symptom of the root problem, which is clinical depression you refuse to address or even acknowledge. But rehab is a start."

He defaulted to the last resort: trying to squeeze out tears. But he was so dehydrated nothing happened, and he probably looked like he was taking a shit right there in the living room. "I'm going to be better. No more drugs. I swear."

She said in a quavering voice, "Just say yes, Bill."

"I don't need rehab," he said. "I need *you.*" *And access to your money.* The thought slipped through the gate before he could stop it, afraid it would show on his face.

She rose and strode out the door, slamming it behind her.

Bill noted with gloating satisfaction she'd left her suitcases. She'd be back. It was a bluff. They were empty. He went to pick one of them up, but he couldn't.

Good bluff.

But then, with horror, he remembered the cassette carrier was in her car. He ran to the window and gaped down at Liz backing the Subaru out and driving away.

He tried to remain calm. She'd be back. She hadn't taken her suitcases. She'd be back.

But…what if she opened the carrier and found the mammoth bag of coke he'd stolen from George's car?

CHAPTER FOURTEEN

George

Sunday, May 25, 1986
Niobe, Kansas
Noon

George stood in the dining room ironing Freddie's white shirts, the steam fogging his glasses, while he suppressed the dangerous desire to burn each and every one. But he had to play along if he wanted to stay hidden. A car approached, its brakes squealing as it came to an abrupt halt, and then footfalls on the walk followed by urgent knocking on the front door.

He pulled the window shade aside and saw Curt's Jeep. What now?

George opened the door and Curt burst inside.

"Three dead girls," Curt said, breathless.

This drew George up short. "What?"

"In that house. In Lawrence. Three *sorority* girls. Murdered.

Fucking murdered, George, in that house you watched burn."

George slapped his hand over Curt's mouth so hard it stung. "Shut up," he hissed.

Curt tried to wrench the hand from his face, but George shoved him toward the front door and through it. Then he let go of Curt and yanked the door closed behind them.

"My cousin is here for the summer," George whispered. "Didn't you see the IROC-Z out front?"

"How would I know whose it is?"

George trudged out to the curb and turned back toward the house. Had the little brat overheard? His face didn't appear in the front windows, so maybe he hadn't.

"Why is he here? Where is he?"

"He's in my grandparents' room." George told him about Freddie's summer job in Salina and his blackmail to keep George's presence a secret. "If he hears this, he'll have even more ammunition, and who knows what the hell he'll do," George said. "Sorry for smacking you in the mouth, by the way."

Curt waved him off. "Let's walk down the street. I'll tell you what I found out."

When they were far enough from the house, Curt relayed a conversation with some girl named Rita, and George's legs went wobbly.

"And," Curt wound up, "this Rita Pavlakis knows—knew— knows Stacia."

"Wait—what?"

"Crazy, right?"

Someone who knew Stacia was here in Niobe County. In Saw Pole, not fifteen miles from here. What were the odds that it was a coincidence?

Very few of the twenty-seven thousand students who attended KU had ever even heard of Niobe County, much less tiny little Saw Pole. It wasn't even on some state maps. Most small-town kids who did go to college went to K-State. KU was for the Kansas City and St. Louis kids. George had been the only one out of fifty-four graduating seniors from Niobe High who'd enrolled at KU. An acute compulsion to run overtook him.

"Are they friends?" George said. "Did Stacia send Rita out here? Did Rita follow me somehow?"

"That's what I was wondering too," Curt said. "Did you notice anyone tailing you the night you got here?"

"I was so out of it after I beat the train, she could have been sitting next to me in my car the whole way for all I know."

"I wonder if you should be staying here, man. Maybe you ought to go on down to your folks' in Havasu."

George attempted to form words, but nothing happened. He didn't know how much more punishment his nerves could take, how many more shocks to the system before he disappeared in a puff of smoke. He rubbed the sides of his face then looked at his hands, remembering the blood on them, and shuddered.

They were silent for several moments, and George looked across the street to the east at the post office, and then at Niobe's Carnegie Library on the north corner.

His hands trembled as he reached for the cigarette pack in his pocket and attempted to remove one but couldn't seem to complete the required fine motor movements, and he finally gave up. "What am I going to do?" He was bone-weary, and his eyes burned.

"Hell if I know," Curt said. "Should we call Bill? He usually kind of takes over, right? We should call him."

That's all George needed—more vitriol from Bill. "After the other night? I don't think so. What we need is more information." He glanced down the street at the library again. "They have newspapers over there, right?"

Curt nodded. "Let's check it out."

"You can't go in there with no shirt on," George said. He took off the long-sleeved shirt that covered his t-shirt and handed it over.

Curt shrugged and pulled the shirt on but didn't button up.

They jogged down the uneven sidewalk, the movement starting up George's circulation again, to the apricot-colored limestone building on the corner. He took the cement steps two at a time and held the front entrance door for Curt.

"Hey, Curt," the librarian called. She was in her early twenties, a solid, freckled brunette wearing brown Sears and Roebuck polyester.

"Hey, Shelly," Curt said. "We need—"

"Got in those books you ordered." The librarian reached under the information desk and came up with two heavy-looking tomes, and George read the titles: *Laser Weapons in*

Space: Policy and Doctrine by Keith B. Payne and *Advanced Weapons Systems: An Annotated Bibliography of the Cruise Missile, MX Missile, Laser and Space Weapons, and Stealth Technology* by Brian Champion, which she laid on the counter.

George glanced from the books to Curt, who looked… sheepish? So many questions circled George's sore brain that he couldn't even put words to them. But this was not the time to ask them.

Instead, he said to Shelly, "Where are the newspapers?"

"Right over here," she said, leisurely strolling out from behind the counter.

Curt collected his books and trailed her and George to the stack of papers. George took the *Star* and *Times*, and Curt gathered up the *Lawrence Journal-World* and the *Wichita Eagle-Beacon*.

They sat on either side of a laminate table smelling of erasers and resin, and George checked the Times first. He found nothing, which wasn't surprising since the Times was a morning paper. The May 24 issue of the evening *Kansas City Star* was emblazoned with this headline: *Lawrence House Fire Cover-up For Execution-Style Murders, Police Say.*

Execution-style?

The air surrounding George seemed to grow thin and cold. His lungs compressed at the lack of oxygen and his vision began to blur.

Execution-style murders were organized crime, international cartel, mafia shit. What exactly had he stumbled into here?

He must have made some sort of noise because Curt looked up from his papers. "What did you find?"

George spun the paper so Curt could read the headline.

Curt's eyes got wide. "Holy shit," he whispered.

George took the paper back and kept reading.

The subtitle of the article was *Murder Victims Identified As Sorority Sisters.*

A shockwave ran through the city of Lawrence today as police announced the identities of the southeast Lawrence murder victims. The three Zeta Gamma Rho sorority sisters were last seen at a fundraiser Saturday morning.

The victims were identified as Jennifer Rickart, 20, of Deerfield, IL, Michelle Wilkes, 19, of Concordia, KS, and Kimberly Laurent, 25, of St. Louis. (For more on the victims, please see p. 1B.)

Execution-style murders. Sorority girls. These two things did not go together. But at least Stacia wasn't one of the dead girls.

Stacia wasn't one of the dead girls.

What did that mean?

But then his eyes were drawn back to the name Kimberly Laurent. There was a Laurent family in Niobe, but she wasn't one of them. They were a family of all boys.

George turned the paper to section B. Above the fold was a picture of two girls, arms around each other's shoulders, holding red plastic cups, their mouths open in laughter, their eyes alight. They were flawlessly beautiful, like so many of the Greek girls he'd seen and known over ten years. George viewed the bright spring day out the window. His eyes stung with the glaring light. Why were these three girls murdered execution-style? They were way too young to be involved in anything that would get them murdered. This had to be a mistake, or a pissed-off boyfriend who wanted it to look like something else.

George inhaled deeply and unfolded the paper to the second half of the story.

And got the shock of his life.

He stared at a college graduation picture of the third victim. Stars began to swim in front of the black-and-white image of Kimberly Laurent, 25, of St. Louis.

"George? George!"

The tabletop beneath the paper smashed into his forehead.

CHAPTER FIFTEEN

Curt

"Is he having a fit or something?" Shelly asked.

"He's all right, Shel." Curt stepped between her and George. "Don't worry. Sorry about the ruckus."

"Should I call an ambulance?"

"Naah. He's fine. He's coming around. Thanks."

Shelly reluctantly returned to the information desk but kept watching them.

George's eyes fluttered and then he sat up.

"You okay?" Curt whispered.

George stabbed a finger at a portrait in the newspaper. "I know her. I know her!"

"Will you mellow out? We don't want Shelly coming over here again."

George whispered, "I know her."

"Who?"

George licked his lips, turned the paper to face Curt and

laid his index finger on the black and white picture. "Kimberly Laurent. One of the—the victims."

"For real?" Curt as good as barked out, and Shelly peered at them again. Curt got goosebumps at the coincidence that just couldn't be coincidence.

"Yeah. The article says she was a graduate student at the J School, and that's where I know her from. This girl was in class with me my last semester at KU, back in '81. She was a junior that year, and I remember because I asked her if she was related to—"

"The Laurents in Niobe," Curt said.

"Yup. But she isn't. Wasn't."

"You sure it's the same girl?"

"No question. I remembered the name, but also . . . I mean, look at her. You don't forget a face like that."

Curt agreed. The girl was a fox.

"You think this Kimberly Laurent is the reason you're being framed or set up or whatever? Did you date her?" Curt knew the answer but asked all the same.

"Hell, no!"

"Did you ask her out? Follow her home or anything?"

"I hardly said three words to the girl."

"But you were acquaintances. That's why Stacia framed you. Somehow she knew that you took a class with Kimberly, that there was a connection."

"But…how could she know? That class I had with Kimberly was five years ago. None of this makes any sense, and what was

Kimberly Laurent doing at that house on Friday night anyway?"

"What were any of them doing there?" Curt said. "Buying dope, of course." He lowered his voice. "Remember that colossal bag of blow?"

George swung his head in disagreement. "No way."

"Why, because they were sorority girls? They do drugs like the rest of us."

"No, that's not why. Kimberly was as straight as the day is long. Super-ambitious, smart, totally wanting to take on the world."

"I thought you said you didn't talk to her?"

George's face reddened. "No, I didn't talk to her. I listened to her. You know. Talking to other people."

"That's a little creepy, George."

"Anyway." George took his glasses off and polished them on his shirttail. "I don't know about the other two, but no way *she* was involved in drugs. That's all I'm saying."

"So why was she there?"

"I don't know. But something else has been bothering me. If Stacia took the time and trouble to put all that evidence in my car to frame me not only for the fire but for these three murders with the intention of turning me in to the police...why hasn't she yet?"

"I've got this horrible feeling that the girl who told me about all this—that Rita girl—might be in town to—I don't know, either take you in or take you out."

"Seriously? You think she's a hit-man?" George looked skeptical.

Curt felt a zing of irritation. This was a perfectly reasonable possibility. "Why, because she's a girl? It's looking like Stacia's the one who killed those three girls, blew the house up, and planted the evidence in your car. If a girl can do that, a girl can be a hit-man. Hit-woman. Hit-human."

"But why would she be posing as an engineer on a construction project out in the middle of nowhere? And how would she know that you and I know each other? It's too convoluted and coincidental even for you. And if she were a hit-woman, she probably wouldn't waste her time posing—she'd do the fucking job and motate the hell out of here as soon as possible."

"Okay, so maybe she's not a hit-woman. But I'm telling you, she knows something. I could tell by the way she was acting. Maybe she's trying to figure out how much we know, if we're liabilities. I'll tell you this. I'm going to find out what she's up to."

George stood. "I've got to get out of here."

"I hear you, man. I want to make some copies of these articles before I go. I'll meet you back at your grandparents' house."

George staggered out and Curt stood at the copier and copied the related articles in the *Star*, the *Journal-World*, and the *Eagle-Beacon*. When he was done, he stacked the papers back where they'd found them, then gathered up his copies, and stopped at the information desk.

"Everything okay?" Shelly raised an eyebrow.

"Yeah, George is a little high strung."

"Your other three books are coming in from the KU library," she said. "Should be here by the end of the week."

"Thanks for ordering me those books, Shel," he said, gathering up the hardcovers and his newspaper copies. "I'm out. Keep on keeping on."

He turned toward the door as it opened, and in stalked Rita Pavlakis, still in her Secret Service sunglasses. When she saw him, her stride faltered.

"Well, speak of the devil," Curt said.

Rita tilted her head toward the books and article copies in his arms. "What've you got there?"

"Little light reading," Curt said, putting the copies beneath the books. "And what are you doing here in the middle of the day?"

"It's my lunch hour," she said. "Thought I'd check out the town library."

Curt frowned at her. "Anything I can help you find?"

"I'll be sure to let you know." She strode past him to the newspaper stacks.

She turned back to him. "I know where you live, after all."

CHAPTER SIXTEEN

Bill

Sunday, May 25, 1986
Hays, Kansas
2:10 p.m.

Bill walked to the mechanic to pick up the Mustang, then toured the neighborhoods, hoping to catch a glimpse of Liz or the Subaru, but all he surveyed were kids running through sprinklers and families talking to neighbors.

When he returned to the apartment, Liz's suitcases were gone and there was a note on the table.

Bill—I've opened a credit account at Dillons for you so you can buy food and another one at the Tiger Oil on 3rd, but you won't have access to cash. Don't forget to eat and sleep. Please think about what I said. -L

How was he going to get the cassette carrier back? He had to find her, but she'd taken her address book and he couldn't call any of her friends. So he took stock of how much cocaine he had left.

Friday night in Niobe, Bill hadn't locked the McWhiskey's bathroom stall securely, and Curt had almost caught him in the act. Bill had just got his pocket mirror and stash put away when Curt busted in on him. The look on Curt's face showed he knew exactly what Bill was up to, but he said nothing. Which was a relief, because Bill didn't share coke anymore. He rationalized that Curt preferred pot, so no real harm there.

Then after Bill had walked the cassette carrier out to the Subaru from the garage behind George's grandparents' house, he'd found an empty M&Ms package in Liz's car trash bag. He scooped several grams from the jumbo baggie of coke into the candy pack, rolled it up tight, and stuck it in his pocket. He sealed the big baggie and put it back into the bottom of George's cassette carrier before going back into the house to confab with Travis, George, and Curt.

Now he transferred the coke from the M&Ms bag to a clean baggie after snorting a meager amount. He had enough cocaine to last him several days if he rationed it carefully. And once he got the big baggie back from the Subaru, everything would be fine. Or at least, closer to fine.

Bill drove to the nearest gas station payphone and dialed the one number he'd memorized and arranged a meeting, then sped to the parking lot of an abandoned business to meet Hoover, who made him wait, as usual.

Summer was on its way—the sun blazed unhindered by

clouds, and the temperature climbed above ninety degrees. The high humidity conspired with Bill's sweat glands, and by the time Hoover cruised up in his red Volkswagen Rabbit two and a half hours later, Bill looked like he'd walked through the nearby carwash fully clothed.

Expressionless behind his mirrored aviator shades, Hoover stuck his arm out the window, palm up, and Bill laid the moist bank envelope containing $4000 cash in his hand. The dealer thumbed through the bills. "Where's the rest of it?"

"I'll have it for you by Friday."

"You said you'd have it for me today."

Bill shifted from foot to foot. He couldn't think of anything to say.

Hoover drew on his cigarette and flicked it, narrowly missing Bill's leg. "I'm not a fucking bank, man," he said. "I've told you that."

Now, that was hilarious. Because in addition to selling drugs, he was what passed for a loan shark around here. In between paychecks, Bill borrowed money from Hoover, and he could never quite catch up. One day he tallied everything up and, added to his maxed-out credit cards, the sum was staggering. Which was why he'd started to cash in the municipal bonds a little at a time.

"Listen." Although no one else was around, Bill lowered his voice. "This is going to sound bogus, but the fact is, I've come into possession of a large amount of product myself. I'll give it to you, and you cancel my debt, even though it's worth considerably more than what I owe."

Skeptical, Hoover said, "Do you have it with you?"

"No, that's the problem. It's in my wife's car and she's—well, she's left, and I don't know where she's gone, but as soon as—"

Hoover held up his hand. "I'm not interested in your personal problems. If you don't pay up, my *investor* will want me to give up your name. And your wife's. And you really, really don't want that."

Since he could summon up nothing resembling emotion at this point, Bill parroted Hoover's words. "I do not want that."

Hoover lit another cigarette and revved his engine. "Call me Friday." He roared away, the hot blast from his exhaust roasting Bill's legs further.

Bill cruised home and collected the mail from the bank of mailboxes by the apartment complex's front office. Overdue bills. Advertising circulars. A letter from the dean advising him of his suspension with pay. He scanned the list: Tardiness or absence without notice. Erratic behavior. Abusive language toward colleagues and students. He balled the letter up and pitched it into the garbage.

With no summer school classes to teach, what was he going to do?

He retrieved his Beretta handgun case from beneath sweaters and blankets on the highest shelf of his side of the closet. He unlocked it, removed the weapon and the false bottom, and noted his depleted stash. The only thing in there besides a box of bullets, some empty bottles, baggies, and vials were three codeine pills, a finger of premium Hawaiian Electric sinsemilla marijuana, and a barely touched bottle of Quaaludes. He'd thought he had more of a variety left over.

Since Liz was gone, he piled the drugs in his sock drawer. He was restless, so he dragged the streets looking for Liz's Subaru. Cars nowadays were interchangeable—clunky, utilitarian, eastern European, without the elegance and power of the '60s muscle cars like his beloved 1967 Mustang. He kept a careful eye out but didn't see her car.

Around sundown he turned down a side street from campus and glimpsed the Subaru in a gravel parking lot next to a large old house with a newer addition built on. He parked two houses down and ambled casually into the lot, hands in pockets. He drew close enough to read the license plate. This was Liz's Subaru, all right. He surveyed the street. A few kids were walking nearby but paid him no mind. Bill peered in through the back passenger window and spied the cassette carrier. Relief washed over him. He tried all the doors, but they were locked.

He kept glancing up at the windows on the house and detected no life inside. Why hadn't he brought a coat hanger? Of course it would be locked—this wasn't Niobe or Saw Pole, after all. Here he'd spent all this time searching for the car but hadn't been prepared to find it. He looked for a fence with wire or some other sort of long thin implement to try to jimmy the door.

"Bill Altenbach?"

The voice startled Bill like an M-80 tossed through a window. He whirled around. A guy with John Lennon glasses, a mustache, and semi-long hair, thirty-five years old or so, stood there. He smiled and held out his right hand. "I'm Pete."

Bill made no move to shake it.

Pete's hand dropped. "How you holding up?"

"How am I...?" Bill said, incredulous. "Do I know you?"

"No," Pete said. "But I know you. I'm a friend of Liz's."

A dozen things went through Bill's brain at once. Friend? The real reason Liz left him? Why an old hippie?

"What are you doing here?" Pete said. His tone wasn't confrontational at all, merely curious.

But Bill would be the one asking questions. "Is this your house?"

"No," Pete said, still smiling. "It belongs to the diocese."

"The—"

"This is Canterbury House, the campus Episcopal Student Ministry. I just work here. I'm the director. And a priest."

Bill viewed the addition to the old house and recognized it as a chapel. He swallowed. "Is Liz around?"

Pete's eyes lingered on the Subaru, and Bill's paranoia doubled. "I don't think she wants to see you."

"I'd like to hear her say it."

"I'm pretty sure she already did, Bill."

This comment loosed magma in Bill's chest, but if Liz was inside that house, she might be watching so he clamped his jaws together to keep it from leaking out.

"She said you're having a tough time," Pete said.

Bill started to leak anyway. "If she gave a shit about what kind of a time I'm having, she wouldn't have left me and frozen our bank accounts."

"Oh, I think you know she gives more than a shit about you," Pete said, unruffled. "You didn't leave her any choice, did you? She agonized over her decision for months."

Bill's face effloresced with heat. Months? She'd thought about leaving him *before* she found out about the missing money?

It sounded as though Liz shared more of her inner life with the priest than with Bill, which flustered him further. When had the transference occurred?

And didn't this guy know anything about the golden social rules of skating the surface, of denial, of fabricated ignorance regarding others' business? This, not to mention the profanity, was not churchy behavior as Bill understood it, rendering him uncharacteristically speechless.

"Liz said you could use a friend," Pete said.

"And of course, by 'friend,' she means *counselor*."

"No," Pete said. "She means friend. I've found her to be a straight shooter."

Bill seethed. "And she volunteered you for the job."

"Truthfully," Pete said, "I've wanted to meet you for some time. My undergrad major at CU Boulder was quantum physics."

It was as if he'd been handed a big, steaming bowl of cognitive dissonance.

"And I wondered if you'd read the Davies and Brown book yet," Pete said.

He was speaking of *The Ghost in the Atom: A Discussion of the Mysteries of Quantum Physics* by PCW Davies and JR Brown that had been released earlier in the year.

"You...wondered..."

"I'd love to hear your take on it," Pete said. "My wife's reading it now."

"Your...wife?"

"Remember? Episcopal, not Catholic. It's all kosher."

The priest had misinterpreted. If he had a wife, maybe he wasn't Liz's lover.

Pete was still talking. "My wife said Davies' introduction explains the field better than anything else she's read. If you'd like to borrow it when she's done, you're welcome to it."

"Uh...thanks."

"All right," Pete said. "I'll tell Liz you came by." He advanced toward Bill, who stepped back, as if Pete were about to slug him in the gut. Instead, he produced a business card from his wallet. "Here's my contact info," he said, holding it out.

This was Bill's only link to Liz, so he accepted the card.

"Good meeting you," Pete said.

"Later days and better lays," Bill said.

Pete cocked an eyebrow at him then went back inside the house. As the screen banged closed, Bill realized he could have asked Pete to get the Subaru keys from Liz, saying he'd left something in the car and no one would be the wiser.

Damn it.

He couldn't do it now, because if Pete told Liz about it after Bill left, she might investigate. He had to get that cocaine out of there before that happened.

He looked at Pete's business card and thought he should have given Pete his in return, but Pete obviously already had his number.

Monday, May 26, 1986
3 a.m.

Thanks to a generous helping of vodka, Bill had a good, bracing buzz on. It was time. Before he left the apartment for the night's mission, he swallowed the three codeine pills and hunted for the extra set of Subaru keys, but of course Liz had taken them. Or maybe he was too drunk to find them.

He'd learned his lesson and fished a wire hanger out of the closet and angled it into a hook. He wasn't exactly clear on how to use this to jimmy open the door but had seen it in movies and on TV, so he figured there must be something to it. He carried it out to the Mustang and tooled through the silent, shadowy streets of Hays to the campus ministry house, which was entirely dark.

He parked down the street and slogged to the gravel lot. He made as little noise as possible, proceeding slowly. Liz's car hadn't moved.

He tried the doors again, and they were locked. So he worked the coat hanger but couldn't force it any farther down than an inch. He shoved so hard the sharp end stabbed him in the meaty part of his palm. He studied his hand, the blood welling up, and he poked at it. It didn't hurt, not with the opiates rafting a river of vodka through his bloodstream.

Lightning blazed. He tilted his face to the first drops of rain. His frustration and desperation flared as more drops fell. He had to get that cassette carrier out of there before the thunderheads fully let go. His right hand was slick with blood now and he could gain no purchase on the wire hanger. He flung it into the woods behind the house.

He scrabbled around on the ground but could find nothing large or heavy enough to be suitable. He ran to the wooded area and groped the soil, hands muddy and bleeding. And then glory! A rock the size of a bread loaf. That would do.

Bill raced back and hurled the rock at the driver's side window. It bounced off the chrome frame. *Plink, plink.* More rain began to fall. He hoisted the stone above his head and slammed it down on the glass with all his might. The crash, thank God, coincided with a thunderclap, and the hole was big enough to stick his arm through and unlock the door.

A tempered wave of jubilation rose as he extracted the carrier from the floor of the car like a firefighter pulling a baby from a burning building. He unzipped it, fumbled inside, and removed the bag of coke.

"*Yes!*"

He kissed it and put it in his shirt. The carrier fell from his hands and tapes spilled on the ground. He slammed the door and ran for his car.

A huge trident of lightning cracked open the sky and the deluge began.

The lot was wider than he remembered. His heart galloped at full bore, but the codeine and vodka reached critical mass and conspired to melt his muscles. He ran in slow motion, each foot step heavier than the last. Almost there. And then his toe caught on the concrete lip of the curb and he went sprawling. He landed on his stomach and face, knocking the wind out of him, and he couldn't move.

Lightning flashed, illuminating the rain that pooled around him.

"*No.*"

He pushed up to his knees and tried to reach inside his now soaked shirt, which clung to him like a diver's suit. His hands had lost the ability to grip, trying to snatch his shirttail out of his waistband. The shirt finally came free. He reached up under it and hooked his fingertips into the bag.

It came apart in his hands, the powder dissolving and disappearing.

The ruined bag flopped to the ground and was instantly sucked under water.

He clawed at the bag. He had to save it. He could dry it. He could—

Lightning flashed, revealing the deflated bag swimming in

murky brown water, tinged with the red of his own blood.

The cocaine was gone.

CHAPTER SEVENTEEN

Bill

Monday, May 26, 1986
Hays, Kansas
6:30 a.m.

"Bill?"

The morning sun beat down. His head, face, and knees hurt.

"How long have you been here?"

The skin of his face was stiff. He touched it with his fingertips, which came away with flecks of dried blood. The hand itself throbbed and Bill vaguely remembered the coat hanger injury. His pants and shirt were damp, and he probably resembled a spook house zombie.

He tried to lift his head to ascertain who was speaking to him. When he did, bits of rock came up stuck to his right cheek. He squinted up at the silhouette of a man with longish hair holding out a hand to him.

He ignored it and attempted to push upright, but his arms had little strength in them. He needed to rest a while longer.

Then the previous night came flooding back like a nightmare.

His mind snapped to attention and turned toward the Subaru. The surge of adrenaline that accompanied his recovered memory helped him get to his feet, his legs still not sure they were up to the task. "I was coming by last night to check on Liz, and I spotted a guy trying to break into her car—he actually already had broken in, used a rock to bust out her window, as you can see, and—" Bill swallowed, swaying on his feet, and went on. "I tried to stop him, but he—he took the same rock and bashed me in the head and knocked me out."

Pete's eyes tracked back and forth from Bill's face to the car, his hands now in his pockets as Bill struggled to stay upright without aid.

"Why don't you come on in and get cleaned up?" Pete said.

"No, I've got to get to work," Bill said.

"On Memorial Day?"

Bill swallowed again. "I don't want to bother Liz."

"She's not up yet. It's just after six-thirty."

But she would be any minute, and he had to decamp before she found out what he'd done. "I need to go."

"I suppose you do," Pete said, an innocent response that elicited an unreasonable flash of rage in Bill. "Your nose is bleeding there."

Bill reached up and touched his upper lip, pulled his hand away, and looked at the fresh blood. Then his eyes sought out the split, waterlogged bag on the ground, all traces of life-giving powder gone, the loss of which portended a swift and steep descent into ruin, one without end.

Pete advanced on him. "Maybe it's time to give in."

Bill turned away and strode toward the Mustang as if he hadn't heard, the words and tone making his hackles rise. It was the kind of thing his dad had always said to him when he was a kid, being stubborn about one thing and another.

A memory from his childhood bubbled up. His family was in Colorado on vacation, hiking in Rocky Mountain National Park, and he was four. The only reason he knew this was because of the photos from the trip.

But he recalled one moment so clearly it could have happened last Tuesday. They were coming down a mountain, and Bill had to go down backward, gripping a boulder with all his strength, and he believed he would fall hundreds of feet if he let go. From behind him, his dad kept saying, "It's okay, Billy boy. Just let go. That's all you have to do."

Bill couldn't see his dad with his face mashed against the boulder, he could only hear his voice. His terror was visceral, mind-erasing, heart-arresting. He didn't have a good grip on the boulder to begin with, and now his dad was telling him to let go! Why didn't he care if Bill fell and kept on falling forever? But it didn't matter if he let go or not, he was losing his handhold, sliding off the boulder. This was it. The last thing he'd ever see was the blue mountain sky and the soaring pines.

Gravity took him.

Bill fell straight into his father's arms.

"See?" Dad said, his smile huge. "I told you you could do it! All you had to do was let go."

And four-year-old Bill wondered why his dad hadn't told him he'd catch him.

Maybe because it was 50-50 that he wouldn't. A coin flip.

But Pete wasn't his dad, and Bill wasn't four.

No one could catch Bill now.

CHAPTER EIGHTEEN

Curt

Tuesday, May 27, 1986
Saw Pole, Kansas
11 a.m.

The hound was the world's worst guard dog. He didn't budge when vehicles approached, or when folks knocked on the door. He couldn't have given less of a shit about keeping intruders out. It was nearly lunchtime before he finally wandered out of Curt's bedroom, jowly and indignant, and flopped to the kitchen linoleum.

Curt put *Bush Doctor* by Peter Tosh on the turntable and cranked up the volume to drown out the sound of the tractors and backhoes breaking ground on phase two or whatever it was of the project across the road. He wondered what they would be installing now. Yes, a cable television receiving station was the official explanation, but why all the vehicles going in and out? Why wouldn't anyone answer his questions or give him a tour of the buildings at the other end of the property?

As he sang along with Tosh and Mick Jagger on "Walk and Don't Look Back," Curt heard pounding on his front door. He turned down the volume on the stereo, went to the door, and swung it open.

There stood Rita Pavlakis in her Raybans. Curt looked beyond her. "Where's Emerson?"

"Just me today," she said.

He spastically swallowed. She may not have been a hit-woman or a cop, but she was way too interested in what he knew about the murders. And she knew Stacia, who might have killed three people.

Stacia, who wasn't dead. Who was probably looking for George. Who might be sending out other people to look for him.

"Can I come in?" she asked.

He tried to think of a non-creepy way to ask if he could frisk her for weapons but gave up. "Yeah," he said. "Okay."

"No slumber party last night?" she said as she traipsed over the threshold.

"Nope. Just me and the hound." The dog strolled from the kitchen into the living room and glanced sleepily from him to Rita, then dropped in a dusty heap by the coffee table.

"Speak of the devil," Curt said.

"You speak of the devil a lot." She bent down to scratch the dog's ears. "Hi there," she said to him.

Curt gathered books and magazines off the couch and shoved the cushions in with his knees and gestured toward it. She didn't sit. Just stood there.

He itched to ask her what she'd found at the library but wanted to keep her as far from the subject of the murders as possible, so he didn't say anything.

She removed her sunglasses and Curt got a look at her eyes for the first time, and all thoughts of the library, of federal agents, of hit-persons evaporated. Her eyes were a pale, opalescent green. He leaned toward her for a closer inspection, and she leaned away from him until she took a step backward to keep from falling over. But she didn't take her eyes from his. Then she blinked, and the air between them shimmered. She turned aside.

Her light eyes contrasted strikingly with her dark hair and tan skin. She was a stone fox. His pulse doubled.

Mother of God. She's the perfect person to send, because she could shove a shiv between my ribs while I was still trying to remember how to speak English.

He hadn't noticed any of this the other day when she first showed up or at the library because of those damn sunglasses, like Clark Kent pretending he wasn't Superman. Now Curt's brain tried to reclassify her, but nothing fit together.

She began moving around the room, studying his belongings, her hands clasped behind her back as if she were on a field trip at the natural history museum in Salina. Or looking for evidence of a crime…or an address book, or maybe photos of friends…

"We'd like to pave the stretch of County Road 15 from Saw Pole to our gate," she said.

"We who?" Curt said, thinking of Stacia and her pals.

Rita's eyebrows came together. "S.H.A. Who did you think I meant?"

"That's what I thought you meant."

"We wanted to ask your opinion."

He had to repeat her words in his mind in order to respond appropriately. "Yeah. Pave the road. That, uh, that would be pretty sweet." He watched her glide from exhibit to exhibit, the muscles in her calves flexing beneath her dark skin. His brain was at war, half attracted to this girl, half believing a hot chick conspiracy was at work—hot chicks murdered, hot chick luring George to the scene to frame him, hot chick here now trying to squeeze him for information.

"We'll need to run it past the county board of commissioners," she said. "But I'm guessing they'll like the idea, especially since S.H.A. is footing the bill. But you know how these things go—there's always at least one bitter old crank saying no to everything."

Was he imagining a suspicious tone in her voice? A little too much interest in his possessions?

Rita moved her glossy lips silently while inspecting the silk-screen tapestry with a robed wizard and the first three lines of "Stairway to Heaven" in fancy calligraphy.

"So I know it's a lot to ask," she said, "but would you be willing to come to a commission meeting and give a rah-rah speech in favor?"

"Sure," he said. No harm saying yes. Didn't mean he'd actually do it, because who knew if this was a real request?

She paused at the bumper sticker pinned over the window that said "Reality is for people who can't handle drugs" and turned to scrutinize him. Drugs like cocaine, she was probably thinking. But that was moronic. No way could she know about that baggie under the passenger seat in George's car.

Could she? *She could if she knew Stacia planted it there.*

Rita rook no notice of the Jack Daniel's mirror or the 1981 *Nature of the Beast* April Wine concert t-shirt. But she did a double-take at the framed black-and-white photo to the right of them. She squinted and leaned forward, and Curt's eyes landed on her ass, which was, of course, prime.

"Where did you get this?" Her voice was bright and excited, much different from her earlier tone.

"The picture?" He walked to it and stood next to her, his arms crossed. Was this photo incriminating in some way? He could not begin to imagine how. So he told the truth. "At an auction in Cawker City when I was eleven. It's the first hypersonic aircraft."

"I know!" She indicated the jumpsuited pilot standing next to the plane with her pinky. "That's my dad!"

This insane declaration pulled Curt out of assessing her looks and intentions and produced the same kind of full-body rush he'd experienced when lightning struck the elm tree by his bedroom window two summers ago. He owned a picture of her father. How was that possible?

It wasn't.

"Oh," he said. "I'm *sure* it is."

Rita turned to face him, and her expression—mouth and eyes wide in Christmas-morning wonder—supported her claim. Goosebumps raised on Curt's arms as he got a closer look at those eyes.

"For real?" His hands fell to his sides. "That's really him?"

"Yes. He was a test pilot in the Air Force. This was one of the main reasons I wanted to become an engineer in the first place."

Her eyes searched Curt's face, as if she were reassessing him as well.

He attempted to work up his earlier skepticism as he examined the photograph. But in the pilot's tiny face he recognized Rita's likeness—the strong nose, the high cheekbones, the dark hair and light eyes. Chills again. "They got the X-15 up to, like, Mach Six, right?"

"Six-point-seven."

That was exactly the X-15's top speed. Without thinking about it, he lifted the frame off the wall and held it out to Rita. "Here."

She raised her hands as if he were sticking her up instead of offering a gift. "No," she said. "It's yours."

"You already got a copy?"

"No, but—"

"Then it's yours. You'd give me a picture of my dad if you had one, wouldn't you?"

She didn't take the photo, just blinked at him, her lips parted. And then her eyes clouded and narrowed, and she turned away from him, their connection fractured as quickly as it had formed. But it wasn't severed completely, he knew. Even though they weren't looking at each other now, they *were*, and it was so intense, he had to catch his breath. The presence of this *thing*, whatever it was, filled the room.

She left him holding on to the frame. He felt like he'd just gotten off a fast-moving carousel, dizzy, trying to reorient himself to the real world. He reluctantly hung the picture back on its nail and steadied himself with one hand on the wall.

Rita dug in her purse and without looking at him said, "Can I use your bathroom before I take off?"

"Sure. Let me show you where it is."

He led her through the kitchen and into the narrow hallway leading to his bedroom. He flipped on the light and found himself face to face with her. He sensed something like an oscillating current passing between them. He couldn't look away from her. They were fixed like that for a moment until she said, "Is that the bathroom?"

He didn't reply, just gazed at her dilated pupils, the flush that covered her exposed neckline. She went into the bathroom and locked the door. And he imagined going in there with her and lifting her onto the sink, and...

He walked into the kitchen and leaned back against the counter, trying to sort out all the conflicting emotions and thoughts. He had to focus. He needed to find out if Stacia had sent Rita here to find George.

But…there was something else here, something separate, apart from George's situation. That had nothing to do with George.

When she emerged, she walked briskly down the short hallway without looking at him.

Curt blocked the exit from the kitchen. She stopped ten feet from him.

"Rita," he said.

"Yes?" Now she looked at him. Just for a second, and then at the toaster.

Damn it. He couldn't think of a clever way to question her without giving himself away. Although this girl knocked him off his game, he decided to try the one thing he did well. He needed to be closer to her to do it.

Her gaze flicked from his chest to his eyes and away again. She skipped sideways. "Don't you own any shirts?"

"Huh?" He turned so he was still facing her, to stop her from sidling out.

"You've never worn one when I've been here, and…"

"So you're here for a week? Where are you staying?"

"The Grand Niobe Inn," she said. Her fingers twined and untwined the gold chain around her neck, a tremor in her hands.

Slowly walking toward her, he said, "Pretty damn grand, ain't it?"

"Grand," she said. "Just grand."

He was only two feet from her. "What room are you staying in?"

"Six," she said, without hesitation, and then appeared to realize sharing that information might seem improper. "I think," she amended.

"My favorite number."

"Mine's pi," she said, swallowing.

This made him smile. He took another step toward her, close enough to smell her perfume, and she took a step backward—and smacked her head against an open cupboard door. She gasped, and her face scrunched up. At the same time, both their right hands flew to the back of her head, his on top of hers.

"Ouch," he said. "You okay?"

"I think so," she said, looking at his mouth.

They stood unmoving this way, with his hand over the softness of hers, their faces an arm length apart.

Her warm breath smelled of peppermint.

"This is some wicked rock and roll hair you got, *Ri-ta*." He reached out with his other hand and gently tugged one of the loose curls by her ear, straightening it out.

That seemed to pull something undone and the clip holding her hair in place gave way and tumbled to the floor. Like magic, her hair fell free, a mass of dark curls.

They stood staring at each other. He wanted to kiss her so bad it physically hurt. His breath quickened. So did hers. He began pulling her toward him. She didn't resist.

But a car horn blast made them both jump, Curt's hand disengaging from her hair.

"That'll be Emerson," she said. "I've got to go."

Damn that Emerson. So much for getting information from her. Curt stepped back, and she picked up her broken hair doodad and tossed it in the trash.

She strolled toward the door, and he tracked her with his eyes.

She turned back when she got there and fluffed her hair. "Did you see yesterday's *Kansas City Star*?" Her eyes glowed like a cat's in the dark. "The night of the murders, some kids saw a man sitting in his car across the street from the house where the girls were killed. He had a gas can and a gun on the back seat."

That part was true. But had she actually found it out from the paper? Or had Stacia told her? He grew cold and his attraction withered away as Rita walked out the door.

CHAPTER NINETEEN

George

Wednesday, May 28, 1986
Niobe, Kansas
9 a.m.

"We'll be in your area on May twenty-ninth and would love to show you how vinyl siding can dramatically reduce your utility costs!"

George deleted the message from the answering machine.

Beep.

"George. You've got to help me."

Stacia's voice whacked him in the face. He clasped the receiver hard to his ear.

"I was supposed to be in that house when it exploded. I want to tell you what happened and—I'm so sorry I left you there. They wanted to kill me, too, not only those other girls. They're looking for me. I haven't been able to go back to my apartment. Please,

George, I need your help. You've got a—oh, shit. They're—"

A *clunk* sound indicated she'd let go of the phone, and then nothing.

They're what? They who?

George's stomach lurched. How long before his adrenal glands gave out entirely?

Could she be telling the truth? Were there other people out there looking for her? Could these same people be looking for him?

Was that Rita girl Curt had mentioned one of those people?

He pressed two to repeat the message and noted the date it was left: Monday, May 26, the day before yesterday.

Was she just trying to flush him out so she and her cohorts could turn him in to the police? Execute him?

He agonized over this as he only half-listened to the next one.

"Hey, George, this is the Highpoint manager. Just wanted to let you know we're changing out the shower heads in all the units—some kind of ecological water saving crap, so we're planning to start tomorrow—what's that, the twenty-ninth? The twenty-ninth, I think. Anyway, it's cool if you're not home. We'll let ourselves in. Don't worry about cleaning your tub or anything like that, ha ha, but yeah. Just needed to let you know."

How had Stacia found his number? Probably the phone book—he was listed as ENGLE, G, so it wouldn't take a detective to figure out...wait. He listened to the message from the apartment manager twice more and was momentarily stunned. White noise filled his head.

The receiver slipped from his hand and thumped against the wall, hanging from its noose-like cord, the barely audible message coming to him from across a canyon.

He'd left the bloody shirt, the washcloth, and the envelope in the tub at his apartment in Lawrence.

He had to go back. Today. Now. Before the maintenance men stumbled upon the bloody things. But he couldn't go alone. The truth was, he was terrified to go by himself. Couldn't even picture it in his mind. Not only could the cops be looking for him, but probably the *they* Stacia had mentioned.

The they *Stacia mentioned*. What if the voice on the message wasn't the Highpoint Apartments manager? What if *they* or the cops had already searched the apartment and found the stuff in the bathtub, and this was a setup to lure him to Lawrence?

What if the message was law enforcement trying to find him, bring him to Lawrence to arrest him?

George stood frozen with indecision, the three scenarios rapidly cycling and repeating through his head. Two of them resulted in incarceration.

He played the message three more times.

It *sounded* like the manager, who he'd chatted with several times over the years he'd lived at Highpoint. But the more he listened to it, the more uncertain he became.

He stood staring at the Lion's Club calendar on the wall, his eyes fixed on Friday, May 23. The day he lost control of his own life. The day everything went to hell.

Why hadn't he brought the shirt and the envelope with him to Niobe in the first place? Why hadn't he burned them? Why hadn't he used his head that night?

He needed to talk to someone about this. He needed someone to tell him what to do.

Bill would gladly tell him what to do, but that option was out. Bill clearly hated his guts. George wanted to talk to Curt, but he didn't have a phone, and it would take too long to drive out to Saw Pole.

Glancing at the clock on the wall, he hoped he could catch Travis before he left for work. He picked the phone back up and dialed Travis's house.

"Answer, answer, answer."

A female voice finally did.

"Hi, this is George Engle," he said. "Is Travis—"

"Oh! Travis's old friend? He told me all about you. I can't wait to meet you all!"

"Uh..."

"This is Toni, his fiancée...you're going to be his grooms— oh, no. Did I ruin the surprise?"

"No, he asked. I'm in." George tried not to sound brusque as he went through the obligatory pleasantries long enough so she wouldn't be offended when he asked to speak to Travis.

"AJ, put that down," Toni said. To George, she said, "We'll have you over to dinner so we can get acquainted. Hang on, I'll get him." Then she hollered right into the phone, "TRAVIS! IT'S GEORGE!"

George fidgeted waiting for Travis to pick up the phone.

"Yello."

"G-Ho, hey…" George faltered.

"What's up?"

"Is anyone on the other extension? Is Toni on the phone?"

"Babe?" Travis called, his mouth away from the receiver. "Did you hang up? Thanks, honey. Okay, George."

"Are you sure she's off? Your mom's not listening in?"

"No, pard. Neither of my gals is like that. It's just us. What's going on?"

George stammer-explained everything, his breath repeatedly catching, and twice Travis told him to slow down.

Once he got it all out, Travis gave a low whistle. "Okay. Give me your answering machine number and the code and I'll listen to that message. Just sit tight and I'll call you back."

George gave him the number and security code then hung up and smoked and paced for the next few minutes, glancing out one of the two kitchen windows with each pass.

The phone rang, and he picked up.

"Here's my assessment of the situation. Stacia, her people, the authorities, none of them could possibly know what's in your tub, right?"

"They could if they broke in," George said.

"Yeah, but wouldn't they come up with a better way to get you back to town? You're in hiding, so they'd have to—I don't know, say you'd won money or something. And there's this. I listened to that message, and the way the guy talked, the tenor of his voice, he was completely relaxed, casual, and talking about water-saving gizmos. I'd bet the farm that's a landlord, and not one who's being coerced by police to make a fake call."

The muscles in George's belly loosened a little. "You really think so?"

"Yeah. You could always call the apartment complex office and confirm."

His heart soared. It was so simple, so logical. No wonder he hadn't thought of it.

"I'll do that and then call you right back." He hung up and called directory assistance for the number then dialed it.

After he ended the call, he imagined that the manager had never heard anyone so overjoyed at the prospect of getting a new showerhead, and George started laughing uncontrollably. But he wasn't out of the woods yet. He had to go get that shirt and washcloth and envelope. He called Travis back.

"Okay," Travis said. "Here's what we're going to do. We're going up to Lawrence after I get off work. We're going to get that stuff in the tub, and we're going to preserve it for when we bring the authorities into—"

"No," George said. "No cops."

"Okay," Travis said, placating. "We're getting ahead of ourselves anyway. Let's go up there and get the evidence and get out of there, lickety-split. Okay?"

George wanted to cry. "Thank you, G-Ho."

"I'll pick you up at five. Wear a hat to hide your face. And don't worry. You know I'm always packing."

George wasn't sure whether that was good news or not.

CHAPTER TWENTY

Curt

Wednesday, May 28, 1986
Saw Pole, Kansas
2:30 p.m.

Curt's new painting was taking shape. Although he usually worked inside the barn, today he stood out in front of the trailer under the shade of the oak tree. The day was cool and breezy with a bright blue sky, and his boom box played *Heart Food* by Judee Sill for inspiration. The night before, he'd dreamed about the three dead girls, and he needed the sunshine and colorful paints and hopeful acoustic music to scour out his mind. And to begin a painting of another girl that he couldn't seem to get out of his head, even though he wasn't quite sure why.

He'd only attempted a few other portraits, none without a reference image, and none he'd kept. But the vision in his brain was as clear as if a Polaroid sat on the easel next to the 36" x 48" canvas, as if this image had been there all along and he was just uncovering it with his brushes.

"So, you *do* own some shirts."

Curt startled. Rita materialized, walking toward him as if he'd conjured her. It was past lunchtime gauging by the angle of the sun, and he was hungry but had been too consumed with his work to even notice.

"I told you I did," he said. "I can take it off, if you want."

She held up her hands. "Please."

He shrugged, wiped his hands on the rag in his back pocket, and reached behind his head to pull off his t-shirt.

"No, no," she said. "I meant stay clothed."

He let go of his shirt neck and stepped around the easel.

"What are you working on?" She advanced on him.

He caught her by her bare arm and gently stopped her forward progress before she could catch a glimpse. She was wearing a ruffled blue sleeveless blouse that turned her eyes a deeper shade of green.

"I never show my work before it's finished."

He steered her to the picnic table and they sat side by side facing outward. Curt leaned back on his elbows and Rita mirrored his pose. As soon as she was seated, the dog trotted over and sniffed her boots then looked up at her with his heartbroken eyes until she reached down to scratch his ears and ruff.

"Just couldn't stay away, huh?" Curt said.

"When was the last time you were in Lawrence?" Rita said,

sitting back again and fixing him with a hard stare.

"No idea. How about you?"

"Recently?"

He shrugged.

She glanced over at the Jeep. "Is this the only vehicle you own?"

"Why do you ask?"

"Ever own a four-door sedan?"

"You looking to buy a new car?"

She pressed her lips together. "Any of your friends ever go to KU?"

"What's with all the questions?"

"Just thought it was interesting that the first time I was here you came running out of your house at the mention of murder in Lawrence." She aimed her knees his way and draped her left arm on the picnic table.

"Well, I think it's interesting that you showed up at my house when you did." Curt leaned toward her. "Talking about a triple homicide in my front yard under my open window."

"Interesting how?"

"Just a real coincidence that somehow you ended up out in the middle of nowhere only two days after the murders."

Her eyebrows drew together. "I'd say it's a much bigger coincidence that you asked about Stacia, and, as I recall, got violent when I didn't answer you. You physically attacked me, demanding that I tell you whether Stacia was one of the girls who was murdered."

Curt sat forward. "I physically attacked—*you* refused to— and what would Emerson tell me about *you*, do you think?" He pointed at her. "That you're a new employee? That he'd never met you before now? Is that what he'd tell me?"

Rita pointed back at him. "Don't try to turn this on me. Let's stick to the subject. How do you know Stacia?"

He stood up and put his hands on the table, one outside each of her elbows and positioned his face even with hers. "Why are you *really* here?" He looked into her eyes then her mouth and straightened.

"I'm *working* here."

"No. *Here*." Curt stabbed a finger downward. "Here on my property. This is the third time you've come to my house."

She cleared her throat. "I suppose you think it's got something to do with you."

He wanted to smile but resisted the urge. "So explain it to me."

She sat forward, set her elbows on her knees, and looked up at him. "What if one of the murdered girls was your mom, or your sister, or your girlfriend? And what if there was someone out there who had information about the crime but refused to share it—for whatever reason—wouldn't you find that wrong?"

He placed his mom and his sisters into that scenario in his mind. "Well, how would you feel if someone showed up out of the blue and started throwing questions at you and being semi-threatening and—"

"I called Stacia."

Curt's heart stopped.

"No answer. Had to leave a message."

"I thought you said you didn't know her that well." He forced himself to speak calmly. "What did you say?"

She shrugged. "Just told her to call me. Asked if she'd heard about our sisters."

"Told her to call you...where?" A bubble of anxiety grew in Curt's midsection.

"My number in Topeka."

"Did you tell her where you are?" He couldn't stop his voice from rising. "Staying in Niobe, working in Saw Pole?"

"I also have some college friends I might call. One works for the *Kansas City Star* and another for the Lawrence PD."

He turned away from her, his heart beating double-time. He touched the canvas he'd been working on. The acrylic paint was dry enough that he draped the rag over it so she couldn't see. He folded the easel and walked it all toward the barn. Over his shoulder, he said, "I think you'd better leave."

He went in the barn, switched on the lights, and carried his easel and canvas to the far corner.

When he turned, Rita was striding in the door, her fists balled at her sides. "Why did you think Stacia was one of the murdered girls? How did you even know her name?"

"It's a common name."

She was incredulous. "How dumb do you think I am? You had something to do with the murders up in Lawrence."

"No," Curt said, standing taller, towering over her. "*You* did.

Who sent you?"

"Who sent me? S.H.A. sent me."

"So if I call up the company's office in Topeka, they'll know who you are. They'll tell me you work for them and have for years."

She rose to her tiptoes and yelled in his face. "Yes. They will. Go call them right now, and maybe while you're doing that, I'll call the police."

He yelled back, "Well, maybe I'll…" He blew out a breath. "Actually, I can't. I don't have a phone."

"You don't—and then you—and…why in the world don't you have a phone?" She held up her hands, eyes closed. "Never mind. The point is, you're hiding something. You're withholding information about a triple homicide, and that could be a felony. Maybe you're even involved in a conspiracy, which means you could be looking at the death penalty."

"And you're trying to figure out if I'm one more person you have to get rid of, and what lakes are around here that you can dump my body in, and—"

"What?" Her face was so astonished, so bewildered, that it let the air out of his tires. He realized what he'd just said was shithouse-rat crazy.

Okay. Maybe he'd gone a little too far.

"You're not working for the people who killed your friends? You're not like a renaissance person, or anything?"

Rita's eyelids fluttered in stupefaction. "You mean *reconnaissance*?" She put her hands on her hips and fixed her narrowed eyes on Curt. But then she exhaled, and her hands fell to her sides. Her suspicion drained away, making her appear to deflate like a spent helium balloon. She slowly shook her head. "You have no idea what happened either. Do you?"

No, he didn't. Not really. He only knew what George had told him and what he'd read in the papers. And now it registered that she genuinely wanted to understand why her sorority sisters were dead. He hadn't grasped how important this was to her. Now that he did, he sympathized. And he wanted to cheer her up.

"I'm pretty much clueless most of the time, so...no. I'm kind of considered the town idiot around here."

Rita stood staring, eyes distant, tapping her index finger against her upper lip. Then she shook her head again. "I'm going to go now."

She turned and started to walk away, and then she stopped. And she took a step back, and her head slowly tipped upwards, taking in the three large canvases hung from floor to ceiling on the wall.

She went silent and still. Then she turned a slow circle, her mouth open and eyes wide, looking at the dozens of paintings covering the barn walls.

Curt had been so jacked up with all the accusations and yelling that he didn't even register that she'd tailed him in here—into this place he'd never allowed anyone. Now it was too late to do anything about it. The horse was out of the barn. Or inside it, in this case. He tensed so hard his whole body felt vacuum-sealed.

She glanced at him and said, "Town idiot, huh?"

Rita examined every wall, every painting, and the shock on her face was alternately distressing and enthralling, as he watched her eyes explore the shapes and colors all around her. Then she came back to the painting where she'd started, which was also the first he'd ever created, and raised her hands like a religious ecstatic, reaching to the sky with fingers spread like fireworks.

Her full-body reaction was a mirror image of his own while witnessing the Northern Lights here in Kansas three years before. He experienced the miracle of the Aurora Borealis somehow appearing over the center of the lower forty-eight in his every cell. The girl he'd been dating at the time, though, had just shrugged when she saw the transparent ribbons of green and yellow and violet. "Pretty," she'd said, unimpressed, and went on talking to her friend. Curt, on the other hand, was awe-stricken to the point of worshipfulness by the phenomenon. The event compelled him to commemorate it, celebrate it, and that was his first painting.

Now, watching Rita took the experience to an even deeper level. He was sharing this sense of wonder with another human being from both sides of the canvas.

"These are..." Rita gawked around again and back at him, her eyes ablaze. "Who *are* you?"

"Who are *you*? And why are you here?" But he meant it now in a completely different way from the first time he'd asked her.

She turned back to the paintings. "No, really. These are *shockingly* beautiful. They're stunning. They remind me of William Carlos Williams."

"The poet? The red wheel barrow guy?"

"Yeah," she said, pleased. "Exactly. The colors. They're so vivid." She tilted her face up, looking at the paintings again. She turned her attention to him. "You act like no one's ever admired your work before."

"They haven't."

"I can't imagine that's true."

"It is. Because no one's ever seen it before."

Rita's mouth formed itself into an O. She reached out with both hands and touched his shoulders, a gentle replay of his actions the first time they'd met. "I know I barged in here uninvited and everything, but...thank you," she said, and he could tell she meant it.

He drew closer to her, but then her eyes tracked to the left and her eyebrows flew up. He turned his head to see what she was looking at, and it was her silver watch.

"Oh, crap," she said. "It's after two. I've got a meeting. I didn't mean to stay this long. I've got to go." When she pulled her hands away from his shoulders, they left trails of fire in their wake. She walked toward the barn door.

"Drop by any time," Curt said, in a voice that didn't sound like his own.

But she was already gone.

CHAPTER TWENTY-ONE

George

Wednesday, May 28, 1986
Niobe, Kansas
3:45 p.m.

Freddie stood over the couch staring at him. George slid on his glasses. He must have dozed off.

"Is there something you want to tell me?" Freddie held up the gun and the bloody knife from George's car, now encased in a clear plastic bag. "What are these?"

George sat up so fast he almost fell right off the couch. His stomach plunged through a hole and kept falling. "What the hell were you doing in my car?" He jumped to his feet.

"I came home for lunch because hail's in the forecast and I wanted to put the Camaro in the garage. You told me you didn't know where the padlock key was, and I had to use bolt cutters to cut it off the door, and—"

"Why did you break into my car, you little shit?"

Affronted, Freddie said, "It was unlocked."

"And you snooped under my seats why?"

"What kind of mess have you gotten yourself into?" Freddie asked, the bag rippling in his shaking hands. His face reddened and his eyes glistened.

"It's a big misunderstanding." George tried to speak reasonably, which was difficult with this beehive of apprehension honeycombing his insides.

"Then what's all this?" Freddie said. He held up the copied articles from the *Star* and the *Journal World* and the *Wichita Eagle-Beacon*, brandishing the one with the police sketch of George.

"You went in my room, too?" His hands curled into fists.

"After finding the knife and the gun, I wondered what else I'd find in your room. Now I know why you're hiding here." Freddie didn't look like a man who'd stumbled upon the evidence of a violent, tragic crime. He looked like a kid who'd discovered his brother's stash of porn. Cunning eyes. Gleeful smile. Quivering with exhilaration.

George recoiled. Freddie was *excited*. Horror and disgust twined around his guts.

Staring at the newspaper copies and the baggie, he nearly blurted out, *and what did you do with the coke?* But he stopped himself. Mentioning that would only make things worse, and the desperate hope that maybe Freddie had missed it under the seats somehow still flickered.

George started talking, fast and furious. "It's all a big misunderstanding. This has nothing to do with me. Just let me explain."

His cousin *tsked* and shook his head, pulling his mouth downward into a caricature of concerned sympathy. "Poor George. I could call the cops right now, tell them who you are and where you are. I'd be a big old hero, solving a triple murder case. That would be *choice*." He glanced happily at the sheaf of papers in his hand.

I should have been nicer to him, and not just because he's going to turn me in. This guy has some serious emotional problems. George cleared his desert-dry throat and said, "It wasn't me. I didn't do it. I was in the wrong place at the wrong time."

"But they don't know that, do they? The evidence is in my possession. But I'll tell you what. I might be able to let the whole thing slide if..."

"If what?" George had the horrible feeling that Freddie was going to ask to accompany him on his next murder spree.

"If you give me the Corvette. Sign it over to me."

The words were an icepick in George's brain. *"What?"*

Freddie grinned, the certainty that he would prevail triumphant puffing him up like a hot air balloon. "That car is worth a lot of money. If you don't want to go to jail, you'll give me the Vette."

Frustration and anger swirled in George's thorax. "You have a brand-new IROC-Z. Isn't that enough?"

"I want that car. It's rare, and it's hardcore. Besides, I'm not going to do this for free, out of the goodness of my heart."

Because as it turns out, there is no goodness in your heart, you spoiled little prick.

"I don't have the title. My parents have it." George shook his head, misery compounding misery.

"You need to figure it out. Because if you don't, your parents finding out you're here will be the least of your problems. I'll be locking these away for safekeeping." Freddie shook the bag holding the weapons. "I'll give you some time to think about it. You don't give the car to me, I turn you in." Freddie gave George one last deliriously happy grin. "And then your mom will probably try to commit suici—"

George's hand shot out and gripped his cousin's throat, choking off the last part of that awful word, before he'd even formed the thought to do it. "There's the line, shit stain," George hissed, "and you just crossed it."

Freddie squeaked and released the bag and article copies, which fell to the floor. He clawed at George's hand with both of his, but George felt nothing thanks to the adrenaline that coursed through his veins like jet fuel.

He positioned his face an inch from Freddie's, compressing his cousin's doughy neck. "You might want to rethink your strategy here. You have no idea what I'm capable of. Do you think it's wise to threaten a murder suspect—and insult his *mother*—when you're not quite sure whether he did it or not? Whether he might do it again if backed into a corner?" He gave Freddie's throat one last hard squeeze and let go.

Freddie toppled to the ground, gasping and holding his neck. "You're going to be sorry you did that."

George could have lifted the couch with one hand he was so amped. "Tell you what. How about instead of giving you my car, I let you live?"

All motion in Freddie stopped. He stared at George.

"See, I think you've misread the situation. We're family, and I've let your behavior this week slide. But I'm starting to lose my patience. So it's your choice. You can either keep your mouth shut or...you've decided your own fate. And don't even think about calling your daddy and *telling* on me. Do we understand each other?"

Freddie still wasn't convinced, so George picked up the baggie and took hold of the gun through the plastic. "Do we understand each other?"

Now he was. He nodded spastically.

George set down the baggie, lit a cigarette, and blew smoke at his cousin. "I'm going to *let* you hang on to those things for me."

Freddie knelt on the floor and gathered up the newspaper article copies while keeping an eye on George. His face was red and his eyes were running, but he tried to approximate a tough-guy face. He only succeeded in looking like an angry baby. The sudden rush of power made George smile, filling Freddie's crying eyes with fear as he scuttled into the master bedroom and closed the door.

Life as a murder suspect might not be that bad after all.

But as the adrenaline ebbed and the victory over his cousin dimmed, a thought buzzed around George's consciousness and wouldn't leave him alone. If he could assault a family member without thinking about it, threaten to exterminate him so casually when he was high on adrenaline, could he also stab three girls to death when he was high on absinthe?

CHAPTER TWENTY-TWO

Bill

Wednesday, May 28, 1986
Hays, Kansas
4:45 p.m.

Bill had already snorted his coke allotment for the day, and he was getting itchy. So he decided to break out the sinsemilla and do a couple of hits. But all self-control had abandoned him some time ago, and he smoked every last bit of it down to ash.

He stowed the works in his dresser drawer, and the world softened and warped around him as the phone rang. He picked it up immediately. He was usually a screener, but today he expected two crucial calls—one from his mom returning an answering machine message he'd left this morning, and another from Hoover, who didn't leave messages.

"Hi, Bill, this is Pete."

Disappointment and irritation forestalled an immediate

response, and Pete went on. "Just wanted to check in and find out how you're doing. Last time I saw you, you were in pretty rough shape."

"Better," Bill said, hoping one-word replies would cut the call short.

"Outstanding," the priest said, sounding unconvinced. "The reason I called is I have the cassette carrier you left here."

Don't need it now. Bill said nothing.

"I dried the tapes out and thought I'd drop them by. You going to be around for a bit?"

"Actually, I'm about to—"

"Super. I'll be over in fifteen."

Before Bill could respond, Pete hung up.

The increased pace of blood flow from the shock sped up the absorption of the dope, and it started kicking in hard.

He paced the floor, back and forth, hardly a thought in his mind other than willing Hoover or his mother to call, until there was a knock at the door. Bill opened it, watching light trail from every moving object, and wishing he could enjoy it. Pete grinned at him and wandered in carrying a motorcycle helmet and George's cassette carrier, which he dropped on the kitchen table. He was dressed in baggy shorts and a wife beater, his long hair kept in place with a do-rag.

He unzipped the carrier, pulling tapes out. "Some good stuff in here," he said. "I couldn't find the cases for some of them; that cloud burst might have washed a few of them away. Sorry. Did what I could."

Bill surveyed the water-warped labels and liner notes inside the clear covers, his vision pulsing with his rapid heartbeat.

"Could I bother you for something to drink?" Pete said. "It's warming up out there."

"Sure." Bill walked carefully into the kitchen and drew two glasses of water from the tap. His own muscles kept twitching thanks to dehydration. He sat across from Pete and placed the glasses on the table between them.

Pete was stacking the tapes. He held up Elvis Costello's *King of America.* "This guy is one of the best songwriters out there, in my opinion. Might even rival Bowie." He set that one aside and singled out another, which he plunked down in front of Bill. "But this is the one that piqued my interest."

Bill's heart contracted. The smeary, handwritten song list inside the case was topped by a faded and tattered snapshot of Curt, George, Travis, and Bill sitting with their backs to the camera on the roof of Bill's old Pinto the morning after high school commencement. They'd partied all night and ended up behind the city swimming pool, watching the sun come up. In the picture, they were nothing but black silhouettes. But identification was easy, by height—Bill was the tallest by four inches—and by hair: Curt's was long, George's was uncontrollable, and Travis always wore a buzzcut.

They faced a colorful prairie sunrise, Budweiser cans at their sides. Another classmate—Bill couldn't remember who—had taken the photo with George's camera, the one his grandpop had given him for graduation. When just the four of them were left, after everyone else had punked out, they climbed the fence and jumped into the pool with all their clothes on—the only time Travis had joined them in this act of innocent rebellion.

Bill would never forget the joy on Travis's crazy cowboy face in the growing light. He'd had more fun than anyone.

On the clear plastic cover, George had stuck a blue label-maker label with the title NIOBE HS CLASS OF 1976 SELECT ARTISTS, the first of a two-tape set covering May 1975 to August 1976, their senior year. The song list included their favorites from the albums released during that time.

"Did you say something?" Bill said.

"I said I'd forgotten what an epic year for music this was," Pete said. "Is this you?" He indicated the tall guy on the right.

"That's me. Next to me is George, then Curt, and to the left there is Travis. We called him G-Ho."

Bill's larynx threatened to close up. Smoking pot had been a bad idea, because it gave him amplified Feelings. Sloppy, sentimental Feelings for his old friends coupled with an almost physical sensation of emptiness, and he couldn't halt the litany of questions. Had he fucked it up beyond repair this time? Dismantled their bond for good? What the hell was wrong with him? Why was he like this? His eyes began to water, and he could say no more. Instead, he busied himself sorting two piles of tapes—one to copy and one to make fun of mercilessly. In the copy stack: *Parade* by Prince and *Radio City* by Big Star. In the make-fun-of mound he set *Hell Awaits* by Slayer (although in reality this was a guilty pleasure for Bill and he'd move it to the dub pile after Pete left) and *Different Light* by the Bangles.

Pete went through the rest of the tapes and came to a Commodores cassette. "*Sixty-four*?" he said. "Never heard of it."

Bill shrugged. "Yeah, the only Commodores I own is the album with 'Brick House' on it. I was more of an Earth, Wind & Fire and Ohio Players man."

Pete held up the tape again. "Where did this come from, then?"

"These aren't mine." Bill glanced at the phone. "They're George's. This guy." He tapped the photo. "I'm sure he thanks you for rescuing his tuneage from my mishap."

"You mind if I take a listen to it? Want to see if I recognize anything on it."

"Sure."

The phone remained stubbornly silent. He willed it to ring. It disobeyed.

Pete popped the cassette into the tape deck and hit play.

A hiss like TV snow after channel signoff issued from his speakers, succeeded by several beeps. Then the beeps were intermingled with the white noise and a few instances of three or four rapidly repeating notes that sounded like a cheap, crappy synthesizer. He wondered if this was some funk jazz fusion experimental crap—George liked some weird shit, to be sure. He made a mental note to ask about it when he saw him next.

If he saw him. If George would ever speak to him again. His throat tightened even more.

"That reminds me of some of the prog rock from the '70s," Pete said. "I was at this club in 1973, and—"

The phone rang, and Bill ran to the bedroom extension. "Hello?"

"Well, Ethel Rue finally threw out her good-for-nothing son," his mother Marge said, water running in the background.

Although Bill had been frantic for his mother to call, the sound of her voice silenced him.

"Hello? Is anyone there?"

"Hi, Mom," Bill said, and heard the quaver in his own voice. He had to remind himself that this call was not only necessary, but absolutely critical. Everything would be okay after he'd done what desperation was forcing him to do. Something he'd never have done back when he was…what? A decent human being?

"I told her—I've been telling her for years." The garbage disposal screeched in the receiver.

"You told her," Bill said.

"Says his back hurts. Says he can't work." She snorted. "Lazy, I say. But you know how mothers are with their sons."

Bill hoped he did. Even though the priest was in another room, he lowered his voice. "Mom, I need a loan."

Silence but for the splashing water in his childhood home's kitchen sink.

He looked at his reflection in the bureau mirror, forced the face to approximate a smile, inject enthusiasm and hope into his voice. "Liz and I are buying a house."

"Is that right?" she said, cautious.

He plowed on. "You're going to love it—three bedrooms. A basement. Wrap-around porch."

"How much?" she said.

"One of the rooms is for you."

"How much?"

"I need…I need twenty-five thousand dollars."

The water on the other end of the line ceased running. This time there was not just an absence of sound but a void: negatively charged, absolute.

He tried to swallow but had no saliva.

"Bill," she said, slowly. "You know I don't have that kind of money."

He shut his eyes. Could look at his reflection no longer. "I thought maybe you could…take out a mortgage on the house."

A long pause. "I don't feel comfortable…it's the only thing your dad left me. Where would I live if…"

"Of course I'd—we'd just make the payments," Bill said, clenching his fist and banging it into his thigh, harder and harder.

"But you still haven't paid me back for the—"

"And you can always—you can always live with us." Bill raised the fist and bashed it twice against his temple.

She didn't say anything.

The word *evil* rolled through his brain, whirled and tumbled, the glossy black letters boomeranging inside his skull, and he viewed this from thirty-thousand feet above the earth.

He dug his fingernails into his neck. "I'll go to the bank with you, Mom."

"Bill," she said, and the tone of her voice signaled she knew he was lying, and she was hurt and confused. "Put Liz on the phone."

"She's not here. And it's…a surprise for her…for our anniversary, and I don't want her to—"

"Bill."

"What?"

"She's gone, isn't she?"

He spluttered, trying to work up indignation, but he was too tired and high to put on a good show. This was a fucking disaster. "She'll be back." His voice was a croak.

"I love you, son. Goodbye."

The line went dead. He hung up and went back in the living room.

"Everything okay?" Pete said.

Bill nodded, his movements now mechanical and only approximating true human reactions. "My mom," he said. "She's having some…health issues." He heard his own snide tone, the sarcasm, and turned leaden with self-pity. Bill himself would be suffering from *health issues* if he didn't find the money he needed.

The phone rang again, and Bill snatched it up. Maybe she'd changed her mind.

"Hello?"

"Have you got it?" Hoover said.

Bill twisted away from the priest's prying eyes. "I need a little more—"

"What happened to the 'large amount of product'?"

"I've had a little setback, and what I—"

"Not so high and mighty now, are you, Professor?" Hoover said. "Always treating me like white trash, like you're a king and I'm some peasant who'll park your car for you. If you don't have the money for me by tomorrow night, I'm going to send my associate over there to kick your ass, and when I say kick your ass, I mean break some bones. Count on it. Don't call me again."

"Hoover, wait! I can—"

The line disconnected, and Bill stared at the receiver as if he expected to see Hoover's face there. He hung up and stared. He needed money right now, so he'd have to sell something. Scanning the living room, he saw nothing of value. He owned nothing of value.

Nothing except his white 1967 Mustang.

But…he loved the Stang. Had pined away for one for years before saving enough money to buy one in excellent condition. It was his baby. And once he'd sold it, he could envision the downward spiral: pawning his watch. Finally, his gold wedding band. Selling plasma. And then…

Enough. It wouldn't come to that. He just needed to get a little ahead. And to take a step toward that, he had to sell his car. And the fastest way to do it was to track down the person who said if Bill ever wanted to sell, he wanted to buy.

"What was that all about?" Pete asked.

Bill had forgotten the priest was there and he was suddenly embarrassed. It must be obvious what that had been all about.

"That was…" He was too stoned to come up with a lie. "I need to go to campus and get some things from my office, and…"

Pete scrutinized him. "Should you be driving?"

"Why not?" Bill swallowed.

"I'm sure you've had plenty of practice," Pete said, "but better not chance it, eh?"

Bill couldn't speak. He felt like he was fifteen, busted.

Pete put a hand on Bill's arm. "Maybe wait a while before you hit the road. Okay?"

They were petrified in this pose for what seemed like ten minutes. To make it stop, Bill said, "Okay."

Pete patted the arm and let go. "All right," he said. "Catch you later." He slid on his helmet as he left.

As the door closed, Bill realized he hadn't thanked Pete for bringing him the tapes. His douchebaggery knew no bounds.

No more answering the door or the phone. That was it. He couldn't keep doing this with the priest.

Bill went to the bathroom to take a leak and caught a glimpse of himself in the mirror. Mistake. Pallid skin. Hair matted and oily at the same time. But worst of all, the empty, soulless eyes.

A monster stared back at him.

He went back to the dining room, placed his special mirror on the table, and dumped the remainder of the coke on it. He cut it into lines and snorted every last grain.

CHAPTER TWENTY-THREE

George

Wednesday, May 28, 1986
Lawrence, Kansas
7:30 p.m.

As they pulled up to his Lawrence apartment complex, George remembered the day he'd signed the lease five years before. The complex was near new at that time, beautifully landscaped, with all the modern bells and whistles. It felt like years instead of days since he'd left the leafing trees and well-lit and manicured lawns.

He had to remind himself to breathe. In and out. Every muscle a taut rubber band ready to snap. Never-ending rivulets of sweat rolling down the neck of his shirt.

Travis parked his Gremlin two buildings over from George's. He took his pistol out of the glove box and slipped it into his shoulder holster then donned his security uniform cap and jacket. "Gimme the key," he said. "Stay put. I'll go check it out."

He toured the parking lot, his movements stiff, on constant alert to his surroundings. Then he made his way to George's apartment. After several minutes, he returned, his expression grim. Alarm bells went off in George's head. Travis looked around again and motioned for George to get out of the car and follow him.

He obeyed and met Travis at the entrance to his apartment. Travis whispered, "Brace yourself."

George opened the door. What he saw was not his old apartment. It was a trash heap, a junkyard. Furniture overturned, papers scattered, trash upended.

"The cops," George said. "The cops were—"

"It wasn't cops," Travis said, looking around. "The warrant would be posted, or a note stating the property was searched pursuant to a warrant and stating where a copy of the warrant could be obtained." He touched the door's deadbolt. "Plus the lock's intact. It wasn't cops. It was Stacia and her people."

"How would she have—" Then he recalled something Stacia said that night: *I think we live in the same apartment complex. Highpoint. Right?*

She must know someone on staff here, found out which apartment was George's, and got hold of the master key. He knew first-hand how persuasive Stacia could be without even trying—she could talk some dumb maintenance man or horny janitor on staff here into doing whatever she wanted.

"We have to get out of here," George said.

"They've already been here," Travis said. "There's no reason to come back because they didn't find what they wanted. What would they have been looking for?"

George dodged garbage on the floor. Apparently, the searchers had dumped out every trash receptacle in the apartment. He ran into the bathroom and ripped aside the shower curtain. Travis arrived in the doorway as George investigated the tub. The bloody shirt lay dried and wrinkled in the bottom, exactly where he left it, the washcloth he'd used to clean himself up and his acceptance letter on top.

Travis stared, then pulled a ballpoint pen out of his pocket and lifted the shirt out of the tub. He examined it without touching anything then let it drop. "Whoa Nelly," he said. "This thing really happened, didn't it?"

Faint and nauseated, George nodded silently. This wasn't just some random blood, but the blood of three murdered girls, murdered with that gun and bloody knife now in the possession of his asshole cousin. Now that he knew, it seemed almost sacrilegious to destroy the part of those girls that remained, that had been smeared all over his face and hands.

"So they weren't looking for this," Travis said. "I told you it wasn't this. What were they looking for?"

"Has to be the big bag of cocaine, right?" George said.

"Must be," Travis said. "In any case, I brought an evidence bag." He produced it from inside his uniform jacket.

"We can't carry these things out of here," George said. "I have to burn them."

"George," Travis said. "We can't destroy evidence."

"What if there was no evidence to begin with?"

"What do you mean?"

"I burn the shirt. It never existed. You had no knowledge of it."

"But I did," Travis said.

"No," George said. "You didn't."

Travis lowered the toilet lid, sat atop it, and inched his hat back on his head. He peered up at George. "The shirt exists, pard."

"I know that," George said. "But say we carry it out of here, and you hide it for me. That's what you're thinking, right?"

"I was, yeah."

"Then if the authorities do become involved, and you turn in the shirt *then*, you're going to be an accessory. There will be physical evidence that you were. You will get arrested, and then you'll never become a cop. You need to go stand outside while I burn all this stuff. That way you can say in good conscience that all you did was drive me up here so I could get my clothes. That's all you did. You didn't know anything about the shirt or the envelope or the washcloth or anything."

George could see Travis's brain wrestling with the ethical dilemma, and he hated himself for putting his strait-laced friend in this horrible situation.

Finally, Travis sighed, stood, and squared his hat on his head. He walked silently out of the bathroom and seconds later, George heard the front door open and close.

He pulled the batteries from the smoke detectors, and gathered Comet, paper towels and a can of lighter fluid from under the kitchen sink.

He knelt before the tub and stretched the fabric taut to look at the Head East logo on the back. He re-experienced Stacia's light touch.

Love me tonight.

What a dipshit he was, letting himself believe even for a second that the girl was into him. For blindly and trustingly drinking an unknown substance like a lovesick teenager. What would she have done if he hadn't drunk the absinthe? He hadn't thought about this until now.

She would have shot him. He'd be dead.

His hands shook as he lit his lighter and held it under the letter, which burned easily. Then he doused the shirt and washcloth, and a muffled combustion noise accompanied the growing yellow-blue flames. He poured until he'd emptied the can. He watched the shirt and cloth burn.

The disintegration took longer than George thought, and when the fire went out, he turned on the shower and let the water run. Much of what was left ran down the drain. Some solid material remained, which he tore up into small pieces and flushed down the toilet, one at a time, followed by the buttons. Then he scrubbed with Comet until the tub gleamed as it never had before while he lived there, which was even more striking with the current trashed state of the apartment

George opened the front door and looked out. "It's done."

Travis stood at attention. He shook his head, his lips a thin line, and reentered the apartment. He stood with his arms crossed, and George saw how hard this was for law-and-order Travis.

"Thank you, G-Ho," he said.

Travis grunted.

"I need to find some stuff and pack it up to take back to Niobe with me before we go," George said. "And I need to get my mail."

"You got a PO box?"

"No." George pushed up his glasses. "The mail boxes are over by the front office and club house on the other side of the complex. I'll run over there and—"

"I'll go. You pack. The less you're seen the better."

"Yeah, okay," George said. "I really appreciate it." He pulled out his keyring, singled out the mail box key, and gave it to Travis. "It's number one fifty-seven."

"Be right back," Travis said. He removed his side arm from his holster and held it out to George. "Here."

"What am I going to do with this?"

"Protection. Take it."

George would argue no more with Travis after all he'd sacrificed to help. He accepted the pistol and cradled it like a newborn kitten.

"I'll be right back." Travis walked out and shut the door behind him.

George inspected the pistol then stuck it down the back of

his jeans like he'd seen characters in movies do. The cold metal dug into his back as he walked around inspecting his belongings strewn about the living room: his record albums with the discs torn out of the sleeves, two of them splintered on the carpet, the rest of his cassette collection with cases open, the tapes flung around as if a toddler had thrown a tantrum in here.

This sight depressed him to the point that he couldn't seem to make himself pack the clothes, cassettes, and papers he'd intended to take. So he sat in the one open spot on the living room floor against the wall and lit a cigarette. He closed his eyes and tilted his head back, exhausted.

To keep from obsessing about his situation, he turned his thoughts to fantasies of spending evenings at little dives in the towns he would be visiting as a traveling K-Mart portrait photographer, the tourist attractions he'd visit, the stories he'd have to tell when he was an old man.

George sensed a pressure change in the room as the door and his eyes opened at the same time.

Two strange men stood in the doorway.

A gut-punch of adrenaline made his limbs jerk. And then he noticed the matching navy-blue work shirts they wore and the red metal toolbox one of them carried. George stifled a gasp, provoked by the realization of how close he'd cut it in destroying the shirt.

The workmen looked around at the carnage in awe as if they'd wandered into a war zone.

"Yikes. What happened here?" said one. He was a tall, wiry,

red-headed frat-rat type. The other was an enormous body-builder with gelled black hair. Their shirts sported embroidered name badges. The body builder's said Mike and the frat-rat's said Derrill. Mike's biceps were so huge, George wondered if he'd had to special order his shirt.

"Had a little party," George said. It was the first thing that popped into his mind and it was as good an explanation as any.

"Big party, looks like," Derrill said. He was the one with the toolbox.

"I thought the manager said you all weren't going to do this until tomorrow?" George said.

Derrill glanced at Mike and said, "Figured we'd get an early start."

"Okay," George said. "I cleaned out the tub, so you can get right on it. Bathroom's right through there." He pointed with his cigarette.

The workmen looked at each other and trooped down the hall, then clanking sounds echoed from the bathroom. George resumed his reverie, head tipped back.

A few minutes later, Derrill, the redhead with the toolbox, re-emerged, looking around. "You are absolutely not getting your deposit back."

"Definitely not." George took a hit of his smoke and tapped ashes into an empty Pepsi can.

Derrill strolled closer, now ten feet from George, and stared at him. George's hand went to his recently shorn hair.

"Mike," Derrill said over his shoulder. "Come out here."

The body builder appeared in the hall. "What?"

"Come here. Look at this guy. Does he look familiar to you?"

George had to force himself to keep from ducking his head. He took a hit of his smoke. "I just have one of those faces."

Mike advanced, stood next to the redhead, and joined him in studying George's face, which broiled under the scrutiny. Mike crossed his arms. "I don't know."

Something strange about Derrill's light blue eyes, and it took a moment to realize what it was. They didn't blink, which made George blink twice as much, his eyes watering.

George took a final draw on his cigarette and slipped the butt into the Pepsi can.

He wished G-Ho would get back here so they could book.

"I swear I know this guy," Derrill said.

"I'm sure you don't—"

Mike talked over George as if he hadn't spoken. "Know him, or he looks like someone you know?"

It was as if George were in a store window and they were debating whether to buy him or not.

"You probably want to finish up in there and get on home," George said.

"You think you know everybody," Mike said to Derrill.

Panic spiraled deep in George's guts. He said nothing.

Derrill snapped his fingers. "I know where I've seen you. You hit a guy with your car on Third Street by the railroad crossing last Friday night."

The bottom fell out of the world. George's stomach rose,

threatening to pop out of his mouth. For a moment, Derrill seemed to be speaking in Korean. George let out a noise that sounded like "Wha..." How did they know about that? There'd been no mention of any such thing in the papers. These guys were cops. George had almost fallen for their lure.

"This is the guy, right, Mike?"

Mike nodded. "That's him."

"You didn't think anyone saw, right? You thought you got away with it. But you didn't, George."

They knew his name. Of course they knew his name. They'd found something with his fingerprints on it, and they connected it to his DWI police file. They knew everything about him.

"You had a busy night last Friday, didn't you?" Derrill said. "A lot of people wonder why those girls were killed. Because they were sorority girls, and why would anyone kill sorority girls? But you know why, George. Don't you?"

George started to stand. "You've got the wrong—"

"Don't get up on our account," Derrill said, holding up a hand.

The hand held a gun.

CHAPTER TWENTY-FOUR

George

George slid back down the wall.

"You know why those girls were killed. Don't you?" Derrill repeated.

Mike sauntered over to the front door, closed and locked it.

A tendril of fear slunk down George's spine, a more profound fear than when he'd believed these men were cops. Now he longed for law enforcement to arrive and arrest him.

"One of those girls had something that belongs to us," Derrill said. "And you came back to your apartment, so we figure you left it here. Although we searched the place pretty good. So where is it?"

"Where's—" He stopped talking because he remembered the metal digging into his back was a gun. But he couldn't make himself reach for it.

"You give it to us and we won't kill you," Derrill said. "Sound fair? You give it back, no harm, no foul. We'll forget the whole thing. Deal?"

"But—but—I don't know what you're talking about. I swear to you..." He was stalling, trying to will his hand into motion, to draw the gun. He tried to convince himself he was a badass. He'd scared the piss out of his cousin. He could do it to these guys.

"Where is it?" Derrill drew closer and George tensed all over, his mind a fizzing blank.

"Think a bullet might jog your memory?" There was a metallic *chunk* as he chambered a round.

George reached behind him and pulled Travis's piece. He cocked it and aimed with feeble, shaky hands.

A slow, quizzical smile came over Derrill's face, and he looked back at Mike. "What's this?" He turned back to George. "You threatening me?"

George's hands quaked, the pistol dancing all over the place.

Derrill reached down and wrapped his fingers around it. George tried to hold on but he couldn't, and Derrill slid it out of his sweaty grip. Mike took Travis's gun from his partner and targeted George's head.

George's weakness disgraced him. Who had he been kidding? He was no tough guy.

Derrill squatted before George. "*I'm* the guy you hit with your car, motherfucker." In a lightning-fast motion, George heard a *thok!*, felt the sand of a broken tooth, and tasted cold metal and warm blood as Derrill shoved his gun barrel between George's teeth. "You're lucky you only clipped me, or—"

The front door knob shook followed by knocking. George's heart went into his esophagus and set up shop there.

But Derrill was a rock, serene and assured. "Ask who it is." He eased the gun from between George's lips with almost obscene gentleness then pointed it at his crotch.

"I know who it is." George pulled the bandanna out of his back pocket and pressed it to his bloody, swollen mouth.

"Do it!" Mike hissed.

"Who is it?" George sang out in an unintentional falsetto.

"Let me in," Travis said.

"Hang on a sec."

"We'll kill him, too," Derrill said quietly. "But you first."

If George shouted, Travis would come busting in here like Clint Eastwood. Words and blood spewed from George's mouth, as he hissed, "If you shoot me, you won't get your property back." Trying to keep his voice down made it crack and quiver like a twelve-year-old boy's.

This gave Derrill pause. He glanced back at Mike whose lack of interest chilled George more than Derrill's intimidation tactics.

"You gonna bring it back here?" Derrill said. "Because if you don't bring it back to us by ten p.m. on Saturday, we're going to give the Lawrence P.D. more evidence. Like all those threatening letters you sent to Kimberly Laurent because she wouldn't go out with you."

"*What?* I didn't—"

"Come on, man," Travis called through the door, impatient.

"And her friends, they'll say you were obsessed with her, wouldn't leave her alone. They'll swear under oath you were constantly lurking around the sorority house. How she had to move to that house on Kansas Street to get away from you. But then you found her."

"But—"

"I know what you're thinking: you can disappear again and then you don't have to do anything. But here's the thing. We know where your parents live."

George's eyes widened, and his blood turned to powder.

"Yeah, you heard that, didn't you? If you don't bring our property back by Saturday, we'll drive down to—" Here he pulled a slip of paper from his pocket and read it aloud: "11000 Adobe Road, Unit D, Lake Havasu, Arizona, and kill your parents."

Derrill kept his eyes on George and now got the reaction he apparently wanted. George's chin quivered.

Travis pounded on the door. "Open up!"

"If you don't want to be an orphan, you'll do what I tell you. Come back to the apartment and we'll meet you here again. And if you don't, there'll be hell to pay."

As near as George could tell, hell had already rented a room next door and was listening to its shitty music at top volume twenty-four hours a day.

Derrill slapped George's cheek and gave him a big toothy grin. He stood, tucked the address and his gun away and stalked toward the door, where Mike likewise pocketed

Travis's pistol and opened the front door.

Travis stood aside and let them exit.

"So we can start in here tomorrow?" Derrill said over his shoulder to George. He had the nerve to wink.

"Yeah." George stood. "Thanks for coming by." He followed them on rickety legs and watched them cross the parking lot, climb in a red conversion van—probably the same one that had tried to pull him over Friday night—and sit there. Waiting for George to leave, presumably to tail him, nab the cocaine, and kill him, all without having to wait for Saturday night.

Travis got a look at George's face and said, "What the hell happened?"

"Those two guys—" A familiar face caught George's attention over Travis's shoulder.

Travis turned to look.

Across the parking lot walked a man carrying a twelve-pack of Miller High Life, but for a moment George couldn't make the connection because the context was all wrong. Then it clicked. It was the liquor store lifetime student himself, wearing his usual topsider shoes and Polo shirt.

"Richie?" George said, not loud, but Richie turned in George's direction.

His eyes lit with recognition. "I can't believe you blew off the match on Saturday!" He walked toward them.

George pushed Travis out the door and closed it behind them so Richie couldn't see the mess inside.

When he got close enough, he frowned. "What the fuck

happened to you?"

George touched his lip, which ached. "I—uh, fell."

On a frat-rat gangster's semi-automatic.

Travis cocked a skeptical eyebrow but said nothing.

"What's with the hair?" Richie said. "And the glasses? The last time I saw you, your shirt was all—" Richie cut his eyes at Travis and switched gears. "You look snuffed. Need a brewski?" He cracked open the box and pulled out two cans. He proffered one to Travis, who refused. George, however, gladly popped the tab on the Miller and drank, even though it stung his mangled lip.

"Thanks, man," George said. "Exactly what I need."

"Sure, buddy," Richie said, glancing at Travis, who stood vigilantly next to George.

George had forgotten his manners. "This is my friend, Travis."

Richie shook Travis's hand. "How do you know George?"

"We grew up together."

Richie nodded then turned to George. "Haven't seen you around the store lately, and you know you—you're totally canned. I know what day it is by when you come in after your shift. When you didn't show up at your usual time on Tuesday night, I started to think you'd ditched."

"Just took a little time off." George waved a hand vaguely.

"You're not going to another liquor store, are you? That would be narbo to the max."

Why would he give a damn? He acted like he was the owner

of the joint instead of a peon employee.

"No." George patted his stomach. "I'm trying to cut down on the beer."

"All things in moderation," Richie said, lifting his can in the air. "Well, I'm going to go on home now to veg and watch some *Sledgehammer* reruns."

"Where do you live?"

"Here. In the complex."

"You do?" George said. "Why didn't you say anything about it the other day at the store? When that girl said she lived here?"

Richie went blank-faced for a moment and then said, "Oh, the blonde, right? I didn't want to be a beaver dam on you, bro."

Travis's nose twitched at the crude euphemism, which made George want to laugh, but he squelched it.

"Got some friends coming by for a beer pong-o-rama later," Richie said. "You want to drop by?"

"Sorry, man, but I'm beat. Just going to crash. Thanks, though. For the beer."

"Sure, bud," Richie said. "Go handle that lip." He waved and departed.

George pulled Travis back inside and closed and locked the door.

"So what really happened?" Travis said.

"G-Ho—those were the guys who ransacked the apartment. They're Stacia's henchmen. Goons. Whatever. They're the ones who tried to pull me over on Friday before I beat the train."

"The plumbers? The same guys?"

"They're still sitting in their van out there. They're going to follow us home."

Travis pulled on the bill of his uniform hat, thinking. Then he said, "I'll tell you what we're going to do. We're going to call 911."

"Yeah, no we're not."

"We're going to call them and tell them a suspicious van has been sitting in the parking lot for a long time, and we think they have some illegal gear in there. They've got an illegal cherry light in there you said. That'll detain them long enough that we can get out of town. And that's why I covered the Gremlin in mud—to obscure the license plate in case this very thing happened."

"You would make a hell of a cop," George said. "You *will* make a hell of a cop."

Travis's ears and face lit up like a Christmas tree.

"I'll call. Go patch up that lip." Travis stepped around the debris toward the kitchen phone, picked up, and dialed.

George rinsed his mouth in the bathroom, looking in the mirror and remembering the night just a few days ago that he was spitting out someone else's blood. He switched off the light and went into his destroyed bedroom, where he sifted through the papers that were scattered everywhere until he found his car title.

When George returned, Travis said, "They're on their way. Soon as law enforcement gets here, we're history. I'll do surveillance and then—"

The phone rang. Travis and George stared at each other and waited for the machine to pick up.

"George." That slight southern accent without the teasing tone. Frantic. "You've got to help me. I'm supposed to be dead."

Stacia.

George clutched his hands together, forbidding himself to answer. He and Travis held eye contact as they listened. George's lip throbbed, and the throbbing migrated to his temples.

"Are you there?" Stacia said and waited, traffic sounds in the background. He figured she was at a payphone somewhere. His shoulders started to twitch.

Then he heard soft crying. "I don't know what I'm going to do," she said. "I left something in your car by accident Friday night." More crying. "And some very bad people want it. I did something really stupid, but that's not your problem. I'm sorry I left you there. Here's what happened. I was told to drink the absinthe with my—my—my—sisters." Her cry had changed into sobbing and she couldn't go on for a moment. "And now I know it was supposed to knock all four of us out. That's why I'm still alive. Because I didn't go in that house or take my shot along with the girls. I was supposed to share it with my sorority sisters."

George got a chill. Was this true? If it was, Stacia was in as much trouble as he was.

"If my car had started, I would have been in that house by the time these bad people got there. We were all supposed to be unconscious by the time they got there. George. I'm only alive *because my car wouldn't start.*" Her sobbing intensified.

George's skin erupted in goose bumps. If her car had started, everything would be different. He'd have won the match against I Phelta Thi and he'd be making his supervisory rounds right now.

"You can't imagine what a shock it was when you passed out in the car. I was about to get out and head into the house when I heard *pop-pop-pop-pop* from inside the house, and then these guys in dark clothes came out, black ski masks over their faces. They ran toward your car, and I panicked. I tried to wake you up, but you were out. I got out of the car and I ran. They chased me, but I hid in a neighbor's dog house and then I heard the explosion. Scared the hell out of me, it was so loud, I thought it was the house I was hiding behind." Here she broke down completely.

If she was lying, she was the best liar he'd ever known. He could feel her terror and despair like a miasma seeping through the answering machine.

"George. If you're listening, if you hear this, you have to call me. Please. Come back. Take me with you. I have to get out of here."

Something must have shown on his face, because Travis shook his head at George.

"You have no reason to believe me, but if you'll call me back…I can explain everything to you…see, I needed money for college, and I made some bad decisions and got involved with some bad people."

Travis stepped between him and the answering machine. "Steady, George," he said.

"I'm hiding, but if you get this message, I'm begging you. Please call me at my friend's apartment. I need you, George. I need your help to stay alive. I hate to do this to you after everything I've put you through, but it'll be on your head if I die. My life is in your hands."

George went light-headed at this statement.

"Here's the number where I'm staying." She recited the digits twice. "Please." She hung up.

George let out his breath, and Travis exhaled too.

"Wow," Travis said.

"Could—could all that possibly be true?" George said.

"I don't know, George. One thing I do know, though, and this is going to sound harsh—but you don't owe that girl anything."

"But you heard her. Her life is in my hands."

Travis stroked his chin. "She's mixed up in dealing drugs and killing people."

"I just wonder if I should—"

"No," Travis said, emphatic. "You are not going to call her."

"But—"

"No." Travis walked to the window facing the parking lot and lifted the shade an inch. In spilled alternating red and blue light.

George went momentarily slack with relief. The cops were here. But…

"Wait. What if Derrill and Mike tell the cops about me and—"

"They're not going to. You've got what they want, and they're not going to say anything to anyone until they get it from you. Now let's go. Leave the lights on."

"You don't have to pay the electric bill," George said.

Travis glared at him and George relented.

"Fine," he said.

"Okay. When we get outside, we're going to crawl to the bushes lining the sidewalk."

"What if someone sees us?"

"This is a college town. They'll assume we've drunk our weight in Fighting Cock bourbon."

Travis walked to the door and flipped the deadbolt then slowly opened the door. He slipped out and George shadowed him, both their backs flattened to the exterior wall. George silently locked up, and they got down on their hands and knees and crawled to the bushes. They crawled until they were at the end of the sidewalk and then Travis popped his head up over the Pacer they hid behind.

"They're occupied. Let's go."

They stood and ran bent over toward the Gremlin, and got in. Luckily there were two exits from the parking lot, and Travis steered in the opposite direction of the van and the police cruiser.

George breathed a sigh of relief as he looked over his shoulder out the back window and saw the flashing lights and the two officers standing by the van.

They rode silently toward I-70, and once they were through

the Topeka toll booth, Travis held out his hand. "Can I have my sidearm back?"

Oh, shit.

"Um, G-Ho, I don't know how to tell you this, but those guys took it from me. When they gave me this." He touched his mouth.

Furious, Travis said, "You let them have it?"

"I didn't let them—they took it!"

"And you didn't do anything." Travis punched the dashboard, his face screwed up in frustration. "And now those cops are going to find it when they search the goons."

George tried to think of a way to phrase his question so it didn't sound completely self-serving.

"What does that mean for us?"

"The first chance we get I need to find a payphone and report my piece stolen." Travis angrily pulled his hat from his head and flung it into the back seat. "And I'm going to have to come back to Lawrence and file a police report, and I'm going to have to lie my ass off. Thanks a lot, George. I'm going to have to lie to the police. Do you have any idea what that means to me? I helped you destroy evidence, and now I have to lie. To the *police*."

I'm sorry didn't seem to cut it. "How about this," George said. "I'll call it in stolen. I'll file the report."

Travis turned an infuriated face his way. "You know you can't do that, George! You're a wanted man, even if they don't exactly know it's you."

"Can we wait to report it stolen?"

"Once they run the serial number, they'll know it's mine."

"It's legal, right? It's registered, isn't it?"

"Of course it is! How else would they know I'm the owner?"

They drove in silence a moment and then Travis slapped his palms on the steering wheel, making George jump.

"Damn it, George. You are a shit magnet."

He was. A hot flare of shame swept over him. He never should have involved G-Ho.

On the drive home, Travis remained utterly silent, and George knew better than to try to make small talk. All he could think about was Travis and all he'd had to put up with from George, Bill, and Curt.

Back in ninth grade when the three of them started smoking pot, Travis strongly disapproved. Although he never ratted them out, he began spending more time with the cowboy crowd. So George, Curt, and Bill were surprised when Travis decided to spend graduation night with them, just like old times. That night, George asked Travis why he'd never turned them in for their dope-smoking.

Travis had looked shocked by the question. "You're my best friends," he'd said. "Nothing's ever going to change that. Plus, I'm no fink." Travis had slapped George's back. "Now, when I become a cop for real, I can't make any promises."

George thought about that night now as they drove toward Niobe, and it was midnight when Travis braked in front of Grandpop's little lavender house.

George turned to him, miserable. "I guess you probably don't want me to be a groomsman now."

"Just get out of my car."

He did, bereft, and walked toward the house. Travis started to drive away but stopped, reversed the Gremlin, and parked in front of the house.

George turned, and Travis got out and walked toward him. "You got shit for brains, you know that? I'm really pissed, and I don't know what I'm going to do. But you are *required* to stand up with me at my wedding. If you don't show up, I'm going to hunt you down and wring your neck like a chicken. You got me?"

"I get you," George said. "Thanks, G-Ho."

"I gotta go call the Lawrence PD. I'll see you later." Travis got in the Gremlin and roared away.

The little house was dark as George walked around to the back yard and went into the garage. He grabbed the big flashlight off the shelf, opened the front door of the Plymouth, and got in. He reached under his seat to feel for the baggie. His fingers sought out the yielding softness of the plastic bag but touched nothing. He stretched his hand back as far as he could. Nothing.

He backed out of the car and got on his knees, shining the flashlight beneath the seat. He found nothing but road dust. Freddie must have the cocaine hidden in the house.

George's earlier fear and humiliation fueled his rage as he went into the house and stalked straight into Freddie's room, flipped on the overhead light, and shoved him hard.

Freddie gasped and his eyes flew open. "What? What are you doing in my—"

"Where is it?" George said. "What did you do with it?" He let go of his cousin and yanked open dresser drawers, digging through neatly folded undies, socks, and shirts.

"What?" Freddie rubbed his eyes, a cartoon of a sleepy four-year-old. "Where's what?"

In the bottom drawer, George found the newspaper articles and the weapons, which he removed. "Where is it, you little dick bag?"

Now Freddie was awake enough to display fear. "What are you talking about?"

"The cocaine, asshole. What did you do with it?"

"Cocaine?" Freddie's confusion was genuine.

George froze. His cousin had no idea what he was talking about. Freddie didn't have the coke. He'd dug himself an even bigger hole.

Freddie flushed with righteous indignation, which turned into a faint suggestion of the cunning from their earlier confrontation. "You're a drug addict, too?"

George backpedaled like a man riding a unicycle in quicksand, tried to adopt a joshing tone. "I was just messing with you, cousin."

Freddie considered him dubiously.

"You know me," George said. "I'm goofing on you. Go back to sleep." He switched off the overhead light.

"You're lucky I have to work tomorrow," Freddie said, his bluster returned. "Otherwise I'd—"

George turned the light back on and advanced on the bed, full of menace. "Otherwise you'd what? What would you do?"

Freddie cowered, the covers clutched to his face.

"That's what I thought." George turned out the light and closed the door behind him, bursting with adrenaline and triumph.

But only for a moment, because the cocaine was gone. Where? How? Who?

And then he thought back to the night he'd showed the car to his three friends.

The two who got in.

The one who lugged his cassette carrier out of the back seat and straight to his wife's car.

CHAPTER TWENTY-FIVE

Bill

Thursday, May 29, 1986
Hays, Kansas
11 a.m.

Bill had only two goals for the day, and he was about to complete the first: he'd downed most of the bottle of vodka, which now held at most three more shots. And once that was done, he'd be prepared to tackle the last one.

This morning he'd gotten two phone calls, neither of which he answered—just sat and listened to them as the answering machine recorded their messages. The first call came from chemistry professor Max Greene, declining to buy the Mustang. Bill crumpled. He might have been able to find another buyer, but no one would pay the price he needed to dig him out of his predicament, not by tomorrow, Hoover's deadline.

The second was from George, in a voice Bill almost didn't

recognize. Livid. Incensed. Murderous.

"Bill, you asshole. The people who set me up said I've got something of theirs, and they want it back, or they're going to call the cops on me. Oh, and then kill my parents. And what do you suppose I have of theirs? A big bag of cocaine. Only it's not in my car. Because *you* took it. And if I know you, the whole bag is already gone, which means I'm fucked. And so are you, because if you don't bring me that coke, I'm going to call the cops on *you*. You better call me back, shithead, because I have to get that coke. Or I'm dead."

That makes two of us, Bill thought.

Now at eleven a.m., he held his glass in the air. A toast to George, who had given him the last push he needed to silence all the demons permanently. Bill threw down his final shot, calm, peaceful.

Vodka remained, but he was ready for goal number two.

He went into his bedroom and took his gun case from the closet and opened it. He removed the pistol and pulled out the clip. Empty. The last time he'd shot the Beretta was the previous summer on a camping trip with Curt.

Curt. Bill couldn't think of him, or he wouldn't go through with it.

He set the Beretta on the nightstand then stood unstably and staggered to the dresser. He opened the drawer. Inside, amid the plethora of pill bottles, baggies, and vials, sat the box of bullets. He considered a moment and then snatched it up.

It was light as smoke.

He hurled the empty box against the wall and began digging with frantic determination through the drawer, hoping to find one stray bullet rattling around at the bottom. He yanked out the drawer and dumped everything on the bed. He clawed through the contents. And there it was, one bullet.

The bullet.

Bill plucked it up with sweaty fingers then snatched the Beretta from the nightstand and ejected the clip from the grip. He tried to jam the bullet into the clip, but it squirted out of his hand and fell to the floor. Groaning, he sank to the carpet and pawed the knap. Where the hell did it go? He searched under the nightstand, under the bed, back and forth. It had disappeared.

Fury flooded his mind as he weighed his options. Drive over to K-Mart and buy a box of bullets? He pictured himself in front of the clerk. *"Do you sell single bullets? Barney Fife special?"*

A laugh escaped him. If he left the apartment he'd never do what had to be done.

The bottle of Quaaludes he'd been saving for a special occasion lay in the middle of his other goodies. *This might be better.*

Less mess for Liz to clean up. One last high. And then... peace. Because if he didn't do it himself, Hoover's associates would do it for him, and pain would be involved. He would beat them to it.

Bill stripped out of his clothes and shrugged into a terrycloth bathrobe that Liz gave him last Christmas. He slipped the pill bottle into the robe pocket and staggered a little, drunk.

In the kitchen he selected a glass from a cabinet and found the bottle of Courvoisier some ass-kissing student had given him. He gathered the five letters he'd hand-written and carried everything into the living room, set the bottle and glass on the coffee table, and fanned the letters on the carpet behind him.

Sitting cross-legged on the floor, Bill emptied the bottle of Ludes on to the coffee table and counted them out. Twenty-four. That should do the trick. He opened the bottle of Courvoisier, measured out a civilized amount into the glass, sniffed it, then held it in the air and brought it to his lips.

He should feel something. But he didn't.

A knock sounded on the door, and Bill's head jerked toward the sound, spilling his drink into the neck of the robe. He swiped at it, and his big terrycloth sleeve hooked on the mouth of the Courvoisier bottle. Bill watched it tip in slow motion. Before he could catch it, the liquid inside washed over the table, soaking the Ludes.

He sat suspended, staring, watching his plans dissolve in Cognac.

"Bill, you in there?"

He recognized that canny ex-hippie voice.

A key clicked into the doorknob, and Pete backed into the apartment, a box in his arms. "Liz thought you could use some of her famous chicken enchiladas, and we also put in some—"

Bill sprang to his feet, but it was too late. Pete stopped short when he turned toward the dripping table, the mushy mess, and a stunned Bill in a bathrobe.

"What's going on here?" Pete said, setting the box on the kitchen table.

Bill tried to collect himself. "Had a little party last night. I was cleaning up and…"

He trailed off as Pete invaded the living room and squatted by the five letters. He selected one of them, stood, and read it.

The one to Liz.

Pete finished reading and pushed up his glasses. He strode toward Bill, who braced for a well-deserved punch in the face.

Instead, he felt Pete's arms around him.

"Oh, my friend," Pete said. "My lost, lonely, tormented friend."

Bill collapsed against him and sobbed.

CHAPTER TWENTY-SIX

George

Thursday, May 29, 1986
Niobe, Kansas
11 a.m.

George was counting down the minutes until he could go to Salina day after tomorrow for the traveling photographer interview. He sat on the couch reading Tim O'Brien's novel *The Nuclear Age*. Bad idea. It described a vision of an intercontinental ballistic missile rising from the middle of Kansas. It felt like an omen.

George heard Curt's Jeep pull up, but no running feet this time. He opened the front door before Curt got to the porch.

"G-Ho came to my house this morning," Curt said. "Told me all about your trip to Lawrence. Holy shit, brother. You are in it deep."

He led Curt into the kitchen and recounted his own version

of yesterday's events and his earlier call to Bill.

"He didn't pick up," he said. "I left him a very persuasive message, though. I told him he'd better bring that cocaine back or I was going to call the cops on him. If I don't hear from him by tonight, I'm going to drive down to Hays and wrestle the coke away from him. You want to go with?"

The doorbell rang.

"You expecting company?" Curt said.

"G-Ho's at work, so no." George stood from the table, but Curt held up a hand, a frown on his face.

"Stay here," Curt said, and George complied.

Curt walked out of the kitchen, and George heard him open the door and voices outside, but he couldn't make out what they were saying.

Curt's voice: "I just woke up, so I don't know if he's here or not. Hold on."

George inhaled so hard he needed to cough. He covered his mouth with both hands, trying to swallow the spasm.

Curt re-entered the kitchen, eyes huge, and held his finger to his lips then said loudly, "George? You here?" On the pad by the phone he scrawled *KBI*.

It took a few seconds for George to work out what that meant.

Kansas Bureau of Investigation.

Curt turned and walked out of the kitchen and knocked on the master bedroom door. "George?"

George listened as Curt went back to the front door. "I

guess he's not here."

Fear sharpened George's hearing, amplifying the voices outside.

"When do you expect him back?" one of them said.

"I don't know."

"And what's your name?"

"Freddie Baumann." *Bless you, Curt.* "I'm his cousin. I own this house."

The screen door scraped, and George's heart stopped a second time. Was Curt letting them in?

"Sure, I'll tell him. Thanks. Have a nice day."

The front door closed. Curt appeared at the kitchen door and put his finger to his lips again. They waited and listened. Curt went to the window and peeked out the curtain. "They're still here," he said. "I get the feeling they're not going away anytime soon." He slid two business cards on the table. Special Agent Goulding and Special Agent Iacovelli, Kansas Bureau of Investigation.

George started hyperventilating. Thousands of pins seemed to prick his face. That fucking Freddie. This was payback for scaring him. His threats had backfired spectacularly.

"If I go out the side door," he whispered, "they're going to see me."

"They can't hear you from across the street," Curt said in a normal tone of voice.

George wrung his hands. "I have to go down to Hays. I have to get that cocaine back from Bill, if there's any left, and meet the frat-rat gangsters by six p.m. on Sunday, or they're going to murder my parents." George took a last drag from his cigarette and crushed it out.

"George. Even if you drive down there and go to Bill's house, I guarantee you he's not going to answer the door. He's not going to give it up. He's like a dragon hoarding gold."

"Even if he knows they're going to kill my folks?"

"You've never actually *known* any addicts, have you? Bill's lost to us, man. At least until he hits bottom, and I don't know when that will be. Or even if it'll happen before..."

George felt like he was trying to hold up a collapsing brick wall. "I have to do something. I have to talk my parents into leaving Lake Havasu, and then I have to disappear." He had an instant idea, one that seemed to come from heaven itself. "They wanted to sell the Corvette to pay for a cruise to Alaska."

"They wanted to sell your car? What kind of shit is that? "

"I appreciate your outrage on my behalf," George said, "but right now I need to get them out of Havasu." He reached into the cabinet above the phone. He found the Salina yellow pages, picked out a travel agency, and dialed it.

"I hope there's not a tap on this line," Curt said.

George hadn't thought of that but hoped an Alaskan cruise wouldn't arouse any interest in police. "I'd like to book two people on the next available cruise to Alaska."

"One moment, please," the female travel agent said, to the accompaniment of a clacking keyboard. "Yes, sir, the next Voyage of the Glaciers aboard the Sea Princess embarks from the Port of San Francisco on Monday morning. Is that too soon?"

"Perfect." Hope sprouted in his chest. "How many days is the cruise? And how much does it cost?"

"The cruise is eleven days, and the cost is one thousand ten dollars per person plus taxes and fees."

The sprig of hope was trampled. George's heart sank. He had maybe $300 worth of credit available on his Mastercharge.

Curt tapped him on the shoulder and mouthed, *How much*?

George waved him off and said to the travel agent, "Thanks anyway."

An American Express card appeared on the counter in front of him as if by magic. Curtis A. Dekker, it said. George stared at it.

"Hold on a second, ma'am," he said into the phone and then put his hand over the mouthpiece. "Curt, there's no way you can—"

"George, it's the only thing I *can* do. I can afford this. Let me do this for you and your folks."

George regarded his friend a moment longer.

"Ma'am?" he said. "I'd like to go ahead and book that trip."

The travel agent took down his parents' information, then George read Curt's credit card number to her. George wrote down all the cruise details before hanging up. He turned and shook Curt's hand with both of his. "Thank you, man. I'll pay you back. I promise."

Curt patted George's back then peeked out the window.

"The KBI are still here."

While Curt kept a lookout, George called his parents. It took roughly fifteen minutes to talk them into packing up and taking off for San Francisco the following morning. He told them he'd seen the error of his ways for not letting them have the Corvette and to consider it an anniversary gift. They fervently protested, but the lure of the Alaskan frontier was too much for George's dad in the end.

George figured when he didn't show up in Lawrence by ten on Saturday, Mike and Derrill would hit the road but wouldn't arrive in Lake Havasu City until three in the afternoon Monday at the earliest, when his folks would be safely out to sea.

He just had to pray that when they returned, they wouldn't be greeted with the news that their one remaining son had been murdered.

CHAPTER TWENTY-SEVEN

Curt

Curt peeped out the curtains again. The KBI sedan was still there. He nodded at George.

"I'm going to have to go out the window." George shifted from foot to foot.

"Listen, George," Curt said. "You can't come back here. You need to stay with me at my place. Nobody'll know to search for you out in the Nowheres."

"But—"

"We don't have time to debate over this. Pack your shit up and drive out to my place.

I'll meet you there later. Now go jump out the back window and I'll distract the fuzz."

"The *fuzz*?" George said. "I think people stopped saying that in 1968."

Curt didn't take the bait, just lifted his shoulders, hoping to encourage forward motion in George, whose indecisiveness normally didn't bother him that much. But today, impatience prickled at his skin and brain.

George eventually headed to the spare room and returned with a duffel bag. "Ready?" he said, looking scared.

"Godspeed," Curt said and watched George knock the screen out of the master bedroom window and climb out. Curt went out the front door and pretended to lock up as if he owned the joint. Then he crossed the street to the KBI car, which was stationed in the shade of a sycamore tree. Curt bent to look in the driver's side window. "Hey, guys," he said.

They nodded at him.

"I just remembered that George said he was going to a job interview in Salina."

One of the agents sat smoking a cigarette, and the other waved smoke away while drinking a gas station paper cup of coffee. They looked at each other then back at him.

"Anyway, you can stop back by around dinner time. He ought to be back then."

"Thanks," Special Agent Goulding said.

The echoing rumble of the Stingray starting up behind the house drew both agents' eyes in that direction.

"I guess you all can't tell me why you came all the way out here to talk to him, can you?" Curt said.

"Not really," Iacovelli said.

"Didn't think so." In Curt's peripheral vision, he saw the Corvette turn from the alley onto the cross street, not thirty yards away. He forced himself not to watch it drive toward

Main. He straightened, blocking their view of the sports car. "Later, gator," he said.

"Bye," said both agents.

Curt turned, crossed the street, and got in the Jeep where the dog napped on the front seat. Curt drove downtown. When he was out of sight of the cop car, he turned around to determine if they'd shadowed him, but of course they hadn't.

He pulled up in front of McWhiskey's and coaxed the dog out of the Jeep and onto the sidewalk, where he flopped down in the shade of the awning. What a good dog. Curt went inside.

Mac stood behind the counter watching a soap opera on the television in the corner next to the ceiling. Only three patrons were there, all sitting on stools, heads turned toward the TV.

"Hey, Mac," Curt said. "How's it going?"

The bartender grunted, caught up in his show.

"Can I use the phone?"

Without taking his eyes from the screen, Mac plunked the phone down on the bar in front of Curt.

"Thanks, man."

He dialed Bill's number. The phone rang and kept ringing. He was about ready to hang up when the answering machine picked up.

"I know you're there, Bill," he said. "Pick up. Pick up." He waited but Bill didn't answer. "I know you're not working. I know you're not doing anything but putting that shit up your nose, and I don't care if Liz hears this." He waited again. He didn't want Liz to hear the next bit though. "You remember that thing George told us about?" Curt's eyes shifted to Mac, who wasn't listening, but he lowered his voice anyway. "The KBI is here, and they won't leave. I think it might be a good idea if you return the—that thing you took from George's car or the *s* is gonna hit the *f* for George. You can bring it to my place, because he'll be staying with me until everything is resolved."

Silence. Nothing. Bill was a total goner, his friends, his family, his life were imperceptible to him inside the smog. He was the fourth of Curt's friends who'd gone down this road in one way or another, but the only one with college degrees and a professional job.

"Leave me a message at McWhiskey's if you change your mind." Curt hung up. "Thanks, Mac." He dug out his wallet and put a twenty on the counter. "For your trouble."

He walked out of the bar and spotted a white sedan with Shawnee County plates. Topeka was in Shawnee County, and S.H.A.'s headquarters were in Topeka. He crossed the street and walked into the Hometown Café.

The sounds of clanking utensils, the sputtering grill and cutlery against stoneware took Curt back to his childhood, even though he'd been coming here almost weekly his whole adult life. Fly paper flapped in front of the giant air conditioning unit that was mounted to the molded-tin ceiling and sounded like a jet engine. The scents of baking yeast rolls and frying chicken filled the air.

He immediately spotted the back of Rita Pavlakis's head bowed over one of the black, fluted-chrome edged tables, her curly dark hair untethered. She was sitting alone. Curt relished the idea of sneaking up on her for once.

He nodded to several of the diners as he walked over to Rita's table, where a book lay open. Curt pulled out a chair and sat down to her left. "What are you reading?"

She glanced up, startled. She actually looked…glad to see him, which produced not only butterflies in his stomach but worms, roly-polies, a whole ant farm. And then she looked self-conscious and slid her forearm over the book's cover.

Now he was really curious.

"Can I see?" he said.

She hesitated, then relented and lowered her hands to her lap.

He pulled the Niobe Carnegie Library book toward him and read the title on the plain white cover. *This is Just to Say*. William Carlos Williams.

His gut thrummed as she blushed, embarrassed.

"So what are you having?" he said.

"Hamburger, fries, chocolate milk."

"Best chicken-fried steak in the county here," Curt said. "Next time you come, you have to try it."

She smiled. "So," she said. "Truce?"

"Truce," he said.

"Good. Because I've found out some interesting things about the case in Lawrence."

"Tell me everything."

She scooted her chair forward and beckoned him closer. He

leaned in, happy for an excuse to sit this near to her. "This is just between you, me, and the lamppost," she whispered.

He made a rolling motion with his hand. "Okay. And?"

"I'm serious," she said, her face grave. "Because if this becomes public knowledge, it could destroy my sorority."

Her subdued expression sobered him, even though he didn't give a shit what happened to her sorority. But he did care about Rita's feelings. A lot, as it turned out. "All right. Cross my heart. Tell away."

"I spoke to my friend in law enforcement. It looks like some of my sorority sisters—including the girls who were killed—were involved in drug trafficking. And of course our mutual friend Stacia."

"You mean the three who were killed were *involved,* or just buying?"

"They were dealers, the authorities think. Well, two of them were. The third, it turns out, was a journalism grad student undercover trying to gather info for her master's thesis on the drug traffic along the I-70/I-35 corridor."

"Which one?" Curt said, but of course, he knew. It was George's journalism class acquaintance.

"Kimberly Laurent," Rita said. "I also asked some of the sisters about Stacia. Like I said, I didn't really know her. She was a freshman when I was a senior, so we never lived in the sorority house at the same time. In the 'to no one's surprise' department, turns out that Stacia has a police record. The girls I talked to said she was thrown out of the sorority for some crazy, wild behavior."

"That sounds about right. What else?"

"The investigators are trying to determine if Stacia and the two who were killed were an anomaly or if the problem in the KU Greek system goes a little deeper."

Curt reclined in his chair, skeptical. "Do you think that's possible?"

"I don't know." She straightened, and he was sorry he'd withdrawn from the confidential circle. "It's not like Greek kids don't do drugs, but…I don't know. It just seems…like a seismic shift, you know? I've always had it in my mind that drug dealers were…"

"People like me, right?" Curt said.

She looked away.

"Right?"

"I guess. Maybe not quite like you. I mean," here she leaned in again, and as if magnetized, he did too. "I've never *really* known anybody like you."

"To be fair," Curt whispered, "I've never known anyone like you, either."

Their foreheads were as good as touching.

Just then, Heather the waitress, a tall, pretty girl he'd tumbled with once or twice, ambled toward their table, a big smile on her face. "How you doing, Curt? Who's this?" She looked Rita up and down with amusement.

"This is one of the engineers working on the project across from my place," he said.

Heather's eyes danced. "Better watch out for this one. He's a bad one."

Rita spoke to Heather while looking directly at Curt with a suggestive glint in her iridescent green eyes. "We're just... *friends.*"

The way she said it melted his shorts a little.

"Can I get you anything else?" Heather asked Rita. "You want some pie?"

"I'd take a slice of lemon meringue," Curt said.

"Coming right up," Heather said and walked toward the kitchen.

He turned his attention back to Rita. "What do we do with all this information?"

She put her chin in her hand. "To start with, if you know anything, and I mean anything that could help the police, you've got to come forward. If a drug ring is murdering sorority girls, you need to help out in any way you can."

"Okay," he said. "If I find anything out that could help, I promise I will get in touch with the police. All right?"

She gave him a sideward glance. "Okay."

They sat in silence a moment.

"So tell me about being a civic engineer," Curt said.

"*Civil* engineer."

"Yeah. That's what I meant. What exactly do you do?"

"I design construction projects," Rita said. "Like the one outside Saw Pole. When I was a kid, though, I dreamed of designing theme park rides for Disney or Universal or even Six Flags."

He looked at her in surprise. "Yeah? What got you into that?"

"When I was in elementary school, I built these elaborate amusement parks for my hamsters." She gave an embarrassed laugh.

"Far out." Curt's face broke into a smile. "That is the best thing I ever heard."

Heather returned with Curt's pie, a fork, and a cup of black coffee. "You know I know how you like it," she said, winked again at Rita, and walked away.

Curt rolled his eyes and took a sip of the coffee before he dug into the lemon meringue.

"I went to K-State for a semester." Oops. That was not what he meant to say. Didn't know why it had popped out.

"Just one semester? Why'd you quit?"

"Oh, hell, you don't want me to go into all that."

Curt had two more bites before Rita said, "All what?"

He sighed and pulled a napkin from the spring-loaded chrome holder on the table. He wiped his mouth. Now he had to tell her, because he hated when people started a story and then acted all coy.

"It had something to do with a horse."

"A…horse?"

"You want some of this pie?" He'd lost his appetite.

"Sure." She picked up his fork and took a bite. Her eyebrows came together. "Wow. This is really good."

Curt held his breath. He hoped the pie would distract her.

She finished it off and then took a drink of his coffee. He watched her lips touch the same spot on the cup where his had. "Yummy." She pushed the plate away. "So, a horse."

Well, shit. It hadn't worked.

"Yeah." He sighed. "I had this horse named Natchez that I broke and trained myself. Couldn't take her with me to school, of course, and my dad said no way he was tending to another animal that he couldn't sell or eat, so my girlfriend kept her on her folks' farm in Saw Pole."

"Okay," Rita said. "Are we still talking about K-State? Because I'm not making the connection here."

"I'm getting to that," Curt said. "See, Natchez was a great horse—she was an Appaloosa, and the gentlest, most beautiful horse you've ever seen, right, but with a real wild streak. So Jeannette—that was my girlfriend—"

"High school girlfriend?"

"Right. We started going out when I was a junior and she was a freshman." He twirled the salt shaker, trying to think of only the horse. "Anyway, when I came home from K-State at Christmas break, Jeannette was gone."

Rita's hand covered her mouth. "Did she...die?

"No." Curt spat the word out like a chunk of rotten apple. "She ran off with some, like, traveling salesman. A guy in his thirties, right? It was like something out of a bad movie. Just up and left the horse and didn't say a thing to anyone. Just disappeared. Who does that, right? Leave an animal like that— an animal who depends on you to care for it—without a second thought? I sure as shit wouldn't have left Natchez with her if I'd known she could do something like that."

Rita crossed her arms and shook her head.

Heather appeared tableside and filled their shared coffee cup but didn't say a word before disappearing again.

Curt took a sip then set the cup in the saucer. "There was nobody to take care of Natchez, so I dropped out. Didn't go back for second semester."

"And what became of her?" Rita asked.

Curt crossed his arms. "A couple of months after I quit school, she was playing in the pasture, running around and having a good time, and she dropped dead, boom. Aortic aneurysm."

A touch on the arm from Rita startled Curt out of his rememberings. He turned his head toward her.

"I'm so sorry about Natchez," Rita said. "That's awful. But what I meant was, did you ever hear what happened to your girlfriend?"

Curt didn't respond for a moment. "I'll never own another horse, I'll tell you what. Can't go through that again."

Rita regarded him and said nothing.

Why had he told that stupid story? He hadn't even thought about that period of his life in quite a while, the series of events that had robbed him of enthusiasm and light, had changed him into whatever he was now. Those ancient feelings of helplessness overwhelmed him as if he were wearing a lead-weighted vest in frigid, murky water, sinking, sinking...

A warm touch shocked him back to the present. He looked down at Rita's slim hand over his then up at her face.

She smiled at him, and he expected her to tell him her own sad tale or say *we've all been there* or some shit like that, but instead, she said, "When are you going to start showing your paintings?"

"My…"

Now that he was back, she squeezed his hand and let go.

"That's the ultimate goal, right? Make a career out of painting?"

"A career?" He said it like he wasn't sure how to pronounce a foreign word.

"Well, yeah," Rita said. "If you don't do that, what are you going to do?"

"I'm doing it." He sat straighter, back in control.

She cocked an eyebrow at him. "You were a farmer before you sold your land to S.H.A., right?"

"Yeah," he said.

"Do you miss it?"

"Sort of, I guess," Curt said. "Some parts. It's a hard life, though, you know?"

"Is that why you sold to us? Too hard?" She didn't say it snotty, but it landed like an accusation.

"The price was too good to pass up," he said. "See, what happened was, my dad was driving a combine about four years ago and fell off it and broke his pelvis, and then he got pneumonia and almost died. Afterward, he couldn't farm anymore, so he signed the land over to me, because even though I'm the youngest, I'm the only boy in a family of six kids."

"You have five sisters?" Rita said.

"Yup. Callie, Cammie, Carrie, Cassie, and Cathy."

Rita laughed. "Good grief. What was it with '50s and '60s parents naming their children like that? My brothers' names are Russell and Ronald."

"Of course they are."

She smiled. "You inherited the land, and—"

"Yeah, so this guy came out to the trailer one time and asked if I wanted to sell, and he offered me a crazy price. Twenty-five hundred an acre. And then this financial planner guy bought me stocks and bonds and whatnot, and long story even longer, the money more than quadrupled."

Rita gathered her hair on top of her head and let it fall again. "You sold us over a hundred acres. Which means you're worth…"

Curt hesitated, because there was no good way to say it without sounding like some kind of gasbag, one of those K-State city kids who was so impressed with his dad's money he found a way to work it into every conversation. But Rita had asked, so he decided to answer. "About a million and a quarter." He shrugged and choked back saying, *So, see, I don't need a career.*

Rita whistled. She sat gazing at him, her head tilted, and said, "You know, when I saw your paintings the other day, I was really surprised. I wasn't expecting this."

He wasn't sure if she was talking about his paintings or

something else altogether. "What were you expecting?"

"I don't know," she said, a playful smile on her lips. "Maybe black velvet paintings of Elvis and Jesus shaking hands?"

Curt busted up laughing. She did too, in spurts, trying to hold it in, trying not to be too amused by her own joke. But the dam broke and she yawed forward, clutching his shoulder, and pretty soon they were both hooting and hollering like a couple of rednecks at a cock fight.

He hadn't laughed this hard in a while, and as he wound down, he said, "You're funny. I don't know any funny girls."

"But do you know any funny *women*?" she said, raising her eyebrows.

"Now I do," he said.

This conversation, this *woman* added up to a whole new life experience for Curt. Unusual. Strange. Like trying some exotic food, the sensation shocking and unlike anything you've ever had before, but the more you chew, the better it tastes.

Heather made her way over to them again and said, "Everything okay over here?"

"I'm good," Rita said. "You want anything else, Mr. Dekker?"

He wanted something, all right, but it didn't involve food. He shook his head.

Heather laid Rita's bill on the table and said, "Y'all have a good day, all right?" and walked toward the kitchen.

Rita shifted her knee into contact with Curt's and left it there, and he started tingling all over.

"Well, look who finally showed up for work!" Heather yelled

from the kitchen. "Hi, Gracie! Your boyfriend's having lunch out there...with a *date*."

He hadn't considered whether Gracie would be working today. In fact, he hadn't thought about her at all.

Curt glanced toward the order window where Gracie's furious red face popped up. He turned his eyes to the ceiling.

She came hurrying toward them with a glass full of ice and water, her eyes brimming with hatred aimed straight at Rita. She came to a halt at their table and, inches from Curt's face, yelled, "This ought to cool you off, you son-of-a-bitching bastard!" She dumped the water right in Curt's lap, slamming the empty glass on the table.

Rita let out a gasp as Curt jumped up so fast his chair went tumbling over. The ice water had cooled him off, all right. The crotch of his pants was now dark and soaked. Perfect.

"You go to hell!" Gracie said to Curt, and then stuck her tongue out at Rita before ripping her apron off and running out the entrance door. The diners paused briefly, solidified in restaurant poses as they surveyed the theatrics, and then returned to eating.

Curt righted his chair, wiped the seat, and then sat down. He couldn't look Rita in the eye. He wanted to break it all down for her, but what would he say? *Yeah, that's the half-naked girl who called me an asshole that you saw at my house. I bang her when I've got nothing else to do.*

"Poor thing." Rita shook her head. "Does she—"

Heather walked back to their table, her face wreathed in

223

smiles. "Wow, she's super mad, isn't she? I guess I shouldn't have said anything."

"Yeah, well," Curt said.

Heather leaned in closer and whispered, "You hear the KBI is here in town looking for your buddy George? They say he's the one who did the triple murder up in Lawrence."

Curt turned to Rita, whose posture had gone rigid. Oh, shit.

"Oh, now, Heather, you're just—"

"They're searching the Baumann place right this minute. God's truth." She held up one hand as if she were being sworn into office.

Curt's lungs deflated. So quickly she was a blur of movement, Rita threw her purse over her shoulder and bolted out of the restaurant.

"Guess she got smart right quick," Heather said.

"I'll be back to pay her bill," Curt said. "I'll be right back."

He jumped out of his chair and ran out the front door.

Rita was standing at the driver's side door of the white sedan trying to put the key in the door lock and failing.

"Rita," Curt said.

"Stay away from me," she said.

"Let me explain," he said.

Rita gave up trying to unlock the car and turned to face him, her eyes ablaze, her keys clenched in her fist.

"You *knew*," she said. "You promised me, you crossed your heart, promised you'd tell me anything you knew about the murders. And all along you knew what he'd done, and you

224

pumped me for information so you could—"

"Wait," Curt said.

"I can't believe I almost—"

"Just hold on a minute."

"You are a—"

"Stop," Curt said, loud. He didn't want to hear what noun she was about to use on him. His hands and legs shook.

She quit talking.

"I promised you I'd call the *authorities*. I didn't promise to tell *you*."

"What are you, a lawyer? You're just playing with words. Because you didn't contact the police either, did you?"

"Well, no—"

She threw her hands up.

"Listen," Curt said. "I didn't contact them because my friend George, the guy she was talking about in there, was framed. All he knew was that he woke up across from that burning house and—"

"He was *framed*? That's your explanation? The KBI wouldn't be here unless they had some pretty substantial evidence."

"He's guilty until proven innocent then." Curt's damp pants chafed his legs and the heat agitated him further. "You don't know anything about what happened, or what George has been through since then."

"You're right. I don't. Because you didn't *tell* me. You were only collecting intel for your pal."

He rolled his eyes. "This isn't a spy movie, Rita. I don't

collect *intel*." He scrubbed both hands over his face. "As I recall, you were the one who kept showing up at my house. I didn't ask for this. You were the one who came to *me*."

She was about to say something, but stopped, his logic apparently preventing her from going on.

"Look," Curt said, "George couldn't hurt a flea. He was in the wrong place at the wrong time. It's the story of his life. He couldn't murder people and blow up a house if he tried, because he can't do *anything*. The people closest to him fucked him over years ago and now he's stuck. These things just *happen* to him. He can't do anything about it. He's powerless. He can't change what he is."

It was out of his mouth before he recognized he wasn't talking about George anymore.

She scrutinized him. "Can't he?"

"No," Curt said, dropping his gaze. "He can't. He's tried."

"So instead he *wants* everyone to think he's a bum."

"He doesn't *want* that," Curt said, blood pressure rising. "That's just the way it is."

"Sure he does," Rita said. "Because then he only has to react, right? He doesn't have to *act*. He has no control over anything, no control over his own life, which is so comfortable. He'll never have to live up to anybody's expectations. Right?"

Curt took a step toward her, his hands fisted, his voice climbing to a shout. "Don't stand there and talk about him like you know him. You *don't* know him. And you never will."

Curt expected her to yell back at him, but she wilted, her

green eyes red. "Yeah," she said. "I guess you're right."

He blinked at her, feeling as if he'd been hollowed out. He opened his mouth to say something, but words failed him.

She turned away, unlocked the car door, got in, and sped away.

Curt went back in the restaurant to applause, and Heather yelled, "How about some just desserts, Curt?"

CHAPTER TWENTY-EIGHT

Curt

Thursday, May 29, 1986
Niobe, Kansas
8 p.m.

Curt sat on a stool with his back to the bar in McWhiskey's and stared at nothing. He'd had eight beers already, and he wasn't anywhere near done.

After the Hometown wait staff applauded him right out of the restaurant, he'd collected the dog and went for a long drive, thinking about everything. And then he came back to town and planted himself on this barstool and hadn't moved for hours.

To be fair, he'd thought Rita was a spy for Stacia until very recently, and he hadn't told her about George because you don't rat out your friends, no matter what. But if it weren't for George and all his problems, Curt would be with Rita right now, because she wasn't a spy. She was…Rita, the first person who'd ever seen his art. Who made him laugh. Who'd built amusement parks for her *hamsters*. Whose dad's picture somehow ended up on Curt's wall years before they ever met.

The worst of it was, he had a feeling that he'd been given a brief glimpse of his true destiny, and George had fucked it all up.

But he had to concede that even without all the drama, the Gracie scene would have scared Rita off. All his careless, selfish behavior had come home to roost and it was shitting all over his windshield. There would be cosmic consequences, beyond just missing the chance to get with Rita.

But the great thing about booze…the more you drank, the more righteous and justified in all your actions you became, and he was approaching that magical intersection.

He surveyed the seven chicks in the bar. He'd slept with five of them.

Of the two he hadn't screwed, only one was a viable candidate. The other was about eight months pregnant, and that was not Curt's scene at all, especially since her boyfriend or husband or whatever was there with her. So that left the one chick he didn't recognize, sitting in a booth with Hot Rod Wentz and Starvin' Marvin. Maybe he'd go home with her tonight. Except he wasn't in the mood, and she probably still lived with her parents. Not like that had ever stopped him.

The door opened and there stood George, wild-eyed behind those big stupid glasses, looking around until his eyes lit on Curt. He dashed toward him. "There you are."

"Here I am." Curt raised his beer. He drained it and tried to slide it onto the bar but missed, and it fell. George caught it. At least he was good for something. Curt snorted and swiveled toward the bar. "Mac," he said. "Beer me."

Mac scowled at him and then at George. "The feds are looking for you, boy."

"It's not the feds," Curt scoffed. "It's the KBI. And he knows."

"Does everyone know?" George said.

"Of course they do. Look around. Everyone's staring at you."

George ducked his head. "Those agents must be from the Great Bend office. That's only ninety miles from here, and they'll be back, probably tomorrow. I went out to your trailer and you weren't there, and it was locked, so I got worried."

"You got worried? You needed the key."

"Come on," George said. "Let's go."

"Fuck that," Curt said. "I ain't done. Two more, Mac."

Mac filled two glasses at the taps and sloshed them across the bar, foam spilling and soaking the napkins in the vicinity.

George eyed Curt, on his guard. As well he should be. "Let's grab a booth."

"Yeah, sure. Why not?" Curt coasted off his stool, slopping more beer on his shirt. A shirt which he did indeed own. He staggered over to the first booth, which was occupied, but he said, "Clear off."

"Cool out, Dekker," Hot Rod said.

"Not you." Curt focused on the girl he'd never met. "You stay. On your knees. "

THE THROWAWAYS

The girl giggled, but Hot Rod stood so fast his belt buckle tipped the table, spilling beer and sending the napkin holder to the floor. "That's my niece you're talking to," he said.

"That doesn't mean you can watch."

Hot Rod slammed Curt against the wall, the impact driving the air out of him and ringing his bell. The beer glass slipped from his hand and shattered on the floor.

"Good God, Curt. What the fuck's wrong with you?" George turned to Hot Rod and said, "He's waxed. He didn't mean anything." He tugged on Curt's arm.

Curt shook off George's grip.

Mac loomed over the table and said, "I'm gonna throw the bunch of you out of here if I see any more of that shit." He aimed at the broken glass on the floor. "Pick that up."

A red-faced Hot Rod said to his companions, "We're outta here."

His niece smiled at Curt and licked her lips. Hot Rod caught it and yanked on her arm and dragged her out the door.

George gathered up the biggest pieces of broken glass. Mac wheeled out a mop bucket and a trash bag, into which George deposited the shards.

"I'm magic," Curt said. "We've got a booth."

George looked at him like he was crazy. They sat opposite each other and Curt reached across the table and took George's beer glass and drained it.

"Mac! Gimme another draw!" Curt called out.

"Get off your goldbricking ass and come to the bar," Mac

said. "I ain't your waitress."

"I'll go," George said.

He bought two more draws of beer at the bar.

George seated himself and placed one of the glasses before Curt.

"Have you ever noticed," Curt said, "you never ask me how *I'm* doing?"

"What are you talking about?" George shoved up his glasses. "I asked you—"

Curt wagged a finger at him. "You said 'What the fuck's wrong with you.' Not the same thing at all."

George pursed his lips and said, "So how are you?"

"I'm funkadelic, my friend." Curt aimed finger pistols at him. "I am fucking *funk-a-del-ic*." He took a long drink.

"You don't seem funkadelic."

"How would you know? Bill was right. You don't know anything about me anymore."

George's befuddled, offended expression would have made Curt laugh in days gone by.

"I know everything about you," George said.

"Is that right? So you know that my dad hasn't spoken to me in two fucking years. Right? Since you know everything about me?"

George's mouth fell open.

Curt would not have blabbed this if he hadn't been drunk. But he was, so what the fuck. "No, you don't, because all we do is talk about you and your problems."

"Your dad—why?" When Curt didn't answer, George said, "We used to tell each other everything, remember? What happened to that?"

As soon as he said it, the look on his face acknowledged he'd made a grave mistake.

"What happened to that?" Curt said, straightening up in his seat. "You fucking disappeared off the face of the earth, that's what happened, and then—"

"I didn't disappear," George said. "I was busy."

"Right," Curt said. "Like you were too busy to come to Bill's—"

"Haven't we already covered that?"

"You flaked out on us, just like Bill said, and—"

"I didn't—"

"You think for once you could let me finish a fucking sentence?" Curt shouted.

CHAPTER TWENTY-NINE

George

George had never been so shocked. This was the very first time, in the twenty-some-odd years they'd known each other, that Curt had raised his voice in anger at him. Apparently most of the people in McWhiskey's were experiencing the same surprise, because everyone fell silent and stared their way.

In as pacifying a voice as he could muster, he said, "Calm down, man."

"Don't tell me to calm down like I'm your pet or some shit. I'm sick of you guys treating me like I'm a retard."

"Come on, man, you need to—"

"You shut up!" Curt said. "You don't get to tell me what I need to do. I've been busting my ass trying to keep you out of trouble and all you do is ask for more more more. I gave up something I didn't want to give up because I'm protecting you, and it's gone forever, and you don't give a shit about anyone but yourself. The *only* time you ever open your mouth is to tell everyone how *not* to feel. 'Don't be mad. Don't be sad. Go with the flow. *Calm down.*'"

George stole a glance around at the gawking faces. He shrank into his seat.

"I thought this experience might snap you out of your trance, dig you out from the shit pile your parents heaped on you, but I was wrong. Somehow you're still as passive as you've ever been even after everything that's happened."

George jutted out his chin, his face blazing hot. "Not true. I'm interviewing for a traveling photographer job on Sunday, and then I'm going to be on the road like Kerouac, living like a—"

"You're not going to do that."

"Yes," George said, attempting to inject his voice with authority and resolve. "I am."

"Gimme a break," Curt said. "This is no different from any of your other schemes, your plans, trying to deke us out with your big fake stupid stories. You're never going to do *anything*. Because you know what you are, George? You're beige. You're just—you're not even there."

Beige? George attempted a carefree laugh, but it came out sounding like a yip. Only a liquored-up hippie-dippie college dropout would come up with a bullshit tag like that. He snorted and looked away.

"Oh, no you don't," Curt said. "I can see what you're doing, you're dismissing me like you always do. But you know I'm right. Your parents got their wish—a son who's afraid of *everything*, afraid to do *anything* but make up shit about what he's going to do someday and never does. Nothing going on around you affects you in any way you're so far inside your head. Everything just goes right through you. Like I said. *Beige.*"

Suddenly, George had the sensation of riding a fast-moving train, only instead of rocketing him forward, it was standing still, the world rushing around him, past him, through him. Like vapor. Like neutral wall paint. *Beige.*

George felt stripped, raw, exposed, as if Curt had peeled his skin off with a dull butter knife. And now he wondered if that's what it felt like when your own father didn't speak to you anymore, pretended like you didn't exist.

Curt's dad hadn't spoken to him in two years. *Two years.*

Curt watched the bar crowd, as downcast as George had ever seen him.

George drank down the rest of his beer and pushed his glass aside. "Why doesn't your dad speak to you anymore?"

"I don't want to talk about it."

"But I do," George said. "Tell me."

"Naaah," Curt said. "It's old news."

"Dude. What happened?"

Curt waved a hand in the air and his head sank onto his folded arms.

Now that George thought about his time in Niobe, he realized that Curt's happy-go-lucky nature was tempered with a new sadness, and George hadn't even noticed. He never noticed. When Curt's true love Jeannette had run off with another guy while Curt was away at college freshman year, Bill had called from Hays to tell George and said they should meet in Manhattan to cheer their friend up from this devastating blow.

But George was busy with school, and he'd thought, *old Curt. He'll be fine. Nothing really affects him.*

Then Curt quit college, never to return.

"Tell me," George insisted, determined. "I'm not moving from this spot until you tell me about the situation with your dad."

Curt sat up and sighed but still said nothing.

He would wait for however long it took. He'd wait until the cops came and got him, if he had to.

Curt took a few swallows of his beer then fixed his eyes on George's. "So you know I sold our land, right?"

George didn't, but he said, "Right."

"It was for a lot of money. I mean, a *lot*. Like, a suspicious amount—but we'll talk about *that* another time. After I got the check for the land, I go up to the big house to tell my folks, and before I can say anything, Dad cold cocks me with his cane. Starts beating me with it."

George drew in a sharp breath. Curt's dad had never beaten him. He'd know about it if he had because Curt held nothing back when they were kids.

Curt nodded. "You know how that land was in our family for over a hundred and ten years, and of course, you know, farming is next to godliness for my dad. So he's all, 'You're nothing but a bum, and you're going to buy drugs and sit on your lazy, worthless ass' and blah, blah, blah. Says I don't deserve to be a farmer. The only reason he didn't crack my skull open is because Mom stopped him."

"Good God," George said. "What the fuck?"

"Yeah, you know how Dad and I were never close—six kids and farming three hundred sixty-five days a year and all that—and he was a hard ass, but I'd always thought he was a decent enough dad. But then the older I got, the more I annoyed him, how I *was*, you know—nothing like him."

"Right," George said. He'd always known that Curt's sunny, empathetic disposition confused Curt's phlegmatic, old-school father.

Curt took a drink and continued. "So after Mom takes his cane away, Dad tells me to get off what's left of his property—the four acres around the farmhouse—and says he'll shoot me if I ever step a toe over the line. And then he says—he says—" Curt began to choke up.

George knew this was partially because Curt was drunk, but it was also genuine, and a quiet anger at Curt's father built up in George's guts.

Curt visibly steeled himself, blinked, and then cleared his throat. "He said to me, he said, 'You're no son of mine.' And then I got it, you know? He gave more of a shit about the land than about me."

And George thought, *You've always known that.* But he didn't say it. Wouldn't help. "I'm sorry, man. I'm sorry I didn't know."

"This happened like right before your grandpop's funeral, and so when you were here I didn't think it would be cool to talk about it since, you know, we were at a *funeral*, and plus I was like, what am I complaining about? George's folks can't even see him."

Because I'm beige. I blend in. I'm invisible.

Curt was too drunk to notice he'd picked carelessly at George's oozing wound, but in spite of that, and even in the midst of his own deep suffering, Curt was always thinking about everyone else. This was his special gift.

The telling of his story had kept Curt somewhat coherent, but now that he was finished, it was as if he was wired up to an I.V. of Everclear. George couldn't understand a word he had to say anymore.

"Let's go home, man." George got up from the table.

Curt got to his feet precariously and George corralled him around the shoulders.

He settled their tab at the bar with Curt propped up against it.

Mac's normally surly expression was replaced by concern. "What's up with this guy?" he asked.

"Rough day," George said. "Sorry about the broken glass and the ruckus."

Mac waved his hand. "He's never caused me any grief before. Just get him home safe, will you?"

George nodded and draped Curt's arm over his own shoulders. He guided Curt out of the bar.

"Come here, boy!" Curt slurred.

George had been so frantic when he arrived, he hadn't seen Curt's dog napping on the sidewalk against the building, lying on his side, his huge floppy ears spread out at odd angles on the cement like beach towels.

"Come here, boy!"

The dog lifted his head and looked at Curt and George, but he wasn't going anywhere.

George put Curt in the passenger seat of the Stingray, and then addressed the dog.

"Are you going to make me carry you too?"

The answer was clearly yes.

"It's not my fault Curt doesn't know your name, dog," George said. "But at least it's not *beige*."

He gathered up the hound, carried him to the car, settled him on Curt's lap, and headed toward Saw Pole.

CHAPTER THIRTY

Bill

Friday, May 30, 1986
Hays, Kansas
2:30 p.m.

Bill woke up wrapped like a mummy on the living room couch, while Pete lay stretched out asleep on the recliner. Bill sat up and Pete's eyes opened.

"How are you feeling?" Pete said. He brought the recliner upright, rubbed his eyes, and put on his old-hippie glasses.

"Okay." Bill was shaking, his flesh rippling, and he ached all over, feverish and clammy. The coffee table was no longer blanketed in broken glass and mushy Ludes and Courvoisier.

"How long was I out?"

"What do you remember?"

He didn't answer.

"Off and on for about twenty-eight hours," Pete said. "I'm

guessing withdrawal is kicking in hard about now."

"Have you been here the whole time?"

Pete nodded. "Do you remember anything from yesterday?"

Bill sighed. "Unfortunately, yes."

Pete said nothing, just gazed at him, waiting.

Bill didn't want to remember, but blurry moving pictures leaked into his consciousness anyway: puking into the toilet, his nose bleeding and bleeding, Pete sitting on the edge of the tub begging him to go to the hospital, Bill refusing. Blubbering uncontrollably. Talking, talking, talking. Confessing everything: how much money he owed, how he'd lied to Liz, cut her out of his emotional life, how his emotional life had all but disappeared. About watching himself from a distance powerlessly as his desiccated soul evaporated entirely. "I remember I told you everything."

The priest nodded. "Do you remember what happened before that?"

Bill couldn't answer him, remembering the gun and the lost bullet. His desperation. Writing the suicide letters.

"Remember our deal?"

"Vaguely." This part was a little hazier.

"You agreed to, one, trade places with Liz. She's going to come back here, and you're going to move in at the Canterbury House, and you'll be assigned chores there in exchange for room and board for as long as it takes."

Bill had to bite back a sarcastic reply.

"Two, you're going to select a counselor and a drug program

within the next week from my resource list. And three, you'll be working on the church's house renovation for the refugee family so you can sweat that shit out of your system. And four, you and I are going to put together a payment plan to your pal Hoover." Pete rolled his eyes at the goofy nickname. "Five. You're going to tell Liz everything you need to tell her. And you need to tell her *everything*. And of course, six, you'll be attending our Sunday night worship every week." He grinned. "Overwhelmed yet?"

"Every day of my life."

"But first, lunch. I'll heat up those enchiladas. After that, hospital. After that, everything else."

"All right," Bill said.

"Why don't you go shower and then we'll eat."

Countless things went through Bill's mind, swirling, dipping, tangling themselves up. He just wanted to *do* and not think. So he went into the bathroom and took a long, hot shower then dressed in gym shorts and a t-shirt. As he sat on the edge of his bed to put on his shoes, in plain view, right there on the floor, lay the bullet he had lost.

Pete knocked on the open bedroom door. "Lunch is about ready."

Bill turned his head toward the priest, his mouth open, his scalp tingling.

"What is it?" Pete stepped farther into the room, his concern obvious.

Wordlessly, Bill bent over and picked up the bullet and

held it out to him.

"Where was it?" Pete accepted and examined the bullet.

Bill pointed at the floor. His ears rang and his skin buzzed. "It was right there. It was right there *the whole time.*"

"And you couldn't see it." Pete pushed his glasses up, a ghost of a smile on his face.

The gears of Bill's mind went into overdrive. There was a perfectly rational explanation, after all. He snorted. "You saw how drunk I was."

"No. Don't try to logic yourself out of it. Is it possible that you were *prevented* from seeing it?"

Bill couldn't answer. Even skunked out of his mind, he remembered a clear image of the carpet and scrabbling around on it, searching for that bullet, which had not been there. Nothing wrong with his vision. It wasn't possible. But it had happened.

"Think on that for a while," Pete said and handed the bullet back to him. "Come on. Let's eat."

Bill slipped the bullet into his shorts pocket and followed Pete to the dining area adjacent to the little galley kitchen. He seated himself at the table in front of one of the place settings Pete had laid out, at once nauseated and famished. The bullet in his pocket seemed to have a magnetic pull, and Bill couldn't stop thinking about it.

Pete wiped his hands on a towel and hung it up as the timer dinged. He removed the enchilada pan from the oven and served the two of them. He sat and placed a paper napkin in his lap before bowing his head and praying aloud. Then he dug in.

The undeserved kindness of this man combined with the strange appearance of the bullet made Bill's eyes cloud and throat begin to close up. So he escaped to the kitchen to hunt for the hot sauce he knew wasn't in the refrigerator.

"God ain't done with you yet," Pete said, "so you'd better get used to this kind of thing."

Bill turned back toward Pete and thrust his hand in his shorts pocket. He closed his fist around the bullet. Then he let go, sat at the table, and cut into his enchilada.

CHAPTER THIRTY-ONE

George

Saturday, May 31, 1986
Salina, Kansas
2:45 p.m.

"You mean I've got the job?"

George was sitting in the conference room at the Arnold Group in Salina, across the table from the K-Mart portrait photography interviewer. This was by far the easiest interview he'd ever had.

"Yes, if you want it," the HR manager said. "You'll need to be in Kansas City for training Monday morning. Here's the address." He pushed a card toward George. "You can fill out a W-4 then so we can pay you. Where do you plan to be based?"

"Corpus Christi, Texas." It was the farthest city from Lawrence in the territory, and it was on the Gulf of Mexico. He'd never seen the ocean.

He hadn't felt this happy, this free, this optimistic since he was accepted to KU Law. That seemed like years ago, so much had happened in the interim. But this was even better, somehow. It was adventuresome. It was wild. It was spontaneous. His buttoned-up brothers would never have done something like this, something they wouldn't tell their parents about. George was the free spirit brother. He was the wild card. Maybe he'd finally found himself. Maybe that's who he was.

This morning he'd driven a massively hung-over Curt into Niobe to pick up his Jeep.

"Sorry for losing my shit like that last night," Curt had said.

"I deserved it."

"No. I'm just ratched up about that girl Rita."

"Wait," George said. "Did you...go out with her? I thought she was just—"

"I don't want to talk about it." Curt would say no more.

They hadn't seen any sign of KBI cars around town, so the agents must have gotten what they needed and gone back to HQ to analyze the evidence. Then George headed to Salina for his interview.

Now he hit the Salina K-Mart and spent most of the cash he'd borrowed from Curt to buy underwear, shirts, socks, and toiletries, and a pair of jeans for his trip to Kansas City and beyond. He could buy more clothes as he made more money. After that he stopped at a gas station before heading to Saw Pole. While the car was filling up, he plugged a quarter into the payphone and dialed his answering machine.

The first message was from his mom. "George, I'm not sure we should go on this cruise. You don't make enough money to pay for all this. So I think we'll—"

George hung up and savagely punched in his parents' phone number, the mixture of rage, frustration, and terror feeling like it would blow the top of his head off. Before his mother could even complete "Hello?" he was shouting into the receiver. "Damn it, Mom! There are no refunds. It's *nonrefundable*. I've already paid for it. If you don't go, I'm out two thousand bucks!"

"But George—"

"And don't tell me you'll miss a golf tournament or a tennis match." His hands shook with such violence the receiver rattled against his ear. "I bought you the fucking cruise, and you're going to go!"

"You know how I feel about that kind of lang—"

"I don't give a shit, Mom!" Having to hold back the true reason they had to go, the sheer effort of it, was making George hypertensive, feeling as if his heart would explode out of his sternum. "We all know you'd go if the twins had given it to you. But they can't because they're *dead*, Mom. I'm all that's left, sorry to say. You're going, or I swear to God, I will not speak to you again. So if you want to lose your only remaining child, your leftover son, stay home and play bridge and don't go on the *fucking* cruise."

She gasped.

George had broken the cardinal family rule: Thou shalt not make reference to the twins' death, only their golden, glorious, supernaturally gifted lives.

His dad got on the phone. "What the hell did you say to your mother?"

George tried to speak calmly. "Dad. Mom's saying you may not go on the cruise." He went over the litany of reasons they had to go.

"Well, now, thanks to you, I'm not sure she's in any shape to go."

"You know what?" George fumed, angrier than he'd ever been with his father's enablement of his mother. "If you let her manipulate you out of going on your dream trip to Alaska, then you don't deserve to go. So don't go."

He gasped. He'd gone too far. If they didn't go because they were mad at him, they would die. And he'd be responsible. He breathed in through his nose, exerting all his will to be calm, reasonable, and persuasive. "Dad. I'm sorry. I didn't mean that. I've been really stressed out and I'm—I'm taking it out on you. I want you to go on the cruise. Please, Dad. Please. It would mean a lot to me. Put Mom on the phone and I'll apologize to her too. I'll send her flowers. Tell me what I have to do to get you to go on this cruise."

His dad sighed and lowered his voice. "I'll smooth everything over with your mom. Give her a call tomorrow. She should be...better by then. All right?"

Practically teary with relief and gratitude, George said goodbye and hung up.

The high white clouds raced overhead as he jetted north on

state 81 and turned west on 110 toward Saw Pole. A flock of birds rose from the cluster of transparent green-leafed oaks on either side of Ross Creek as he blasted over the bridge. Just on the other side, the car jolted and jerked to the right. The sound of hard rubber flapping against the pavement made him pull to the side of the road next to a stand of cottonwood trees.

Flat tire. He hadn't changed one since college. It was the right front, and he hoped he hadn't gone far enough to mangle the wheel too much. He got out of the car and went to survey the damage. The tire was in shreds. He pulled the scissor jack from the compartment behind the passenger seat, then sat on the ground to pry the chrome rally wheel cap off.

The hubcaps were like big snub-nosed bullets. He worked his fingertips under the edges and pulled. The cap popped off into his lap.

A dark brown mass nestled in the concave center of the cap, and for a moment he thought it was a wasp's nest. But wasp's nests typically weren't bound up in clear plastic.

He fished the mass out of the well and hefted it in his hand. It weighed about a pound, he estimated.

What was this?

And then recognition clobbered him over the head. He'd seen a photo of this substance once before in a *Time Magazine* article.

A car rushed by him now on the county road and George shoved the gunk back in the hubcap well. He stood and watched the car vanish into the distance, grateful the driver hadn't stopped to help.

He walked to the back right tire and pried the hubcap loose. Then he quickly did the same to the remaining tires. All held identical plastic-bagged lumps.

George was transporting four pounds of black tar heroin.

CHAPTER THIRTY-TWO

Bill

Saturday, May 31, 1986
Hays, Kansas
3 p.m.

Ants marched in a steady procession under Bill's skin, and he had to sit on his shaking hands to keep from scratching himself raw as Pete drove him to Canterbury House.

"I don't know if I'm up to this," Bill said. "It's too soon."

"That was our deal," Pete said, and pulled into the gravel parking lot where Bill had broken into Liz's car. "The sooner you do this the sooner you can get well. Secrets will drive you back to using."

Bill sighed, but it came out a moan. He got out of the car and tagged behind Pete toward the chapel building. His guts knotted up in much the same way they had the last time he'd approached a church with Liz waiting inside, but for another reason entirely. The irony did not escape him.

The ancient herbal aroma of the sanctuary censer met him as he crossed the threshold, and it was cool and dim, the only light coming from an overhead skylight. All this pleasantness annoyed him. Pete led him down the aisle and into a back meeting room papered in colorful '70s pop-art posters with slogans like *Hang in there, baby!* and *Sail On, Sailor/Mustard Seed Faith.* Liz sat in a metal folding chair on the other side of a white Formica table.

At the sight of her and without warning, a convulsive sob erupted in Bill's throat, violent and gut-wrenching. He clapped his hand over his mouth, trying to contain it, but it heralded a tsunami, all control gone, his shoulders shaking, snot running unchecked.

Pete put an arm around him, pulled out a chair across from Liz, and helped him into it, then handed him tissues from a half-empty box on the table. Bill wondered how many other meetings like this had taken place in this room, its cheery posters now seeming sad and desperate.

Bill hoped this was not going to be the new normal for him, emotions springing out of him seemingly from nowhere like caffeinated grasshoppers.

When he'd calmed down enough and his vision cleared, he saw tears welling in Liz's eyes and he started crying all over again. He wanted to go to her, but Pete had warned him not to force himself on her in any way. He could touch her only if she initiated physical contact.

Pete sat at the end of the table and squeezed Liz's hand. She smiled thankfully at him with trembling lips.

He turned to Bill and said, "Liz has requested that I be here today as support and to be a witness."

Pete had alerted Bill he would stay for the meeting, but hearing it put in that way disturbed him, and he flashed on a possible future scenario in which he and Liz sat on opposite sides of a table with lawyers present. His stomach cramped. All the things he would have normally said in this situation— cracking jokes at every word—died in his throat. There would be no deflecting anything today.

"Bill?" Pete nodded encouragingly at him, as if to say, *Tell her what she's won!*

He opened his mouth. He wanted to run out of there, vacuum up every grain of possible cocaine in the apartment, and snort it all right this instant. He attempted to speak, which set him to coughing.

"I'll get us some water," Pete said. He rose and left the room, leaving panic in his wake.

Bill could do nothing but stare at Liz's small, delicate hands, which were tightly clenched together. He couldn't stand the silence, not with these ants marching under his skin. "Do you suppose he did that on purpose?" he finally said, still watching her hands wrestle each other. How he wanted to scratch. This craving nearly eclipsed the primary one.

He was struck by her drawn and pale but beautiful face and realized he hadn't truly looked at her in months. She smiled faintly but distantly at him. There would be no banter. Not today. Maybe never again.

Pete returned with a sweating pitcher and three glasses. He filled them all and handed them out. "Sorry," he said, pushing up his Lennon specs. "Accosted by a student." He sat and gestured at Bill. "Please," he said. "Continue."

Continue staring? Continue itching? Continue wanting to die?

Bill tried to meet Liz's eyes and almost succeeded. "Liz," he said. Just saying her name summoned tears from both of them again. "First, I want to say how—how sorry I am."

She covered her mouth with her hand.

"I'm…I am…addicted to…I'm a drug addict. Cocaine addict. Addicted to cocaine." Getting the words out took a supreme effort, ellipses between each one, as if he'd never spoken whole sentences before. "I've been doing it daily for about sixteen months. But I've started a—"

"No," Pete said. "No talking about all the great things you're going to do until it's all out on the table."

Bill glared at Pete with such a violent rush of hatred he might have punched the priest under other circumstances. He picked up his water glass and squeezed it, hoping it would shatter and cut him, flooding the table with his blood, because that's what this felt like. The heavy glass held fast, so he drank without stopping, his hand shaking and sloshing water down the front of his shirt. He set down the glass and wiped his mouth.

"To pay for the…the cocaine, I've taken out several credit

LS HAWKER

cards without your knowledge. And maxed them all out. And I've…destroyed our credit rating. We're…I'm deeply in debt to my dealer. I owe…" He pulled in a breath and found he couldn't release it, had forgotten how.

"Go ahead, Bill," Pete said.

"Give me a minute, will you?" he snapped, rubbing his sweating palms together. "Sorry. I'm a little…I can't seem to…"

The glasses danced on the table to a rhythmic thumping, and Bill realized it was his knee spastically jittering against the table. He used both hands to stop it, clenching his teeth together hard enough to shatter them before he got everything out.

"Tell her how much," Pete said.

He couldn't say it. He gave in to the itching and raked his nails down his arms until Pete grabbed his left hand and forced it to the table.

"How much do you owe?" Pete said.

Bill closed his eyes. If he couldn't see, he couldn't be seen. That's what he believed when he was a tiny kid, and maybe it would work now. He whispered it: "Sixty-seven thousand dollars."

A squealing noise, like a strangled scream, emanated from Liz's throat.

He opened his eyes. Liz's tear- and mascara-smeared face was a shifting kaleidoscope of facial expressions: horror, confusion, disbelief, betrayal, and back again.

Pete put his hand on her forearm. "Is there anything you

want to say to Bill, Liz?"

She was shaking her head slowly. "How," she said. "How did this happen? How could you do this to us?"

"And what else, Bill?" Pete said.

Bill's head pivoted toward the priest. "That's it," he said. "That's all."

"No, it's not."

"Yes," Bill said, emphatic, giving Pete a warning glance. "It is. There's nothing left to tell."

Pete's voice dropped to a growl. "Bill. Tell her or I will."

"I…" Bill swallowed convulsively. "I thought about…"

Pete started to open his mouth to finish Bill's sentence, so Bill shouted, "Killing myself. I thought about killing myself."

"Thought about it?" Pete said. "You did more than think about it. You made a plan. You were in the process of carrying it out, five suicide notes next to you when I came into the apartment, and…"

Everything in the room faded away and Bill was transported back to freshman year of high school after George's mom's first suicide attempt. School was out for the summer, and Bill would later learn the trigger had been the first anniversary of the twins' death.

The day after, Travis, Bill, and Curt picked George up at his grandparents' house, and they walked downtown to the Isis Theater where John Wayne's *The Cowboys* was playing. They were all too young to confront this kind of grown-up suffering, this kind of parental abandonment. They never discussed what had happened. Instead, every day for the next week, they repeated the ritual. Pick George up, walk downtown, watch the Duke boss a bunch of snot-nosed kids around and give them the experience of a lifetime.

George's tortured, bewildered expression during that week would haunt Bill's dreams for years to come. It was the same expression Liz wore now.

"What happened to you?" she asked. "And where was I?" She dissolved into tears.

Her hand darted forward, and before it made contact, Bill assumed she was reaching out to slap his face. But she grabbed his hand and squeezed, painfully hard. He didn't flinch. He welcomed the pain.

"I didn't know," she said. "I didn't know how unhappy you were."

"It wasn't you," Bill whispered.

"But you had to carry this all alone. I didn't know how alone you were."

Bill gaped at her, stunned. He sat like a statue, afraid to move, but he wanted to take her in his arms so badly it almost stilled the ants.

Liz cried for quite a while, holding his hand, and his shriveled corn kernel of a heart began to soften, and it hurt like hell. Finally, she took her hand back and Pete gave her a tissue.

"I know this doesn't help," Bill said, "but Pete got me into an outpatient drug rehab program through the hospital. If all goes well, I'll graduate in August. I went to my first Narcotics

Anonymous meeting yesterday, and I'll be attending meetings every day for the foreseeable future. I know it doesn't help, but I wanted to let you know that I'm trying."

Then Pete explained how Bill planned to pay Hoover back.

Liz kept nodding and dabbing her face with the tissue, and he began to think that maybe everything was going to be all right. He had forgotten the sweetness of her heart. He'd forgotten he loved her. As if a wind had blown a toxic mist off the lake of his mind, he remembered that now.

"As long as I was high, I believed I was in control," Bill said. "Counterintuitive, I know. Until I didn't anymore, no matter how much blow I did. I don't know when that happened. Or even why. I've just never…felt like I belonged anywhere."

"But you *did* belong somewhere," Liz said.

Past tense. She didn't say *do* belong somewhere. Terror seized him.

"I'm glad you're trying to clean up, and I love you, Bill, but I don't know if…I just don't know. I don't know if we ever should have gotten married in the first place. I don't know if the damage can be repaired. It's possible we're no good for each other."

But we are. You are. He sat dumbstruck, focused on her, and now that there was a valid reason to cry, he was dry-eyed.

"Would you be willing to try couples' counseling?" Pete asked Liz. "Bill is willing."

She stared at the table and drew circles in the condensation on it with her fingers. "I always thought I was willing," she said.

"Now, I don't know."

This was a cruel joke. That's all she'd ever talked about, and now she didn't know. His knee started jittering again and he didn't bother to stop it. So many things he wanted to say, but his past insincerity would color anything he said now.

"I'll call you," Liz said. She lifted her purse from the back of the chair and walked toward the door then stopped and turned back. "Oh. I almost forgot." She reached in her purse and pulled out a folded piece of notepad paper. She held it out to Bill. He took it, and she left.

Bill stood holding the back of his chair with one hand and the notepaper with the other.

"You okay?" Pete said.

"I could use a gram of cocaine and a fifth of Stoli," Bill said. "But other than that…"

"Not funny," Pete said. He looked at his watch. "We can postpone our other errand if you need to. You said the dean may or may not be at Rarick on a Sunday, so…That was difficult, I know."

"Let's get it over with," Bill said. As they walked toward the chapel parking lot, he unfolded the paper—would his hands ever stop shaking?—and read in Liz's small, neat handwriting: *Curt called. KBI looking for George. Searched the house. George staying at Curt's.*

"Oh, shit," Bill said.

"What is it?"

"Friend of mine's in trouble. And I made it worse.

Unsurprisingly." He pocketed the note.

Pete drove them to campus, and Bill's exhaustion left him without thought or impulse other than to scratch. Maybe he'd used up every ounce of emotion he'd been allotted for the rest of his life.

The quad was empty of students, although landscapers were hard at work mowing the grass and planting pansies and petunias. Bill and Pete walked toward the nondescript buff-colored stucco façade of Rarick and entered the building. Bill led the way to the dean's office, heart stutter-stopping the whole way. The dean wasn't there, and Bill was both relieved and apprehensive, because he was going to have to face him at some point.

"Guess we'll try again tomorrow," he said. The ants were chanting: *one more gram. Then we'll get clean.*

A short, stocky female student with an afro and big glasses came their way down the hall. "Excuse me," Pete said. "Have you seen the dean today?"

"Nope." She pointed behind her. "But try the Computer Science lab. He hides in there sometimes because it's the coolest room in the building."

They walked into the CS lab, but no dean. Bill had thought she meant *cool* as in *bitchen* but realized she'd meant temperature, with the two brand-new air conditioners humming in the windows. Every horizontal surface was piled high with perforated computer paper, yellow legal pads with mathematical equations and algorithms, issues of computer magazines and comic books.

Bill searched the work surfaces for a pad of paper and a pen. "I'll leave him a note to make sure that I—"

His eyes landed on one of the computers. He gasped.

Pete turned. "What is it now?"

Bill pointed mutely at the machine.

Pete walked toward it and bent to read the logo, holding the stem of his glasses as he squinted at it. "It's a…Commodore 64." He looked back at Bill.

"Remember the cassette at my apartment? *64* by the Commodores?"

Pete's eyes narrowed and then widened. "Right. We thought it was *the* Commodores. But it was…"

Bill flashed on the noises the tape had made on his home stereo—static, beeps, synthesized notes. "We were listening to data."

"Huh," Pete said, straightening.

And then another thought bludgeoned Bill over the head. In his angry phone message, George said that Stacia's people said he had something of theirs—the cocaine.

But it wasn't the cocaine at all.

The A/C units contributed to his sudden attack of goosebumps. "I have to go home."

Pete headed for the door. "Fair enough. I think there's some leftover lentil stew in the Canterbury—"

"No, I mean home. To Niobe. My hometown."

"Bill," Pete said slowly. "You need to go to a meeting. And

leaving now, at the very beginning of your program, could—"

"I know, but that Commodore data cassette—my friend George needs it. I have to get it to him right now, now that I know what it is." He handed Liz's note to Pete.

"This friend is wanted by the KBI?" Pete said, his expression calcifying.

"It's not what you think. I'll explain on the way back to Canterbury."

Bill gave the quickest synopsis of George's situation he could in the drive time between campus and the ministry house.

"Brutal," Pete said as he parked in the lot by the chapel. "But my friend, I fear that it's too soon for you to leave the nest. You're in dangerous territory right now. You're in withdrawal. This is the time to take care of yourself."

"I know," Bill said. "But—" He paused and watched several ideas in his head link together, a sensation he hadn't experienced in a while. Cause and effect. Action and reaction. "George needs my help, and correct me if I'm wrong, but acting unselfishly reinforces sobriety." When Pete didn't reply right away, Bill put a hand on his arm. "George is not a coke guy."

Pete pushed his glasses up. "I'm not your babysitter. Either you will, or you won't. It's up to you."

Bill *wanted* to do drugs, but right this instant, he wanted something else more. He wanted, he urgently desired to get the cassette to George, because he had the feeling that if he did this thing, it might bring him closer to being worthy of Liz.

Was this feeling irrational? Yes. Illogical? Absolutely. But it

LS HAWKER

was a spark of something, and he wanted to hold on to it. And that pushed his baser desires aside—for the moment.

"All right," Pete said. "We'll try the dean again early in the week. When will you be back?"

"As soon as I possibly can," Bill said. "Tomorrow at the latest."

They exited Pete's car and Pete placed his hand on Bill's shoulder. "Listen. You know you've been given a second chance. And God's going before you. You have my phone number on you?"

Bill patted his back pocket. "Right here."

"You call me if you need to, even if it's the middle of the night. My poor, long-suffering wife is used to it."

"Do me a favor," Bill said. "Call Liz and let her know I'm coming to the apartment to pick something up. I don't want to scare her."

"Good idea."

Bill wanted to hug him, but he settled for a handshake then got in the Mustang and headed toward his apartment.

He knew leaving this soon after his rescue wasn't the best idea he'd ever had, but he'd already lost his wife. His friends were all he had left.

264

CHAPTER THIRTY-THREE

George

Saturday, May 31, 1986
Near Ross Creek, Kansas State Highway 110
5 p.m.

After George had put the heroin back into the hubcaps, he got to work changing the tire—no small feat, the way his hands were shaking, the way he could barely hold a thought in his head. After he tightened the last bolt, he stowed the jack and wrench, and slid into the driver's seat. He stared through the windshield.

He had to dispose of this heroin before he got pulled over and sent to prison forever. But he couldn't dump the junk into Ross Creek and poison the town of Miranda downriver.

But then, a thought occurred to him. *Bill may have the coke. But I have* this. George had no idea whether the value of each was even close, but maybe he could convince Mike and Derrill to take this in lieu of the missing cocaine. Would that spare his parents? Would they kill him anyway? He had no choice. He had to risk it.

He could take it to them on his way to Kansas City for photography training.

But where had the heroin come from? How did it end up in the Corvette?

Immediately, he thought of Stacia, but just as quickly discarded the idea as ridiculous.

He ticked off the other feasible explanations for his discovery one by one.

Uncle Howard was a heroin dealer, hiding his stash in Niobe for later sale?

Not remotely possible.

Freddie?

Nope. The way he'd reacted to George's threats showed he'd never have the stones to pursue a life of crime.

A local drug dealer discovered that the Corvette was stored in the Niobe garage?

But why wouldn't a dealer just steal the car?

Behind door number four was the only logical answer, crazy as it seemed. Unbelievable as it seemed.

His long-dead brothers. Vic and Chad.

How could it be? They were fraternity boys, sparkling clean, athletes, heroes.

But had they even known there was four pounds of heroin in their car? Had someone else—a rival, maybe?—planted the drugs in the Corvette?

It was a very expensive frame job. But then again, so was George's.

He needed more information. To look for clues, maybe a letter from his brothers explaining that they'd confiscated the heroin from a dealer and were taking it to the feds as a public service, he popped open the glove box. George inhaled the recognizable scent of his brothers' Aramis cologne, one he hadn't smelled in fifteen years, and it blasted him backward to adolescence. He sat a moment, eyes closed, allowing the sensation to linger and dissipate.

Inside the glove box he found a leatherette folder with the owner's manual and various other paperwork, even gas receipts from 1971, maybe the last gas they bought before their final day on Earth.

He unfolded a yellowed letter-sized piece of paper. BILL OF SALE it said at the top.

Kindred Chevrolet, Smithville, MO.
CASH PRICE OF CAR INCLUDES INLAND FREIGHT, GAS AND ANY ADDITIONAL COSTS: $5296.
Make year: 1971. Model: Corvette Stingray LS5.
Color: Bridgehampton Blue
Paid in full: Check #472
Buyers signature: Victor Engle.
Co-buyers signature: Chad Engle.

George sat gazing at his brothers' signatures. He started up the Vette and headed toward Curt's place, not listening to music, not doing anything but having his world turned upside down. Again.

George grasped that he'd never known his brothers at all. But how could he have, being nine years younger than them? If he'd been closer to the same age, would they have confided in him? He'd never know.

But of one thing he was certain: No one had given them the car. George now understood how ludicrous it was to think that an alumnus would give a student an expensive sports car for being a *tennis player*, especially for a team that had never even been close to a national championship. Yet everyone had bought this lie without a second thought.

No, the twins had purchased the car themselves.

And where would two jobless college seniors get five thousand two hundred ninety-six dollars?

From selling drugs. That's where.

The precious, perfect, golden Engle twins had been heroin dealers.

CHAPTER THIRTY-FOUR

George

Saturday, May 31, 1986
Saw Pole, Kansas
6 p.m.

As George turned on to County Road 15, he felt relief that this was all still a secret, because if people in town found out... although why would he care if they did? But it was time to come to terms with the fact that he was as invested in the myth as his parents. He'd basked in their golden glow the way name-droppers and star-fuckers everywhere did, attached himself to their accomplishments and charisma like a blood-sucking leech.

And this self-revelation was much worse than discovering the truth about his brothers.

He felt something else, something that, if he put words to it, would shame him far beyond his most embarrassing secrets. But it bubbled up anyway, unbidden, unwanted. It was validation.

His brothers hadn't been any better than George, and in point of fact, had been much, much worse. And his parents had no idea.

But following that thought was a horrible sadness. He had loved Chad and Vic, revered them almost, and now he realized that reverence was misplaced and even unfair to them. Carrying around the worship and adoration of other human beings was a heavy and unfortunate crown to wear. They hadn't asked for that.

He also knew, no matter what they'd done, he would have loved them anyway. And he still did. They were his brothers.

It was 6:00 p.m. when he arrived at the trailer. He parked behind it so the Vette couldn't be seen from the road then walked around to the front carrying his K-Mart bags.

Curt was sitting in a lawn chair against his green and white mobile home. The grass in the yard was sparse, but George spied a bag of grass seed by the curled-up hose next to the latticed stoop. The hound dog lay at Curt's feet as Springsteen's *The River* moaned from the boombox.

"I got the job," George said.

"Congratulations," Curt said, his tone matching his despondent posture. Man, he was really messed up over this girl. It seemed like Jeannette all over again.

"How are you doing?"

"I'll live."

"You want to talk about it?"

Curt half-smiled. "No, man. Thanks, though. I appreciate it. For real."

"Let's have some beers," George said. "That'll make you feel better." He went in the trailer, dumped his purchases in the guest room, and returned to the yard with two Michelobs from the refrigerator.

George sat in the lawn chair next to Curt's and popped both bottles with a rusty opener hanging from a string attached to the stoop lattice. He handed Curt a bottle then explained what he'd found in the Corvette's hubcaps and the bill of sale in the glove box. Curt came to life during the telling.

"You think your folks know?" he said.

"No way in hell. No way."

"Are you going to tell them?"

"You know, I can't think about anything else other than making sure they stay alive," George said. "If they don't go on that cruise, and if Mike and Derrill won't take the heroin in trade, then..."

Curt propped his elbows on his knees. "Your folks will go on the cruise," he said, ever the encourager. "Your dad said he'd take care of it."

"But you know my mom," George said, twisting his hands around his beer bottle.

Curt nodded.

"Please, God, make them go." He lit a cigarette and they stared grimly at the construction project across the road. He used his cigarette as a pointer. "What's the story over there?"

Curt perked up a little again. "You really want to know?"

"Yeah."

"They've told everyone it's a cable TV receiving station," Curt said, "but I think I've figured out what it's really for."

George couldn't help but smile.

"No, for serious." Curt set down his bottle. "At first I thought it was a SETI installation, but the dishes aren't big enough. So I did some reading, and I think it's a DARPA research facility."

"What's DARPA?" George attempted to keep a straight face.

"The Defense Advanced Research Project Agency. They're testing weapons for Reagan's Star Wars program."

George nearly choked. "Oh, come on, Curt. Congress will never approve SDI. The budget's more than a billion dollars. They won't even fund research."

"And Reagan—or any president, for that matter—would never do something without Congress's approval, which he doesn't need if it's a black project, because they'll use a black budget." Curt snapped his bottle cap at the field to the south.

"Curt. There's no conspiracy, no black projects here—the government doesn't run secret installations and pretend they're for cable TV." He could barely contain his mirth. "They don't test things within sight of civilians, with nothing but a chain link fence protecting them."

"One of the books says you only need twelve-hundred and fifty feet between testing facilities—missile silos, even—and inhabited buildings."

George remembered their morning of newspaper research at the library. "That's what all those library books are about, right?"

"Yup," Curt said.

"Wait. Did you say twelve-hundred fifty feet? Seriously? That's fucked up."

"Yeah, but there haven't been, like, any explosions or anything. But a whole ton of weird shit has been happening out here."

"Like what?" George flicked ashes to the ground behind him.

Curt leaned forward, his face earnest, his eyes alive. "Like these sharp green beams of light. Almost exactly like the laser light show in the Steve Miller Band Book of Dreams concert. Remember?"

This couldn't be true, but George was enthralled nonetheless. He nodded.

Curt continued, setting down his beer and rubbing his hands together. "So every once in a while, my hair will stand on end for no reason. The first time, I hit the deck, you know, thinking lightning was about to strike. But when I went outside, there wasn't a cloud in the sky."

George raised his eyebrows.

"Swear," Curt said. "Then sometimes the trailer will rock like a hammock. Of course, living in a mobile home, that isn't so unusual. And sometimes I hear this low, metallic hum that makes the whole, like, atmosphere shimmy—like a heat mirage."

George nodded again.

"So that's why I've been hanging out at the library reading about ground waves and lasers and Tesla coils."

"Tesla coils?" George tried to keep his face impassive.

"Yeah," Curt said. "Nobody's ever around when it starts up except me and the dog. But they've been running night tests this week, so maybe you'll get to see something."

"Except I'm clearing out tonight," George said. "Training starts Monday."

"So why not leave tomorrow?" Curt said.

George shrugged. "I just feel like I want to get going. I'm going to drive the back roads to Kansas City after dark."

"Oh. That's good, I guess," Curt said. All the liveliness that had picked up steam during the discussion of SDI drained from his face. He slumped back in his chair and he concentrated on picking the label off his Michelob. "But I kinda got used to having you around. I mean, I knew you weren't going to, like, move back here permanently or anything, but…"

"I'll be back." George looked at his own bottle and used his thumbnail to copy Curt's label-picking. "We'll see each other again."

"Awesome."

George had never heard Curt say the word in that flat of a tone before. But of course, Curt didn't believe George, who opened his mouth to say something when a distinctive car exhaust *phut phut phutted* toward them.

Curt raised his eyebrows at George and they both stood as

Bill cruised into the yard in his Mustang.

What was he doing here? George's trepidation doubled.

Bill got out of the Mustang, looking uncertain, but Curt sprinted toward Bill and threw an arm around his shoulders. "I knew you'd come. I knew it!" He turned to George. "I called him and told him—or his answering machine—about what happened with the KBI and told him to bring the cocaine back, and here he is!"

"Whoa, wait," Bill said, holding his hands out. "That's not why I came."

George crossed his arms. Of course it wasn't.

The dog wandered over to Bill looking baggy and sad, and greeted him with a thorough sniffing then sneezed.

"I need to tell you some things," Bill said. "First, I'm sorry for being a jackass. No. First, Liz left me. That's first."

This deflated George's indignation, but only slightly. Bill deserved to be left.

"I wish I could say I'm surprised, but I'm not," Curt said. He was the only guy in the world that could say something like that without sounding unkind. "What are you going to do?"

Bill waved his hand. "More urgent at this moment is George's situation."

"Let me get you a beer," Curt said.

"I'm going to have to decline," Bill said.

"I thought your issue was—"

"Coke. Right. Booze is a gateway for me, I'm told. So it's best not to throw myself down that slippery slope."

George couldn't believe that Bill had just come out and said it.

"But we have more important matters to discuss. It wasn't the coke the goons in Lawrence wanted back from George."

George traded a glance with Curt.

"I know what you're thinking." Bill's earnestness was unfamiliar. "That I'm concocting this bullshit story to cover up stealing the blow. But I'm not. I *did* steal it, and then I—anyway, it's not the cocaine they want. It's this."

Bill produced a cassette from his back pocket.

"A Commodores tape?" Curt said. "Come on, Bill, I'm gullible, but I'm not—"

"This is a data cassette."

"Can I see that?" George said.

Bill dropped the tape into his palm. George turned the cassette over then handed it back as Bill shook his arms out and made a groaning sound. "I'm in pretty bad shape. Can't stop moving and I feel like I'm going to burst into flame. This is what withdrawal looks like, kids."

"I think maybe you need to air that out a little," George said.

"Fair enough," Bill said. "I met this…priest and he…well, he kind of saved my life, if I'm being honest. He's helping me get clean. Him and Narcotics Anonymous."

George contemplated this. He'd seen how bad Bill looked ten days ago, but he'd been wrapped up in his own drama. He'd had no idea. But why would he have since he'd been out of their lives for so long? It was just like Bill had said that night—

and Curt reiterated yesterday—George had disappeared. His stomach roiled. Because he was going to abandon them again, leave them tonight, leave them to clean up his mess. Why were they even still talking to him?

"How did it happen, man?" Curt said to Bill. "I mean, one minute we were partying and having fun, and then all of a sudden you were going at it like it was your job or something."

"I don't know," Bill said. "I'm in an outpatient treatment program now, so I'll keep you posted." He took a deep breath. "To make matters worse, I've maxed out all our credit cards on cash advances to buy cocaine. Including what I borrowed from my dealer, I owe sixty-seven thousand dollars."

"Sixty-seven thousand dollars?" George said, awestruck. "How is that even—I mean, holy *shit*, Bill."

"I know." Bill rubbed his eyes.

"Wow," Curt said. "I wish you could have told me."

"I'm telling you now." Bill shook himself. "But seriously, enough about that. Let's talk about the data cassette. The night of the murders, Stacia must have gone into that house to get this, and then when she got in George's car to fill it with the goodies, she left this too."

"That doesn't make any sense," Curt said. "Unless…she meant to put it in there."

"Why would she do that?" George said.

"So you'd find it. You said her message said that she was supposed to be in that house when it blew up. She was supposed to die too, and maybe she knew it and wanted you to find the cassette and give it to the cops."

"She called you?" Bill said to George.

"A couple of times." He detailed her messages for Bill.

"We're missing something here," Bill said.

"And we've found out some other details." George told about learning he took a class with one of the dead girls, his trip with Travis to Lawrence, cousin Freddie, the KBI's visit, everything except the dirt on his brothers. He wanted to keep the spotlight on the immediate problem. There would be time to talk about that later. He hoped.

"There's more," Curt said. He turned to George. "The girl who told me the story in the first place—"

"Rita," George said.

"Who's Rita?" Bill said.

"She knows Stacia. She also found out that your friend, that Kimberly Laurent, she was a grad student in the journalism school who'd gone undercover to learn about the drug trafficking along the I-70/I-35 corridor."

George and Bill stared at each other.

"And apparently there's some connection to the sorority that Stacia belongs to. Some dealers were sorority sisters."

This just got weirder and weirder. It didn't jive with his experience of the Greek kids at KU. But he hadn't been a student since 1982, so things might have changed since he graduated.

"Stacia and her pals killed the girls when they found out Kimberly was investigating them," Curt said, "and then they set George up to take the fall for the murders."

Bill tapped the cassette on his palm. "Kimberly's research. That's what must be on this tape."

George got a chill. Of course it was.

"We need to get the data off that cassette," Curt said, and then his face fell. "I know where we have to go. Holy hell."

"What do you mean?" George said.

"We have to go over there, to the 'cable receiving station.' They got a big old computer lab, probably the only one for a hundred miles around."

Bill looked across the road. "But how do you propose we get in there? Have you acquired some lock-picking or razor-wire scaling expertise we don't know about?"

"Oh," George said. "Rita. She works there, right?"

Curt nodded.

George looked at his watch. "But it's after seven on a Sunday night."

"There's always someone there," Curt said.

"Then let's go," Bill said.

They jogged across the road where an imposing black wrought-iron fence gate, ten feet high, greeted them. The vertical iron slats curved outward at the top and stretched out of sight in either direction. Next to the gate was a card reader, a talk box, cameras, and klieg lights.

Curt pressed the talk box button. He'd obviously done all this before.

"Hello? Anybody there?"

"Can I help you?" a male voice said.

"This is Curt Dekker from across the way."

George watched Bill move his lips as Curt spoke, as if he were a very tense ventriloquist. Under other circumstances, this would have made George laugh.

"We need to use your computers," Curt added.

"Yeah, I don't think so," said the dubious voice.

"It's really important," Curt said.

But the guy remained unmoved. "Can't help you, sorry."

"Okay, then, is Rita Pavlakis still around?" Curt said it in a resigned voice, his posture once again collapsing.

"No," the voice said.

Bill leaned in, impatient, annoyed. "Hi there. My name's Bill Altenbach and I'm a mathematical physics professor at Fort Hays State. I can't stress enough how important this is."

"We're all pretty busy, so—"

Curt said, "This has something to do with Rita. I think she'd want to know about it."

"Listen, buddy, we're in the middle of—"

"You do not want to piss me off tonight," Bill barked in his best angry professor voice. George jumped at the sound of it. "Get me your supervisor. Right now."

Another voice came on the box. "Hi there." It was a woman's voice. "Rita's not here, Curt. She ran out to get us something to eat, but—wait there for a minute. I'll be right out."

"Who's Rita Pavlakis?" Bill said.

"This girl." Curt flicked his eyes in George's direction.

"*The* girl, right?"

Curt nodded.

"And that wasn't her? Who's coming to see us?"

"Nope."

A woman about their age with dark hair in a ponytail wearing large glasses showed up at the gate. She wordlessly appraised each of them then said, "You must be Curt," pointing at him. "I'm Gloria. What's going on?"

"Hi, Gloria," Curt said. "We wouldn't bother you if it wasn't important. We found a data cassette in his car and we need to find out what's on it."

She hesitated. "We've got some tests coming up that—"

"Please, Gloria," Curt said. "I don't know if Rita told you, but some of her friends were murdered in Lawrence and what's on this data cassette might give us some clue what happened and why."

A pause.

"She did tell me," Gloria said slowly. "But—"

"Please," Curt said.

Bill stepped forward, pulled his wallet out of his pocket, and removed his Fort Hays State University ID. He handed it to her through the fence. "I'm a mathematical physics professor at the university. This is incredibly important. I can't stress that enough."

She studied the ID then looked over her shoulder and back. She lowered her voice. "Let me see the tape."

Bill pulled the cassette from his pocket and gave it to her.

She glanced at it, flipped it, then tapped it on her palm.

"I've got a Commodore in my office," she said. "We have a test coming up in a few hours, so I'll give you sixty minutes. No more. If my boss catches you in there, it's my ass. You got me?"

They all three nodded vigorously.

She handed Bill's ID back but kept the tape. "I already know you're no threat," she said to Curt. "We did a background check." She looked at George, who held his hands up.

"I'm nobody," he said.

Gloria considered a moment longer then unlocked the gate with a card key. "Do not make me sorry I did this. You've got one hour." It swung open and they followed Gloria, who trotted quickly over the new asphalt. A two-story brick building rose to their left. The largest satellite dishes George had ever seen sat atop it.

She card-keyed the building's heavy steel door open and escorted them into a blindingly bright white hallway lined with identical blue doors. She walked quickly down it, and they jogged to keep up. At the end of the corridor, she turned left then led them to one of the blue doors and card keyed it. She stepped inside and flipped on the lights, then beckoned them inside and closed the door behind them.

A large L-shaped desk sat at one end of the room, a computer atop it and a printer, as well as a pencil holder, stacks of paper, and a spider plant. Two visitor chairs faced the desk. A familiar and colorful Klee print hung on one wall, and Curt stopped in front of it.

The huge amount of electricity used to power this facility

seemed to transmit over the surface of George's skin, his nerves buzzing with elation and terror at what they might find on this tape. As he tongued his recently broken tooth, he prayed this would somehow release him from having to face Mike and Derrill again.

Gloria dropped into her desk chair in front of the computer monitor and popped the cassette into the Commodore's tape drive.

The machine whirred as she typed, and Bill and George went to stand behind her chair. The square, neon-green letters DIR D: appeared on the screen. She tapped a key and three lines of text, a file directory, rolled up:

BEASTIEBOYS.DOC | 201041 BYTES | 05/23/86
NEWORDER.DOC | 194760 BYTES | 05/23/86
SIMPLEMINDS.DOC | 99023 BYTES | 05/23/86

"May twenty-third." Bill looked at George. "The day of the murders."

"How did you get this tape?" Gloria swiveled around to look at them.

"It was dropped in my car," George said.

"He's being set up for the murders," Bill added. "We're hoping what's on this tape will exonerate him."

Gloria regarded them a moment, skepticism mixed with curiosity showing in her face, before she turned her chair back to her keyboard. "Let's see what we've got," she said as her fingers

LS HAWKER

flew across the keys once more. D> TYPE BEASTIEBOYS.
DOC appeared onscreen then disappeared after she hit the
ENTER key. Within a minute, the screen was filled with square
green letters, numbers and symbols.

Gloria put her face right up against the monitor. She glanced
back at Bill. "Looks like the data's encrypted."

Curt joined them behind the desk, and all four of them
studied the screen, which was covered with lines and lines
of code, a total foreign language. Gloria traced the lines with
her finger. As she did, George felt Bill go stiff beside him, and
he feared Bill was having a seizure. He'd read about that sort
of thing happening to addicts going through withdrawal.
But when he turned to look, something else altogether was
happening. Bill reached out and laid his finger on a repeating
sequence of three characters, then pointed out more repeating
sequences of various lengths.

"You're right," Gloria said to him, pressing both hands to
the sides of her face. "This isn't gibberish. Those are patterns."

"Substitution cipher?" Bill said. He was vibrating with
excitement.

"What's a substitution cipher?" George said.

"Could be," Gloria said, ignoring his question, still staring
at the screen. "Not very sophisticated, which would work in
our favor. Let's find out. I'll print this. It'll take a little while,
but we can tear off each sheet as it comes and can divvy it up
and figure out what it says."

She broke open a brand-new ream of paper, fed the stack

into the printer, and fit the paper holes to the spokes. Back at the keyboard, she typed in a command and the printer began clicking and chugging.

George felt like he was in some kind of hacker movie, but he was going to be no help, and expected a similar reaction from Curt. But he wasn't even listening. He was staring at nothing, and George imagined he was thinking about Rita.

When he realized George was looking at him, Curt said to Bill, "You don't need me, right?"

Bill turned away from the screen and focused on him. "Well—"

"Come back to the trailer when you're done."

Bill held Curt's gaze as Gloria handed him the first page of the printout.

"Get to it, professor," Curt said, fake-cheerily.

Bill nodded, walked around the desk and sat in one of the chairs, making notations on the paper with a pen, equating numbers to letters and vice versa.

"I'll walk you out," Gloria said and led Curt out of the office door.

George stood looking around, feeling useless.

"Okay," Bill said. "It is a substitution cipher." He turned to George. "That means it's like the Cryptoquip puzzle in the newspaper. You know what I'm talking about?"

"Yeah," George said.

Gloria returned five minutes later and seated herself behind the desk. She tore some of the paper, which was still printing, off the printer. "Where you at with the key?" she said to Bill.

"Working on it," Bill said. "Here's what I've got." He slid a piece of paper across the desk.

"All right," she said and got to work.

Bill sat back in his chair and addressed George. "Soon as we've got the key, we'll give you pages to decode. Okay? You with me?"

"Yeah, I got it," George said, Bill's irritability rubbing off on him. "I went to college, you know." He dropped into the other visitor chair.

Bill gave him a smile. "What was it again? Yale? Harvard?"

"The venerable University of Kansas," George said. "Harvard of the Plains. Oxford of the Midlands."

Three minutes later, Gloria slammed her pen down and held her arms up. "Got it," she said.

Bill examined her work. "Yup," he said. "You win."

Gloria made a crowd cheering noise while Bill copied down the key on a separate piece of paper, which he then placed on the desk between him and George. Gloria gave him a stack of printout paper.

Bill reached across the desk and tapped Gloria's stack with his pen. "Halftime's over."

She grinned at him and started marking up her stack.

Bill's intelligence never failed to impress George, but he rarely got to see an actual demonstration of it when it mattered.

George got to work to the accompaniment of the atonal music of the printer. He'd gotten a list of names in alphabetical order with columns of numbers to the right. Employees? Vendors?

A little while later, Bill looked up from his work. "Wow," he said. "I've got an ops manual here. With a table of contents and an *index*."

Gloria paid no attention, just kept scratching at her paper.

George concentrated on marking off letters and numbers as he wrote their equivalents above them.

Gloria sat straight and said, "Quiet," even though neither he nor Bill were making a sound beyond pen strokes. Then he heard it. Footsteps coming down the hall.

She stood from her desk. "Quick," she said, motioning with her hands. "Back here."

"What?" Bill said, looking up. "I'm not getting down on the—"

"Just do it!" Gloria snapped, and he and George scrambled behind the desk and dropped to the floor as she positioned herself in front of it.

The door's electronic lock clicked, and the footsteps walked inside.

"Oh, thank God," Gloria said. She poked her head over the desk. "It's just Rita. Come on out."

George stood and straightened his shirt. A girl with striking green eyes and long curly hair stood holding a box with white paper bags in it, probably hamburgers from Saw Pole's only restaurant.

Bill returned to his chair and pulled his pen from his mouth.

"Hello."

Rita's eyebrows drew together as she took in the strangers. "What's going on?"

Gloria walked toward her. "Rita, this is Bill, and that's George."

George stood by the desk and put his hands in his pockets. "Hi, Rita."

She took a step backward. "Why are they here?"

Gloria took the box from her and set it on top of a bookshelf. "Everything's fine. They brought in this data cassette that George found in his car, and—"

"This is the guy the KBI came for in town," Rita said, stabbing a finger in George's direction.

Bill set his pen down. "They're looking at the wrong guy. Your sorority sisters in Lawrence set George up. This cassette explains why."

"Curt has been trying to help me," George said. "He's busted his ass trying to do that." He used Curt's own drunken words from last night. "And it's cost him a lot to protect me."

Rita's mouth opened but nothing came out.

"Listen. I gave your friend Stacia—"

"She's not my friend," Rita said.

"I gave her a ride," George went on. "She drugged me and left evidence of the murders in my car, including the cassette tape. I never even went in that house." George clasped his hands together, a plea for her to believe him. "But I'm really sorry about your friends. I can't tell you how sorry."

She stared at him a moment then put her hand to her neck as if it was hard to breathe. "Thank you."

"Also, I need to tell you," George said. "I'm not sure how well acquainted with him you are, but Curt's one of the best people I've ever known." George cleared his throat to keep it from choking up. "He'd do anything for you. He's done everything for me."

"Ditto," Bill said. He picked up his pen and bent back over the marked-up page in front of him.

"I guess what I'm saying is," George said, "I highly recommend him." He hoped she understood what he was saying. "Maybe you ought to go over to his place and let him know we cracked the code."

"*We* didn't," Bill said. "Gloria did."

Rita looked around, seemingly in a daze.

"Go ahead," Gloria said to her. "We've got this. Go."

"Thanks, Gloria," Rita said. To George and Bill, she said, "It's been...educational meeting you both." She walked out the door.

Gloria wore a matchmaker's pleased smile as she sat back down in her seat and picked up her pencil.

George sat in his chair and rubbed his eyes under his glasses. At the top of the page, the columns were broken out by months, and the columns of numbers themselves were the easiest to decode—they repeated across the rows, rarely varying. The numbers were small, 10 and up, but no higher than 250.

Allen, Joe.

Alta, Brian.

This was getting boring. All these names meant nothing to him.

He turned to the next page to see if there was any variation, and one row with several columns of three-digit numbers caught his eye. Unlike the majority of the other entries, there was a definite upward trend until several four-digit columns appeared. He tracked to the left-most column to decode the name.

A wrecking ball of sudden insight slammed into his skull, and he blew out a whoosh of air. His heart petrified mid-beat. He checked again. He was not imagining it.

He skipped the rest of the A's. Went to the D's. Then the E's.

The name next to the big numbers?

Altenbach, Bill.

And on subsequent pages:

Dekker, Curt.

Engle, George.

CHAPTER THIRTY-FIVE

Curt

Inside the sanctuary of his art barn, he slid his favorite mellow mix cassette into the boom box and cranked it up. Then he got to work.

All that was left were the eyes, and he spent time and concentration mixing the perfect shade of green, determined to get the proportions of phthalocyanine blue, diarylide yellow, and titanium white exactly right, as if that would manifest her in front of him.

When he was done with this painting, he decided, he was *done* with painting.

He was so deep in his head he didn't hear the barn door open. But pre-sunset light poured in, and a vision stood there. Rita.

He'd thought about what he would say if she came here again. But seeing her standing there, he couldn't say anything.

She didn't move, didn't speak.

"You lost?" Curt finally said, torn between happiness at seeing her and despair that she would soon be gone, and he'd missed his chance.

"I wanted to tell you what's on the cassette."

"Bill can tell me." He went back to painting. There was no point in prolonging the inevitable. She was leaving. Her week here was up. She lived in Topeka, another world, one that didn't mix with his. The sooner she left, the sooner he could get back to his real life.

"It looks like your friend George was telling you the truth."

"Yeah," Curt said. "I know."

"Also, I'm going back to Topeka tomorrow," she said.

Curt couldn't speak.

"I also wanted to say… George told me what you've been trying to do. Why you didn't—"

"I told you that first," Curt said. "You just didn't believe me."

Rita swallowed. "George told me how hard it's been for you. You're a good friend."

There was no point in talking any longer, no point in answering her. She was going to leave, and he was never going to see her again, so it didn't matter what he said.

Curt continued pretending to paint, his eyes fastened to the canvas.

"What are you working on?" She came farther inside the barn. "Can I see?"

"No." Curt stood protectively in front of the easel.

Her face fell, and his heart fell with it.

"So," she said. "Goodbye, I guess."

"But before you go," he said.

Her eyebrows raised in what looked like hope, to his cruel satisfaction.

"You need to take that picture of your dad," he said. "I don't want it anymore."

Her face fell again. "But—"

"Come on," he said. "Let's go get it."

She stayed put, and he blew past her through the door, careful not to touch her.

"Curt," she said once they were out in the yard. "I'm really sorry about—"

"Yeah, yeah," he said. "I know. Come on."

He went up the stoop stairs and opened the front trailer door. He turned to grab the photo and hand it to her, but she wasn't there. She hadn't followed him into the house. He dropped the frame, vaulted through the door, and took all the steps at a jump.

She was gone.

He ran inside the barn and she was standing in front of the easel, the canvas blocking his view of her.

This was beyond humiliating. She'd skinned and exposed him. He wanted to yank her away from his painting and shove her out the door. But when he canted left to grab her arm, the look on her face was the same as the first time she'd seen his art. It was wonder.

She stood with both hands over her mouth, her green eyes

wide and full of awe. "It's…*me.*"

His arms dropped to his sides.

"It's beautiful," she whispered. "I've never…no one's ever… you…"

"I knew I was never going to see you again," he said, wretched, "and I didn't think you'd give me a picture of you so…"

Her eyes then searched the walls of the barn.

"That's right. There aren't any other portraits. You're the only one. *The only one.*" His despair threatened to crush him. He turned away from her. "I just…can't get you out of my head. It was the only thing I could do."

On the boom box, "Coming Up Close" by 'til tuesday faded into "Miracles" by Jefferson Starship.

No. Not now. Not *that* song, with its plaintively moaning organ, its sparkling bells, its swelling strings.

He strode toward the tape player to turn the damn thing off.

But before he could, Rita's cool fingers slid down his arm toward his wrist. Her hand covered his and she pulled it away from the STOP button. She reached forward and turned the volume up.

She took his hand and laid it flat on the middle of her chest, and he felt her heart beating as hard as his. Then she pulled him close, drawing a gasp from him.

She entwined her fingers with his. His right arm slipped around her waist and they were swirling and dancing, like the song said, the strings and brass soaring higher and bigger.

A sunbeam exploded through the window behind him, igniting the motes of dust like sparklers and fireflies, lighting up Rita's wild hair and green eyes. She stopped him in mid-dance, her hands on his shoulders, breathing hard.

"Hey," she said. "Hey, Curt Dekker." Her hands glided up his neck to the sides of his face, her eyes taking in every inch of it, and he experienced it all through his body, felt seen, illuminated from the inside out.

Her eyes wide open, she brushed her soft lips against his. He didn't close his eyes. Couldn't. He pulled Rita into himself. Then they were kissing, and he felt himself vanishing into her, and every kiss that came before this paled, faded, dissipated. And then they were saying things to each other, crazy things, and he'd give her anything, he'd do anything, anything, anything for her, to have her, to keep her.

"I'm sorry I didn't tell you about George," Curt said. "And for thinking you were a spy."

"I'm sorry I didn't believe you," she said.

"What do I have to do to make this happen?" He held her face in his hands. "Do you want me to move to Topeka? I'll move to Topeka."

"I want to be wherever you are." Rita's breath was warm on his lips. "And right now, where I want to be is in your bed."

Curt felt deranged, as if he was suffocating and she was oxygen. "I want that more than I've ever wanted anything," he said. "But George and Bill are going to come back to the house, and...well, that's not cool."

"Oh, no." Rita sighed, her head tipped back, but she was smiling. She opened those eyes, put her lips by his ear, and whispered, "You come to *my* room then."

"But your coworkers will find out about—"

"Let 'em," she said.

His breath caught. "Take me."

"Wait," she said. "We're running some tests tonight, but I'm hoping we'll be done by around midnight. And then…"

"And then," he agreed.

She backed away, holding both his hands. She squeezed them then let go and walked unsteadily out the barn door.

Curt stood smiling stupidly for a few moments before he went back to the painting and thought *Someday this will hang in our living room.*

He put the last highlight on the iris of Rita's left eye, and it was done. He turned the easel around.

"What do you think, boy?"

The dog's eyes opened and just as quickly drifted closed again.

"That good, huh? I'm going in. You coming?"

The dog ignored him, and Curt stripped out of his turpentiney clothes, left the barn door open, and shambled naked in the twilight toward the trailer, listening to the meadowlarks and phoebes. He went inside. It was dark and silent.

He showered and dressed then went out to the living room.

The clock read 8:45, and Curt was aching to drive to the motel in Niobe. To distract himself, he pulled an LP—Neil

Young's *Everybody Knows This is Nowhere*—from his stacks.

It was his second copy of the album. He'd played the first so many times it was just a mass of scratches, hisses, and pops, and there wasn't a single song that didn't skip. He hadn't even removed the cellophane from this new copy yet. He slit it now and pulled out the record, then lifted the smoky-clear cover on his practically brand-new turntable—one of the few things he'd bought after coming into money.

He centered the disc over the spindle and let it drop to the platter.

The front door opened, and Bill rushed in holding the cassette and a pile of computer paper, followed by George. The dog brought up the rear, and George closed the door.

Bill's expression snapped Curt out of the happy daydream he'd been moving through for the last half-hour.

"What did you find out?" Curt said.

Bill slapped the stack of paper on the counter then riffled through it until he got to the pages he wanted. He put his index finger down next to handwriting that was hard to make out at first, but then it slapped Curt like a faceful of icy water.

"What is my name doing in there?"

CHAPTER THIRTY-SIX

Bill

"Don't worry," Bill said, jacked up on adrenaline from the sight of his own name. "Rita and Gloria didn't see this."

"Whoa, whoa, whoa," Curt said. "Why are our names on there? What does this mean?"

"We think it's a customer database," George said.

Bill raised an eyebrow. "Illegal drug customers."

"It can't be," Curt said. "What kind of drug dealers collect contact info from their customers? Nobody ever asked for my name when I bought dope from them."

"Did you ever buy from someone you didn't know though?" George said. "We're talking rural buys, not big-city back-alley dealings. The whole state is like that—small towns."

Curt opened and shut his mouth. "Yeah, I guess not."

"But the rest of it," Bill said, tapping the paper stack, "is an organizational chart, ledger, operations manual—it's Fortune 500-caliber stuff. This cartel—this business empire—controls drug traffic all over Kansas, and parts of Missouri, Oklahoma, and Nebraska."

Curt's jaw went slack. "Holy God," he said. "So those girls were killed because they were mixed up in this. They pissed off the big boss or whatever."

"Yeah," George said. "There's enough evidence on this tape to send everyone involved to prison."

Curt took the cassette from Bill. "We've got to take this to the authorities right now. You want to drive?"

"Wait," Bill said, the implications of Curt's suggestion tripping alarm bells in his head. "If the authorities connect the dots and see our names on there, we could go to prison."

"Bill," George said, "there are thousands of names in here. Do you really think they're going to prosecute each and every one? Maybe we could—I don't know, get immunity or something in exchange for our testimony. You think the cops—the KBI, the FBI, wouldn't kill to get their hands on evidence like this?"

"Yeah," Curt said. "And if it means we can get the goons off George's ass, we should do it, right?"

Bill's head was cloudy as hell. If only they could be guaranteed immunity... "Hey. Let's track down G-Ho and see what he says about it."

Curt brightened. "For sure. And take him with us to the cop shop. He's missed way too much of what's been going on. Guess that's what being a fiancé and stepdad-to-be is all about."

"I need to change my pants," George said. "Got these all messed up changing that tire." The dog got to his feet and followed him to the guest room door, looking up at him as if asking permission to accompany him.

George glanced at Curt, who shrugged. "He kinda thinks it's his room."

"All right," George said, opening the door. "After you." The dog trotted over the threshold and George followed him in and closed the door.

"'Changing that tire'?" Bill said to Curt.

"Long story," he said, swatting the air. "Hope this isn't going to take all night or anything. I got a date."

"You don't say," Bill said. "So Rita came by, did she?"

"Yeah," Curt said. "How did you know?"

"You can thank George for that. Rita is a—well, she's a home run, that one."

Curt nodded. "She's way out of my league. But here's the thing, man. I think this is it."

Bill's eyebrows rose. "Them's serious words, my friend."

"I know. She's wrecked me. I'm sprung. For real."

Liz's face rose in Bill's mind, and he remembered that wrecked, sprung feeling. Of wanting nothing more than to be near her, to listen to her talk, to touch her. But he also remembered his own lies, deceit, and betrayal, which were now etched in her face and eyes. He remembered her recent assertion that they were no good for each other. He wanted a drink. Right now. He wanted coke. *God grant me the serenity…* how did that thing go? He shouldn't be here. It was too soon.

"I'm going to run out and lock up the barn before we go. Be

right back." Curt lifted his keys from the table and opened the front door.

Bill rose from the couch and spied a library book on the end table. He picked it up and read the cover: *The Soviet Perspective on the Strategic Defense Initiative.* What the blustery hell was this doing here? He put it back and turned. Curt had left the front door open. Annoyed, Bill went to close it against the moths and other critters.

Curt was standing on the stoop, his back to the door, and Bill said, "What are you doing?"

CHAPTER THIRTY-SEVEN

George

George detached the tags from his new jeans, shirts, underwear, and socks, and folded them neatly for inclusion in the duffel. He removed the shampoo, toothpaste, toothbrush, deodorant, and shaving gear from their packaging and bundled them in the smaller zippered toiletry bag. He'd drive the Corvette to the cop shop and head to Kansas City right afterward, because now he wouldn't need to make a stop in Lawrence. He'd turn the heroin over to the cops.

In the other room, the front door hinges sang as it opened.

He just hoped that Mike and Derrill—and Stacia—would be arrested before they took off for Lake Havasu. One way or another, though, the three of them were going to prison thanks to Kimberly Laurent's data cassette. He zipped the duffel and took a step toward the door but was stopped by the sound of high-heeled booted footsteps on the kitchen linoleum.

The front door banged closed.

A female voice: "Hey, cowboy."

Then Curt's: "Who are you?"

"I'm looking for a guy named George Engle."

It was *Stacia*, and she was in Curt's living room. She was *here*. No panic in her voice this time. George now had enough panic for them both, and then some. He stood, still as a deer in the crosshairs, listening. The conversation was muffled, so he crept to the open window that faced the road.

A van was parked to the north of the barn.

A *red conversion* van.

Mike and Derrill's red conversion van.

George's mind shut off like a light. The guest room's other window faced the back yard. He pushed the screen from its frame and jumped out.

He ran past the Stingray, across the wheat field behind the trailer.

Stacia and Mike and Derrill were here to kill them all and take the tape. The information on there would put them all in prison, and no way they would let that happen.

George's lungs burned as he sprinted faster than he had since high school football until he came to a Fred Flintstone heels-to-the-ground stop.

Thirty yards ahead stood the Indian-faced stone fencepost where he'd meet Travis, Bill, and Curt to ride horseback when they were kids. The landmark he'd seen the night he drove into Niobe County bringing havoc with him and infecting all three of his friends with it, the friends who'd carried him through the darkest hours of his life.

George pitched forward to his hands and knees and threw his guts up. His stomach felt as though it were turning inside out, the pain searing.

Where specifically did he think he was going to "find help"? To reach the cable TV facility, he would have had to go east. If he was going to Curt's folks' house, he should have run north. But he was heading southwest.

Just away.

Running away.

He was still a coward and a liar, even to himself.

He'd left Bill and Curt to die in his place.

Clambering to his feet, George wiped his mouth and spat. He didn't have a weapon. He didn't have any skills. He didn't have a plan.

But he had to go back.

He had a stitch in his side by the time he got to the gate of the cable TV receiving station. He pressed the intercom call button. Nothing happened.

"Come on, come on," he said out loud.

He pushed it again, then leaned on it and didn't let up.

An infuriated voice, different from the one that answered before, bellowed, "What is it? Oh, come on. Are you kidding me?"

George could hardly force a word out he was breathing so hard. "I was here earlier, and—"

"You kids and your pranks," the voice said. "Get bent, you hayseed redneck."

"I'm not one of the local kids." George's sweaty hand left a snail trail on the intercom. "Please. We need help. There are these two guys in a van across the road who—"

"Are shooting a porno? I'll be right out."

"Will you shut up and listen to me? Over at Curt Dekker's mobile home, two criminals are there to—"

"I'm going to call the cops if you don't—"

"Yes! Call the cops! Get them out here!"

"That's real funny."

"I'm not joking."

"Step off, I said. I don't have time for this. We're on a clock here."

"Okay, I didn't want to have to do this, but..." George searched for company property he could vandalize, but everything he considered would require tools, and he didn't have anything but his pants. "I'm going to steal this camera. I'm stealing it. Call the cops on me."

He banged on the camera, trying to dislodge it from the post on which it was mounted. But it held fast.

George pressed the buzzer again. "CALL THE FUCKING COPS!"

CHAPTER THIRTY-EIGHT

George

George wished he could sneak into the barn, because Curt must have some tools out there—a shovel, a hoe, a rake—but the van was too close.

He took a wide circle around Curt's property, making himself as small as possible, until he reached the back side of the trailer. He hoisted himself up through the guest-room window and tumbled into the room, then looked around for a weapon of any kind. Of course, there was none.

Bill, Curt, and Stacia were still talking in the next room. George tiptoed to the door and reached for the doorknob, but intermittent flashes of red light issued from the window facing the road.

He sidled over to it and lifted the blind.

Oh, shit. It was G-Ho running his dashboard cherry light, but unlike Mike and Derrill, his was legal. Not that that would help anyone. He was going to try to citizens' arrest them for real, because of course Travis recognized the conversion van.

The Gremlin's dome light came on as Travis exited the car, putting his security guard hat on his head.

"Hey, pard," he called as he shut his driver's-side door, extinguishing the only light out there.

George strained to see what was going on outside, but the angle was all wrong. He could only listen.

"Remember me?" Travis called.

George didn't hear what the guys said in return. But suddenly, he heard a grunt and tussling, shoes dragging through gravel, punches connecting with their fleshy targets.

A muzzle flash blinded George, followed a microsecond later by a bang, and then another, then three more, like Fourth of July fireworks.

George's hands flew to his mouth. As if he'd forced air into his own lungs and corked them, he couldn't exhale.

When he could make his limbs move, he staggered to the door and jerked it open. Curt, Bill, and Stacia were looking out the front window, and all three of them turned, frightened and startled, toward him.

"What's happening?" Stacia's voice was high and tight.

"What the hell?" Curt said.

George banged his fists against his temples. "G-Ho. G-Ho's out there. He tried to go cop on them."

Stacia ran to him and threw her arms around him. "Where have you been?"

The front door swung open.

"Everybody get down!" George shouted and pulled Stacia to the floor with him and covered his head with his arms.

Booted footsteps sounded on the linoleum. "I had to shoot a guy. I had to shoot him and disarm him."

George's head jerked up, and there stood Travis, noticeably shaking and white as Styrofoam, but he appeared unhurt. He laid a pistol on the kitchen counter, and George launched himself and near about tackled him in a hug. Bill and Curt gathered around him.

"How did you do that?" George said. "How did you—"

"Where's my boyfriend?" Stacia said, shoving her way into the tight circle surrounding Travis. She tried to get hold of his jacket.

"He's okay," Travis said. "He'll be right in."

"Your boyfriend?" George said.

"They tied him up in the van—kidnapped him to force Stacia to come out here," Curt said. "She says."

Travis opened his mouth to say something else when an incredibly familiar voice rang out from the doorway. "I'm here, baby, I'm here. I'm all right."

And in strode Richie the liquor store counterman, the lifetime student, George's disc golf nemesis.

Stacia flung her arms around him, kissing his face.

"Are you okay?" Richie said to George. "Stacia told me what happened."

"*You're* her boyfriend?"

Stacia and Richie held each other tight, and he grinned at

George over the top of her head and nodded.

"Wait," George said. "When I went back to the liquor store that night, you said you'd never seen her before, and then when I saw you at the apartment complex, you—"

"Yeah, but she came back in the store and I asked her out. It's been kind of a whirlwind Sean Penn-Madonna thing."

"But—"

"G-Ho," Curt said, breathless with disbelief. "You—how did you—"

Some of Travis's color had returned. "When I got off work today, I swung by George's house and the KBI were there, but he wasn't. His cousin Freddie said he didn't know where George had got to, so I went to McWhiskey's and Mac said he overheard a phone call Curt made saying George would be staying with him. So I had dinner with Toni and AJ and then I came out here after we put AJ down." He scrubbed his hand over the top of his crewcut. "And when I got here I saw the conversion van, and I decided..."

Bill seized Travis's face with both hands. "You should have called the sheriff," he said, then planted a kiss on Travis's forehead. "But you're better than a cop. You are a *hero*."

Travis's face and ears glowed red. His gratified expression at the praise from Bill, of all people, brought tears to his eyes, which nearly had the same effect on George.

"This is not the time to celebrate. The guy out there needs an ambulance right now." Travis disentangled himself from his friends. "I need to run out to my car and call the cops and the paramedics on the CB." He pointed at Curt. "Since *you* don't have a phone." He strode to the door. He opened it and took a step toward the stoop.

There was a loud bang, and suddenly, as if lassoed, Travis flew out the door.

George looked from Curt to Bill, stupefied, but they stared, open-mouthed, at something behind George. He whirled around.

That something was Richie holding a smoking gun.

CHAPTER THIRTY-NINE

George

George's mind required a few moments to work out that the bullet's impact had blown Travis right off the stoop, sent him crashing down the steps and into the yard. George ran to the doorway, an unintelligible sound emanating from his mouth as he did so.

"Stop, George," Richie said. "Or this next bullet is going in your back."

George held his hands up as he turned. Richie pointed the gun squarely at George's forehead while Stacia closed and locked the door.

When he could form words, George said, "What the hell did you do? Why did you...*shoot* him when he saved you from the—"

"George," Richie said, impatient. "You're not really that dumb, are you?" He turned to Stacia. "Hey, babe, be a doll and grab Derrill's gun for me."

Stacia took the pistol off the counter then shoved it down the back of her jeans.

George looked from Bill to Curt, his throat spasming and his stomach heaving. Their hands were in the air too, eyes fixed on Richie's gun. Curt bounced from foot to foot, his face collapsing and reconstituting itself over and over. Bill's expression mirrored the sheer hatred it had displayed the night he walked out of Grandpop's house.

George had to swallow continuously because his mouth kept filling with saliva, furious at his body's refusal to help out in times of crisis. "We have to—" *Swallow.* "Call an—" *Swallow.* "Ambulance." *Swallow, swallow.*

It was as if he hadn't spoken. Richie and Stacia didn't react. What an actress she was. Her performance in the phone messages had nearly convinced him she was in trouble, but Travis had helped him resist calling her.

Not that it mattered now. Because he'd pulled all his friends into a deadly situation, and one of them was outside right now bleeding to death. Maybe dead already. He couldn't see through the tears in his eyes.

"Why don't we all sit down," Richie said, using the gun as a pointer. "I need some questions answered."

George obeyed this guy he'd thought was an annoying but harmless liquor store clerk, his head a droning void, and sat in the chair by Curt's stereo. As if by magnet, he felt drawn to the front yard. He had to go out to G-Ho's car and call the ambulance on the CB. He had to. But he was glued in place.

Bill sat on the far end of the couch by the wall, Curt in the middle, and Richie closest to George's chair with Stacia perched on the armrest next to him. Richie held his pistol casually in his lap.

George couldn't take his eyes off the thing that had blown a hole in G-Ho.

"Seriously, man," Curt said. "We should call an ambulance There are two guys out there who need a doctor, like, now."

Richie shrugged.

"But isn't that one guy your...friend?" Curt said.

"No," Richie said. "He's an employee. Easily replaceable. A throwaway. Like the girls in the house. Like you guys."

This statement plummeted into George's consciousness with the heft of a bowling ball. It had the ring of truth, of reality. Richie was absolutely right. George's parents had always known it. On some level, so had he. Maybe that's why he'd never found his path. He was disposable. He *was* a throwaway.

But Bill, Curt, and Travis weren't.

They were not.

"Where's the data cassette?" Richie said.

Bill looked at the kitchen counter.

"All right," Richie said. "Good. We'll leave that there for now." Richie looked from one face to another. "And what's on the tape?"

"We don't know," Curt said.

"He knows." Stacia indicated Bill with her head.

"We're all friends here, right?" Richie said. "No need for

bullshit now. What's on the cassette?" He picked up the gun and pointed it in Bill's direction.

Bill stiffened and at the same time seemed to shrink. "An encrypted document describing your organization and how it operates. Plus a customer database and a ledger."

Richie winked at George.

"How...how did the cassette wind up in my car?" George said, his voice cracking and shaking like a twelve-year-old boy's, still compulsively swallowing, trying to keep from lapsing into dry heaves. *Keep Richie talking. Let's keep him talking.* He didn't know what good that would do, but he couldn't think of anything else. Because once Richie took the cassette, he would shoot them all and be on his way.

"That's on Stacia," Richie said, and the smile drained from her face. "She dropped it when she was planting that shit in your car."

Stacia said, "Babe, we're here now and—"

Richie reached up and squeezed her neck, cutting off her sentence. The whites of her eyes showed all around the irises, the way a steer's did on its way to the kill floor.

Her terror steadied George. She did all this. She deserved to suffer. But she didn't deserve to die.

"Tell us about Kimberly Laurent, the journalism grad student." Bill seemed to be trying to draw Richie's attention away from Stacia.

"Yes, Kimberly," Richie said. "Worst hire I ever made. That's on *me*."

Richie let go of Stacia's neck as he regarded Bill.

Stacia raised her hand to her neck and coughed.

In reflexive sympathy, George cleared his own throat. "How did you find out Kimberly wasn't who she said she was?" He needed to keep his head in the game, even though all he could think about was Travis. Travis in the dirt, dying.

"Stacia," Richie said. "She figured it out."

Her face relaxed a little at this praise, but she remained wary. George was getting whiplash the way Richie switched so quickly from threatening to lovey-dovey with her.

"I recorded the phone calls at the house on Kansas Street," she said. "Kimberly was supposed to be so smart, how could she have been dumb enough to talk on the phone about her research?"

George swallowed. "If it was just Kimberly you were after, why did you kill the other two girls?"

Stacia locked eyes with him. "I didn't kill anyone," she said. "Mike and Derrill did. I just took the cassette once they were done. And they're the ones who set the house on fire."

George didn't believe her.

"How did you decode it?" Richie asked Bill.

Bill shrugged. "Nothing to it, in point of fact."

"He's a professor at Hays," Curt said.

The light of recognition showed in Richie's eyes. "I know who you are. Hoover's told me all about you. You owe me a shit-ton of money."

"You're Hoover's 'investor,'" Bill said. He was in bad shape.

His leg jiggled endlessly as sweat ran off his face. Curt sat next to him by turns kneading his hands together and dragging them through his hair.

"Is that what he calls me?" Richie said. "I'm his boss. I am *the* boss."

"Ah. I didn't recognize the name. On the org chart, you're listed as Richard."

"How many copies of the tape did you make?"

"Here's the thing," Bill said, wiping the sweat from his forehead. "We don't want the cops to get their hands on this any more than you do."

Richie and Stacia both looked askance, at each other and then at Bill.

"And why's that?" Richie said.

"The customer database I mentioned—all three of our names are on it. I say we take it outside and burn it. And then we call it a night."

Richie was nodding, but then he grinned. "Nice try."

George felt as if every inch of him were shriveling, his insides melting like crayons in the sun. And poor Bill. He kept scratching his arms, which were red and raw.

Richie's eyebrows went up. "Oooh. Hoover told me he cut you off. You got them bugs going, huh? Feel like you want to crawl out of your skin, don't you? Well, all is not lost, my friend." Richie lifted a tiny paper envelope from his pocket. "This should take the edge off." He tossed it on the coffee table.

George had seen those little envelopes from time to time,

filled with that magic white powder.

Bill gritted his teeth. "Thanks, anyway."

Richie smiled mock sympathetically. "Does it really matter now?"

Those casual words shrilled like an air horn in George's brain, inflaming his nerves and muscles, collapsing his lungs. This was really happening. When there was nothing left to say, Richie would execute them all.

But he had to hope the idiot inside the S.H.A. facility had called the cops. He perched atop this hope as if clinging to a champagne cork on a stormy ocean. "Richie," he said. "Why do you work retail if you're the head honcho?"

Richie shrugged. "If you don't want to be caught, you hide in plain sight. Position yourself as a loser, a guy with no real ambitions but tons of big talk. Act like you think you're younger and cooler than you are, and people feel sorry for you, avoid you because you're just slightly annoying. People stop being able to see you. That's kind of *your* life, right, George? I'm as invisible as you are. Only you don't do it on purpose. You're just a sad, pathetic, real-life loser."

Invisible. Beige. A throwaway. George the invisible boy, and it would be ever thus. And when Richie shot him in a few minutes, it would be as if he never existed.

"So...sorority girls. Why sorority girls?" Curt asked.

"About sixteen years ago I started working for a competing organization, but this one was cleaning up, and it was because the guys in charge were fraternity boys like me."

"In other words, stick up your ass, nose in the air, better than everyone else types," Bill said.

Unfazed, Richie nodded. "The organization began recruiting sorority girls—" He squeezed Stacia's thigh. "—and fraternity guys as employees, who were able to sell to other Greek kids. The guys in charge were very magnetic, very charismatic. They changed the business model by upgrading from pot and pills to heroin."

Heroin. George sat bolt upright, the breath squeezed from his lungs, and he looked at Curt, whose eyes widened. "Richie," George said. "I think maybe we can work something out here. I might have something you'd be interested in."

"Yeah?" Richie said. "What's that?"

"I have access to four pounds of black tar heroin."

Bill whipped his head toward George, his mouth open. "George—don't."

"It's true."

Bill frowned at George and shook his head furiously, and Curt put an *it's okay* hand on Bill's red, rashy arm, which Bill scratched when Curt took his hand away.

George ignored Bill's continued protestations and turned back to Richie. "I'll give it to you in exchange for our lives. You give us the guns and any other weapons you've got on you, and I'll give you the heroin and the cassette. Then you go."

Richie and Stacia looked at each other.

"Where's this heroin?" Richie said.

"I'll tell you when you give me the guns."

Richie pressed a finger to his chin and rolled his eyes to the ceiling. "It wouldn't be…in the hubcaps of that '71 Stingray out back, would it?"

George's solar plexus tightened as if a python squeezed it, and he saw fireflies in his peripheral vision. A plaited but frayed silver wire drew taut in his mind, sparks flying as it untwined and exploded in two.

"Bingo," Richie said, pointing at George again. "Your brothers, the golden Engle twins were the heroin wunderkinds."

Bill stared, obviously astounded by this information that George hadn't yet shared or even really understood the extent of.

Richie smiled and handed his gun to Stacia, who held it gingerly in her lap. He stood and thoughtfully walked over to where George sat by the turntable.

George tensed and leaned away, clutching the armrests, taking shallow breaths.

Richie looked around at everyone then bent at the waist so his face was inches from George's. George pulled his head back until it hit the wall. "You knew what it was like standing in their massive shadow, right?" Richie said, his voice sympathetic and mollifying, his breath smelling of licorice. "It was cold, and it was *dark*, wasn't it? I'll bet you wished them dead a thousand times." With his face still close to George's, he turned his head to share George's view of the living room, the horrified faces of Bill and Curt. He snaked his arm around George's shoulders and turned his face so they were eye to eye again. "I took care of you, buddy."

As Richie's eyes sought comprehension in his, George inhaled, a paroxysm of breath, as the significance of the words filtered into his brain drip by drip. Not fast enough for Richie, evidently, because he whispered, "Who do you think shot down that power line by their house?" and he winked.

George no longer saw the face in front of his. He saw a film reel unspool before him, everything about his family, his past, his life, his relationship with his brothers, everything splitting apart and rearranging itself. A polar sweat broke out all over him.

Richie watched the dawn break in George, his smile twitching with depraved jubilation, and now he was satisfied that George understood him. He stood and slapped George's back three times.

"Once they were out of the way," Richie said, addressing the room, "I took over. We now have dealers at eighty-two universities in four states. We still use Greek kids exclusively. They can afford expensive lawyers and they're good at keeping secrets. That's the recipe of our corporation's success. Loyalty and fraternity." He turned his head toward Stacia and his face changed. George followed his gaze and saw that Stacia was now standing by the couch, holding Richie's gun in both hands.

Aimed at Richie.

But George could not react. He was paralyzed, incapacitated with a grief so sharp it nearly outstripped the original. Richie had executed his brothers, cementing George's fate when he was just thirteen. Everything in front of him now held no meaning, no danger. Because George was dead already. He observed from far outside himself, from high above the earth.

Richie slowly raised his hands, eyes both amused and frightened.

"I didn't think you'd *ever* shut up," Stacia said. She kept her eyes on her boyfriend, even though she was addressing everyone else. "He never stops talking. Five years of this. Five years of being his *girlfriend*, listening to this bullshit."

"Babe," Richie said in a placating tone, as if she'd done this before, and all he had to do was talk her down.

"Shut the fuck up," Stacia said. "And sit down." She backed up to give him room to get there, to make sure he couldn't take the gun from her. But Richie clearly understood that Stacia wouldn't hesitate to shoot. He sat on the couch next to Curt.

"Here's what's going to happen," Stacia said. "We're going to finish this."

"Babe," Richie said, and he seemed genuinely confused. "Why—"

"You are a dumbass," she said. "Do you really think I'd go out with a guy fifteen years older than me? Who perms his hair? Who goes to a tanning salon? Yeah, you've got money, but I can do what you do. I've been planning this for a long, long time. It's my time now."

"You can't think my people will actually be loyal to you," Richie said.

Stacia's mouth twisted in contempt. "They already are. Derrill was totally on board until that stupid gomer shot him.

But *all* the women are on my side. All of them. Except Jennifer and Michelle. I gave them the option to switch teams. Turned me down flat. So they had to go."

"I'll make you a full partner—"

"Stop interrupting me," Stacia said. "You should have done that years ago. So here's what's going to happen. I'm taking the cassette, the guns, the heroin. George, you're going to shoot Richie and your two friends, and then tragically turn the gun on yourself."

This pronouncement helped him surface somewhat from his state of shock. He was going to...*what*? But he couldn't concentrate.

"But first," Stacia said. "I promised I'd tell you what really happened that night. I stashed the cassette in your car on purpose—I opened your music case and scattered your tapes so you'd pack it up when you noticed your cassettes on the floor. I was going to make you drive me away from there. When you came to, I was going to explain what you'd done, the horrible crime you'd committed, show you the blood on your hands and face and shirt that I smeared all over you, and you were going to turn yourself in. Or get arrested, either way."

She turned to Richie. "But I was going to take the data tape and copy it, hold on to it for leverage, and then take over from you." She rolled her shoulders and went back to addressing George. "But after I put everything on your back seat, I went to get in the front and I saw that Kimberly was trying to leave the house. She was still *alive*. She was still alive with a fucking bullet

322

in her head, can you believe that? I had to go back in there and bash her over the head with a lamp, and when I looked out the front door, there were three teenagers in the park right next to your car. I couldn't let them see me, so I went out the back and ran before the house blew."

She shook her head. "Richie told me you weren't the type of guy to do anything unpredictable, but you were wrong." She nodded her head at Richie. "That's on you. And now," she finished briskly, as if listing chores for her sorority sisters to follow, "after George shoots everybody out here and then himself, the KBI will know he was the one responsible for everything. And I'll go back to work in Lawrence, and you'll be forgotten, Rich."

George knew intellectually that he should be terrified, but the continuous, ten-day adrenaline flood and intermittent shock treatments had finally worn his nerves and emotions away. He figured Stacia planned to hold a gun on him to make sure he did the job, but he'd rather be shot than shoot. When it came down to it, though, he knew he'd do what he was told. He would let his friends down one last ignominious time.

Futility and despair pinned every inch of him to his chair.

"Okay, George," Stacia said. "Sorry for dragging you into all this, but it was Richie's idea to set you up." She said it so flippantly, George knew she didn't have a sorry bone in her body, but plenty of sociopathic ones. Just as she turned, Richie sprang from the couch and tackled her.

But with a strength George wouldn't have thought possible

from such a tiny girl, she rolled fiercely, her arms and legs flailing and then Richie was on his back. She pinned one of his elbows with her knee, but he grabbed at her arms with his free hand as she desperately tried to aim the gun at his face.

"George!" Bill and Curt shouted, overlapping each other.

She squeezed the trigger, and the gun went off with a loud *bang,* but the bullet pierced the floor above Richie's head.

"George!"

The sound of their voices finally penetrated and shattered the hard membrane that had surrounded him. He started as if from a doze.

"The fuck's wrong with you?" Bill yelled. George focused on him as he pointed at the pistol sticking out of Stacia's waistband. "Grab the fucking gun!"

Curt and Bill both rose and charged forward as George reached to pull the gun free.

But Richie beat him to it. He withdrew the gun. He pressed the muzzle under her chin. He pulled the trigger.

CHAPTER FORTY

George

A volcano of organic matter blew into the air, misting George's entire left side, clear up to his hair. Richie lifted one of Stacia's shoulders and removed the gun from her flaccid hand then let her flop back on her face, blood oozing down her hair.

Warm brain, blood, and bone rolled down the side of George's face.

"Sweet Jesus," Curt said, in a terrifyingly high-pitched voice.

Bill made an unnatural dying-animal sound, and George couldn't seem to look away from Stacia's open skull, the sight so horrifying that he was left numb and blank.

Richie now had one gun in each hand and pointed them outward, bouncing like a prize fighter who'd just scored a KO. He sniffed and breathed hard, looking around at everyone, his face glazed with Stacia's blood. "Sit the fuck down, all of you! Now!"

They all dropped into their original seats.

Particles of Stacia's viscera were all over the room—the ceiling, the lampshade, the curtains. George sat quivering in his chair, his skin white-hot and freezing at the same time, his senses intensified. This heightened awareness of life signaled his inevitable death.

"All right," Richie said. "Enough of this shit."

Bill's and Curt's faces reflected George's disbelief and horror at the unfairness of it all.

After Richie slipped one of the guns into the front pocket of his khakis, he wiped his face on his sleeve, removing most of the blood. He snorted and spat on Stacia's back, a thick, red glob of snot and blood. George gagged, but he was too terrified to vomit.

Richie looked around at the interior of the trailer. "The bonus of taking care of business here, in the middle of fucking nowhere, is that you yahoos probably won't be found for days. Weeks, maybe." His laugh was winded and reedy. "So who's going to be first?" He walked to the other side of the room so that he was home plate and the other three were first, second, and third base from where he stood. He casually aimed his gun at Curt. "Any last words?"

"Yes," Curt said. "Do you have any change?"

Non-sequitur Man was making a final appearance, and the look of bafflement on Richie's face would have cracked George up if this had been an ordinary Saturday night. His eyes tracked to Stacia's dead form again, which made him think if he were to live beyond this night, he would never laugh about anything ever again. But he was not going to live beyond this night. None of them were.

"Do you need to make a phone call on your way to hell, or what?" Richie said to Curt, who fell into a violent coughing fit.

An image suddenly developed in George's brain—the vending machine in front of Minnie's liquor store. The image turned into a silent film of thirteen-year-old Curt bent over coughing to distract Minnie so George and Bill could escape out the back of the store.

And suddenly George knew what Curt planned to do. He was going to make for the door to draw fire away from George and Bill. The coughing was just to let them know to be vigilant.

Bill obviously saw it too. He sat straighter and looked at George and then addressed Richie. "Just...indulge me for a second. You've got all the guns. We've got shit. You win, okay? I want to ask you a few more questions before we die."

Curt stopped coughing, and George held his breath while Richie considered. George had to stop Curt, could not let him do what he planned to do. He could not let one more friend of his sacrifice himself.

"Did you know the twins were from here?" Bill asked. "Did you know they were related to George?"

"No to the first question," Richie said. "But I did know George was their little brother. I saw his name on his team t-shirt at a disc golf match. And sure enough. He was the one."

George kept his eye on Curt, trying to will him to stay seated, but Bill did better than that. He reached over and took hold of Curt's arm. George expected Curt to peel Bill's hand off to allow him to spring up, but he didn't. Without looking away from Richie, he patted Bill.

So...why were they stalling Richie? What did Curt think was going to happen?

Richie didn't notice any of this. "After we figured out Kimberly was investigating us, and we made our plans, we knew George would be the perfect guy to set up for the murder."

"Because you knew he took a class with Kimberly?" Curt said.

"We found that out later," Richie said. "Just a happy coincidence. But after George disappeared, we were going to have to go to the *Lawrence Journal-World* office and hunt through microfiche, looking for articles about the twins' unfortunate death from fifteen years ago—surely some mention of the hometown would have come up, but then Stacia suggested I call the KU alumni association."

He looked down at her body sympathetically.

"But they only had George's parents' phone number down in Lake Havasu. No one could tell me where he grew up. It was like he never existed—unsurprisingly. So I called his folks."

Nausea bubbled up in George's stomach at the thought of his parents having any contact at all with this permed jackwagon.

"I pretended to be with the alumni association and told them we were doing a feature on one of our outstanding graduates." He smirked. "They bought it. I was very charming. I chatted them up, asked them to tell stories about you as a kid we could use in the article we were writing about you."

George knew what was coming. He *knew*.

"Guess how many stories your mom told about you?" Richie turned toward George and made a circle with his thumb and fingers. "Zero. Not one."

His friends' heads again turned toward George. Oh, the never-ending humiliation of his family saga.

"But I had to listen to the endless parade of Chad and Vic stories," Richie said. "As if I hadn't played enough second fiddle to those douchebags from the time they floated into Lawrence on their golden chariot. After thirty excruciating minutes and nearly losing my will to live, she got around to saying you'd grown up in some podunk town called Niobe in north central Kansas. And I said to Stacia, that's where he is. He has nowhere else to go."

George's skin was on fire, his feet throbbed, and he wished he could see his parents one last time. He looked at each of his friends in turn, hoping they knew he was sorry. Sorry that he'd drawn them into this, sorry that he'd agreed to drive Stacia, sorry that they'd had to put up with his endless shit over the years.

"When we got to town," Richie continued, "Stacia went in your one shithole bar and asked around. It took less than ten minutes to talk some guy into telling her you were staying out here." Richie held his arms out. "And here we are. Well. Here I am."

Curt started coughing riotously again.

"Somebody get this guy a lozenge," Richie said, and raised the gun again. "Or maybe I should put him out of his misery."

But Bill took the cue and kept talking, louder, to draw Richie's attention again. "Even if George hadn't been related to the twins, he was still the perfect fall guy. Right?"

Curt's coughing eased and Richie laughed. And even though George knew what Bill was doing, he didn't want to hear what was coming, so he read the lyrics to "Stairway to Heaven" over and over. *There's a lady who's sure...*

"You selected George because you got to know him, and you found out he was *nothing* like his brothers," Bill said. "No ambition. No drive. No direction. He's a guy with a bullshit job, a guy who doesn't really do anything or make any kind of impression on you. He's come into your liquor store every week, same day, same time, since you've been working there, right? You observed George for years and knew he wasn't going anywhere. You knew he'd be coming in to buy his Budweiser that Friday as soon as he got off work. I'll bet you could set your watch by him, he's so predictable."

George's face felt as if it would catch fire. Just like Curt had said: *beige.* And because of his beigeness, they were all going to die once Richie got tired of Bill's monologue. Because no cops were coming.

"Even if by some miracle he put together what was happening to him," Bill went on, "you knew he didn't have the balls to fight back."

Richie closed one eye and pointed at Bill. "Hoover's right.

You *are* a smart guy."

"And best of all," Bill said, "you could get retroactive revenge on those Engle brothers who'd overshadowed you."

"Yes," Richie whispered. "One final 'fuck you' to the golden Engle twins. But first…" He took aim at Curt's head again.

"But I have one more question," Bill said, his voice rising with barely suppressed hysteria, "what was in the absinthe? What knocked George out for less than an hour?"

Richie lowered the pistol and smiled. "It was ether."

"Ether?" Curt said.

"I do a lot of reading, like you, professor," Richie said. "I read about how last century the Irish discovered that if they drank ether, it gave them a big head rush for about sixty seconds and then unconsciousness."

George nodded. That described his experience exactly.

Richie shrugged. "It was cheaper than booze. As a bonus, it leaves no trace in the blood," he said. "If George had gone to the cops claiming he'd been knocked out by some exotic substance, his tox screen would have come back negative. He would have wound up in prison. Like he should have. Would have been better than what's about to happen."

"I do have some last words," Curt said as Richie turned the gun on him once more. Curt started talking, but George couldn't understand anything he said.

His heart was threatening to come loose, his whole body in danger of splitting apart, seams popping, stuffing and gears spilling out all over the shag carpet. His helplessness simmered in his gut like a pot of boiling oil.

Details of the room sharpened, the faces of his friends, even the stupid poster of Farrah Fawcett and the ridiculous Jack Daniel's mirror. He swiveled his head in a semicircle, from the kitchen on his left to the turntable with its open cover on his right with a pristine vinyl record. *Everybody Knows This is Nowhere.* He loved that album. He'd never get to listen to it again.

He wished one of his favorite songs was playing now, craved music, a swan song, maybe "Can't You Hear Me Knocking" by the Stones or "Straight to Hell" by the Clash or "Voodoo Chile" by Hendrix.

Or "Love Me Tonight" by Head East.

"—I think things finally got weird enough for me," Curt was saying.

George was so freaked out, his feet buzzed, and the trailer itself seemed to rock. But then the Led Zeppelin tapestry swayed on its nail, as did everything else on the walls.

What was happening? George looked again at the turntable, at the new record on the platter. The brand-new record. The unwarped, perfectly balanced disc.

"Let's do this," Curt said.

A blast of brilliant, blinding light illuminated the room so brightly Richie's bloody face appeared dazzling acid green, along with everything and everyone else in the room. His arms out for balance, he yelled, "What the hell is going on?"

"Richie," George shouted.

Richie turned his attention from Curt to George, who stood, and in that blinding light levered up the Neil Young record and hurled it, disc-golf style, at Richie's face.

The record sailed fast and straight before Richie could even react. The disc edge axed directly into the bridge of Richie's nose with an audible pop.

Ace.

The force and surprise of it knocked Richie into the wall behind him. Blood erupted as Richie's hands flew to his nose, effectively hitting himself in the face with his gun with a satisfying crack. His cheek immediately swelled as he blinked in surprise and pain.

The green light disappeared, and the buzzing and rocking ceased.

George ran at Richie and wrenched the gun from his hand, snapping his trigger finger in the process. Then he trained the gun at Richie's head. Bill and Curt flanked him, and Bill pinned his arms to the wall as Curt pulled the second gun from Richie's pocket and pointed it at him.

Richie babbled, blood running down his face, clearly completely undone by the bizarre occurrence.

"What the fuck was that?" Bill's huge eyes were even huger than normal. "You guys saw it, right? It wasn't just me?"

"I told you, didn't I tell you?" Curt said to George, triumphant. "I told you it was an SDI testing site!"

"An SDI...*what*?" Bill said.

"We were saved by Ronnie Raygun," George said. "So you

knew this green light thing would appear? But—then what did you think was going to happen? How did you know—"

"I had faith in you," Curt said.

"In me?" George said. "But I'm—"

"I was counting on that test to distract Richie long enough for you to do something. And you did." Then Curt hurdled Stacia's body, threw the front door open, and disappeared outside.

CHAPTER FORTY-ONE

Curt

"Grab G-Ho's handcuffs while you're out there, will you?" Bill called out the door.

Curt was glad that Bill was level-headed enough to think of that, because all Curt could think of was G-Ho, and he slipped on the top step and bumped his ass all the way down, but he barely felt it.

The lifeless body of the guy apparently called Derrill was sprawled on the road by the conversion van. Travis had done that. He'd saved them. Had he not taken this goon out, they'd all be dead. Travis lay on his stomach, just beyond the reach of the porch light beam. He looked as though he'd tried to crawl to the steps at some point but was unmoving now.

Curt plopped down on the ground next to him. "G-Ho! You okay?"

He removed the cuffs from the back of Travis's belt.

"G-Ho," he said, tugging at Travis's arm. "I'm going to call for help in a second. I wanted to make sure first that you—"

There was no resistance. Travis's arm flopped.

Curt sprang backward and landed on his ass again, breathing hard, but he felt no pain. He crawled back to Travis. "G-Ho?" Curt touched below Travis's ear for a pulse. His skin was cool and waxy. But Curt discerned a pulse. Weak, but it was there. "Hang on, buddy. I'm going to call for an ambulance right now. Just hang on."

From the open guest room window, a howl arose.

"Hold on, boy," Curt called. "Forgot you were in there. I'm kinda busy. Hold on."

He ran to the Gremlin, threw open the door, and got in. He switched on the CB, which came to life with a squawk. He depressed the talk button on the handset and spoke into it. "Hey, out there, we need an ambulance right now! We've got three people who've been shot."

A voice came back. "Ten-four. What's your twenty?"

"My place—uh, Curt Dekker's place on County Road Fifteen. You gotta hurry. Travis Mussberger is down."

"Travis?" the voice said in alarm. "On our way. What's the location of the gunshot wound?"

"In the back, I think. I don't know," Curt said. "I gotta go. Just get here!" He got out of the car and ran back to Travis, where he flopped on the ground and felt for a pulse again.

"Curt?" Travis's voice was a raw whisper, the right side of his face against the dirt.

"Yeah?" Curt leaned down over Travis's face.

George loomed in the doorway. "How is he?"

Curt gave him the thumbs-up.

George plunged down the stairs. "You call the ambulance? You get the cuffs?"

"Yes to both," Curt said. He squeezed Travis's shoulder and stood so George could take his place. "I'll take them in. You watch over old Gung-Ho here."

He heard the sirens coming closer as he went in the trailer. Bill now had Richie lying prone on the carpet and was sitting on his back.

A red stain surrounded Richie's face, which was mashed into the carpet under Bill's weight. Curt was surprised by how much blood continued to seep out of Richie's nose. Now that the shock had worn off, Richie struggled, but Bill kept him pinned.

"Calm down," Curt said handing the cuffs to Bill. "You're not going anywhere."

"My face itches," Richie said. He sounded like he had a bad cold. "You're cutting off the circulation in my legs. Just let me—"

"Too fucking bad, fuckwit," Bill said, and hauled Richie to his feet. "Put your hands on your head."

Richie scratched at his nose first. "Ow," he said, then raised his hands to his head.

Bill cuffed one wrist and shoved him forward, then pressed his wrists together behind his back. Bill spun him to face them, his back to the wall once again.

"You guys know how much I'm worth," Richie said. "I'll pay you both a lot of money if you tell the cops I was a victim like you. A lot of money."

"Look around you," Curt said. "Does it look like I give a shit about money?" He glanced at Bill, who kept his lips tight and didn't acknowledge Richie's offer. But he had to be thinking hard about it with all the money he owed.

The front door opened again, and the red and blue lights backlit George's form in the doorway.

"Ambulance here?" Bill asked.

"They're loading him up now," George said. He walked to the kitchen counter and picked up the gun lying there. He went into the living room and aimed it at Richie's head. None of his usual shaking hands or sweating and stammering. He was as self-possessed as Curt had ever seen him, steady and determined. This experience *had* changed him, no doubt about it.

"Now get out of the way." George spoke to Bill in a calm, conversational tone, as if he were asking him to pass the salt.

"It's all good," Bill said. "He's cuffed. He's not going anywhere."

"Oh, he's going somewhere," George said, in that same calm voice.

"What are we doing, George?" Curt said.

"I wanted to tell you, Richie, what G-Ho just told me. He can't feel his legs. He can't move them."

Curt's jaw slackened, and a rush of adrenaline sent jets of pain to every nerve ending. His knees buckled, and he fell heavily against the couch arm.

Bill breathed hard, his expression vacant.

The ambulance siren started up along with the engine, and the vehicle pulled out of the yard, headed to Niobe.

George cocked the hammer on the revolver, still aimed at Richie's forehead. "And now I'm going to shoot *you*."

Curt trembled and gasped in torment. "No," he said, "you're not."

"George." Bill's voice was frantic. "Sheriff's on his way."

"I'd better hurry then," George said.

"This is bad," Curt said, "this is very bad. You don't want to do this." He should step in front of Richie, but he couldn't urge his legs into action. Plus, he was afraid any movement would start George shooting.

George never took his eyes from Richie. "Yeah, actually, I do."

"George, think," Bill said. "The nightmare's over unless you pull that trigger."

"You killed Stacia," George said to Richie. "You're responsible for the murders of Kimberly, Michelle, and Jennifer. You might have killed G-Ho and left a little boy fatherless and widowed his mother for a second time. You killed my *brothers*. And now you're going to pay."

Bill and Curt were both statues, their hands out like traffic cops about to be flattened by a runaway semi.

But Richie was smiling through the drying blood on his face. "Don't worry," he said. "He's not going to do it. I know this guy. He couldn't even if he really wanted to. And he doesn't really want to."

George fired the gun.

CHAPTER FORTY-TWO

Curt

Curt's brain was slow to catch up and believe what his eyes had just witnessed. The sound of the gunshot made his ears ring, but not as much as the screaming. Richie fell to his knees, his hands still cuffed behind his back. The bullet had grazed his ear and lodged in the wall behind him. Fresh blood flowed down the left side of his head, and he screamed and screamed. George took aim once more, the calm determination on his face frightening to witness. Curt didn't recognize this George. This George was *anything* but predictable.

"Oh, you thought I missed, Richie?" he said. "No. I'm going to shoot one piece of you off at a time, one piece for every life you've ruined. We're going to be here a while. So get comfortable."

Bill held his hand out. "George, give me the—"

The front door flew open and in ran Sheriff Zoellner and a deputy, guns drawn.

"Drop the weapon!" Junior Zoellner shouted, nearly tripping over Stacia's crumpled body.

But it was as if George hadn't heard. He continued aiming the gun at Richie. Didn't even look at the cops.

Richie's screaming had devolved to high-pitched whimpering, bloody drool and snot hanging from his lips. "Help me," he brayed at the officers. "He's trying to kill me!"

"Drop it!" Junior yelled. He cocked his sidearm.

"George!" Bill shouted. "They're going to shoot you if you don't drop that gun. Drop the gun!"

George never looked away from Richie.

Curt was afraid all the yelling and Richie's mewling would jangle George's nerves and cause the gun to go off. To Curt, it seemed inevitable this evening would end with George dead, one way or another, because he didn't care anymore if he lived, and maybe he was counting on the cops to do the job for him.

"Because of you," George said to Richie, "my mother is crazy. My dad is a fucking zombie. All those things Bill said about me? They're all true, and they're *all* because of *you*."

"No." Bill shook his head violently. "They're not true."

"Shut up, Bill." George remained calm, detached.

There were a thousand things Curt wanted to say, needed George to hear and understand, but all that came out was, "George, look at me,"

"Don't make me do this, George," Junior said, his gun shaking. "Don't make me shoot you."

George couldn't hear any of them. "This next bullet is for

Chad. After that, for Vic. And then—"

In slow motion and without really meaning to, Curt reached out his hand because George's pain was too much for him to bear. He had to touch him, let him know he wasn't alone. When his fingers made contact with George's shoulder, it was as if he'd switched off a radio. George stopped talking, stopped moving, stopped breathing.

"George," Curt said quietly. "Look at me."

George turned his head toward Curt.

Curt smiled at him, his hand still on his shoulder. "Good," he said. "That's good. Can you hear me?"

George nodded.

"Okay. I need you to *really* listen, yeah?" Curt used his quietest, most soothing voice, the one normally reserved for talking friends down from bad drug trips.

All eyes were on him, suspended, mesmerized by what was happening, but they faded from Curt's peripheral vision. It was just him and George.

"You're not going to shoot Richie. You're not going to shoot yourself, or anyone else," Curt said. "Because you know what? Just weeks from now, you're going to start law school. You're going to make something out of your life, because the new life, the *better* life, begins today."

Richie had gone silent, and the only sound now was Curt's own voice.

"You're going to meet a girl, and you're going to get married, and have children, and we're going to be there. We're *here*. Bill and me and Travis, we've always been here, and we always will be. *We're* your family, your brothers, and we're not going anywhere. You're not alone, and you never have been."

George's face crumpled, and his hand fell to his side. The gun slipped to the floor and he sank to his knees, hands over his face. Curt's hand remained anchored to George's shoulder. Bill stepped forward, his eyes spilling over, and took hold of George's other shoulder and held on while George wept.

CHAPTER FORTY-THREE

Curt

Sunday, June 1, 1986
12:45 a.m.

Curt opened the guest room door. He dropped to his knees and hugged the sleepy hound, rubbing his face into the warm fur. He opened George's duffel bag and pulled out a pair of jeans and a t-shirt and threw them over his shoulder. Then he lifted the dog in his arms and walked into the living room, stepping carefully around Stacia's body, and tugged the door closed behind him. He descended the steps and set the dog by his water bowl.

Out in the yard, he tossed the pants and shirt to George, who was standing by Bill and Junior next to the picnic table. George stripped off his bloody clothes and handed them to Junior, who put them in a waiting evidence bag. Curt was glad Junior hadn't slapped the cuffs on George. Benefits of living in a small town, he guessed.

The ambulance was on its way to the hospital with Travis inside, and the deputy was in transit to the same destination with Richie still cuffed in the back of the police cruiser. Junior had called for more ambulances from neighboring towns and police backup which had not yet arrived.

Curt now got a look at the huge bloodstain where Travis had lain. His gut contracted, forcing a grunt from him. He sent up a silent prayer. *Please, God, don't let G-Ho die before we get there. Please.*

Junior looked up from his notepad. "Sorry about your linoleum in there," he said to Curt. He was referring to the vomit on the kitchen floor. The deputy hadn't quite made it to the bathroom. "He's never seen anything like that before. Hell. Neither have I."

"I was going to have to replace it all anyway," Curt said. All the carnage, the dead bodies, the blood and bone, were a shocking sight. Although Junior hadn't thrown up, he was distinctly shaken. He and the deputy were cops, but they were small-town cops.

"I'm going to need you all to come down to the station tomorrow morning. Sorry, George, but I'm going to have to book you when you come."

"I understand," George said.

"Junior," Bill said, "there were extenuating circumstances."

"I know it," Junior said. "But we need to do everything by the book, because if what you've told me is true, a lawyer can help you all get immunity. Maybe throw you in witness protection if need be." He turned to Curt. "You got somewhere you can stay tonight? Maybe for the next several nights?"

"Yeah," Curt said.

"And George, you're going to need to leave the Corvette for now so we can process that heroin."

"I know."

"You riding with me, George?" Curt said.

"Sure."

"I'll follow in the Mustang," Bill said.

Everyone shook hands with Junior before they trooped to the vehicles.

George climbed into the Jeep's front seat and Curt gunned it toward Niobe.

They didn't speak on the drive, the late-spring heat escaping from the ground, ceding to a coolness that would disappear in a few weeks' time.

They pulled up to the hospital, parked, and regrouped near the entrance. Bill made eye contact with Curt. His look said, *Are we ready for this? Can we do this?*

Ready or not, able or not, they had to face whatever was on the other side of the door.

Bill's face slanted toward the sky and his lips moved, but he made no sound. Then he rolled his head on his neck. The three of them entered the hospital and walked down the hall until they reached intensive care. They hesitated and looked at each other, a silent question rising among them.

George stepped forward and went in first.

CHAPTER FORTY-FOUR

George

In the hall outside the ICU, Travis's parents were huddled with Travis's fiancée Toni and Niobe's only Lutheran pastor. None of them even looked up when the three of them came in. An older nurse in blue scrubs, the mom of one of their classmates, came down the hall toward them.

"I'm sorry, boys," she said. "You can go to the waiting room, but you can't be in this area right now. Family only."

Travis's father came down the corridor toward them, his face stoic, his hands in his pockets. "Give us a minute?" he said. She nodded and stepped discreetly away.

"Can you tell me what happened out there?" Mr. Mussberger said.

George explained, as best he could between hyperventilating episodes, the events of the night. It was as if George were standing apart and listening, not telling the story. He ended with, "I'm so sorry, Mr. Mussberger."

"How's Travis doing?" Curt said.

"He's in critical condition," the old man said. "Still in surgery. He needed a transfusion—he lost a lot of blood. There's no…" He couldn't go on for a moment, struggling for control. "There's no reflex response in his legs." The old man placed one hand over his mouth and the other on Curt's arm, shaking his head. He could say nothing. He let go of Curt then turned and trudged back down the hall.

George had to lean against the wall to stay on his feet, gulping air. Curt blinked, his mouth open, and Bill stood shaking his head, the muscles in his jaw working.

The nurse reappeared and said, "We're not going to know anything for a couple of days. No point you all sitting around here. Go home and get some sleep and come back tomorrow. Visiting hours are ten to two every day."

George and Bill followed Curt out the exit.

Out in the parking lot, George and Curt stood with their backs against the Jeep, George bent over, hands on his knees. Every time he blinked his eyes, the vision of Travis lying motionless on the ground appeared.

The three of them were silent staring out at the night. George's breath came faster and faster until he turned and pounded the Jeep's roll bar and shouted, "Fucking G-Ho, dumb-ass gung-ho cowboy! What the hell's wrong with him? Why didn't he call the sheriff when he saw the van?"

Rough hands forcibly spun George away from the Jeep. Bill's red, enraged face was right in his, hands painfully gripping his biceps.

"What the hell is wrong with G-Ho? What the hell is wrong with *you*? You're the one who brought down this shitstorm on us, and Travis might die for his trouble. I ought to beat the shit out of you."

Curt forced himself between the two of them and shoved Bill off George, who stood panting and rubbing his arms. There would be bruises.

"And don't think we don't know what you were up to in the trailer," Bill said. "You were hoping for suicide by cop. At least when I tried to off myself, I didn't get anyone else killed."

"That happened after G-Ho was down," Curt said, "so you really can't—"

Bill talked over him at George. "And after going through it with your mom so many times, you'd think you'd—"

George lunged at him, wanting to rip Bill's face off. Curt pushed them apart again.

"If G-Ho dies, if he's paralyzed permanently," Bill shouted, pointing a finger in George's face, "I will *never* forgive you for this."

Curt shoved him away again.

George could say nothing. Because he would never forgive himself either.

"Bill," Curt said. "Take a second and think about what you're saying."

Bill turned on Curt, teeth bared and eyes blazing, but as his own words sank in, he began to lose steam.

Curt said, "How many people in your life have forgiven you even after all the shitty stuff you've done?"

"I've never gotten anyone killed," Bill mumbled.

"Listen," Curt said. "I will lose my fucking mind if G-Ho dies. But this whole self-righteous act is bullshit, and you know it. Yeah, George fucked up big time. But so did you. So have I."

George hung his head, bereft and miserable. If he lost his friends, there would be nothing left.

"G-Ho is who he is," Curt said. "He could never be anything else. He came to our rescue. But we'd all be lying dead in my trailer if it weren't for George. He saved us."

Bill looked from Curt's face to George's. "We wouldn't have needed saving in the first place if it weren't for George." He got in the Mustang and drove away.

CHAPTER FORTY-FIVE

Curt

After George got out of the Jeep at his grandpop's house, Curt went to City Park and sat in the Jeep by the empty bandstand, unable to go forward or back. He stretched out on the hood, eyes on the giant tin man's head of a water tower and the trees that waved around it like they always did, as if nothing had changed. But he kept seeing the bodies in his mind, the blood and brains, hearing the sobs and the shouts and the gunshots.

Darkness pervaded his mind, his soul. At this moment, he wasn't sure he should contaminate Rita with it.

Maybe he should just spend the night out here and let her go.

But the longer he lay there, the more he understood he had to see her. Had to, no matter the result. He climbed into the Jeep, started it up, and pulled out onto Main Street.

Driving past the old Farmers National Bank, he was startled to see the clock flicker 3:22 a.m., much earlier than he would have guessed after all that had happened. He wished he could take a shower. He didn't know if he'd ever feel clean again.

He traveled north on High Street, followed it past the Sunset Drive-in, and turned into the entrance of the Grand Niobe Inn motel. He parked, walked to room 6, and stood there a moment before knocking softly.

Rita came to the door in a sleeveless t-shirt, her hair large and wild, legs bare, eyes sleepy. But they widened at the sight of him. "Are you all right? What happened?"

Curt had rehearsed in his mind what he would say when she opened the door. Something funny, nonchalant, like, "You are *not* going to believe the night I had." But now that he saw her standing in the doorway, everything fell away. Now that he knew she was here, waiting for him, he was rendered voiceless. And to his utter surprise, he completely broke down, his face dissolving into an agony of tears and fear and mourning. She drew him inside and closed the door behind them. She embraced him, and he buried his face in her hair, crying as he hadn't since he was nineteen.

"I'm sorry," she whispered, kissing his head. "Whatever it is, I'm so sorry."

Rita sat him on a chair and pulled his boots off. Then she peeled back the bedcovers and helped him crawl between them, lying on his side, and she knelt before him and dried his tears. After turning out the lights, she got into bed with him, and spooned herself against his back, her arms around him.

"Where have you been all my life?" Curt whispered.

"Looking for you," she whispered back.

353

CHAPTER FORTY-SIX

Bill

Two months later

Bill looked nervously around the crowd as the Niobe County Brass Band played "Stars and Stripes Forever" from the bandstand for the annual Niobe High School alumni band concert. The city park's trees were dark green, swaying in the breeze, and even though the sun was hot, he could feel a whisper of cool in the air, signaling that fall was on the way.

He glanced at his watch. The concert should be wrapping up any minute, and then it would be time for the ten-year reunion over at the high school. Bill still wasn't sure whether he would go. It all depended.

Something suddenly banged into the back of his knees and he nearly fell forward, but he caught himself before whirling around to see Curt standing behind him. He'd used his own knees to knock Bill off balance.

"Hey, man," Curt said, shaking his hand. "When'd you get here?"

"A little bit ago," Bill said absently.

"Have you seen him yet?"

Bill shook his head.

"He'll be here."

"Where's Rita?" Bill said.

"She decided not to come," Curt said. He elbowed Bill and raised his eyebrows up and down. "But she promised to come to our twentieth."

Bill had to smile at this. "That sounds propitious."

"What the hell does that mean?" When Bill just grinned, Curt said, "Guess we can't sneak behind the bandstand and smoke a doob like we did in the old days. Too bad."

"Is it?"

Curt shrugged and turned around, and then Bill got an elbow in the ribs again.

"Will you cut that out?" he said, and then turned in the direction Curt was pointing.

George approached, holding up a hand in greeting.

Bill gulped.

"See?" Curt said.

George walked up to them, and he and Bill stood blinking at each other, George's face completely impassive. He tilted his head and the corners of his mouth twitched. "So. We even?"

"We'll never be even," Bill said. "You could never even begin to approach my level of assholery."

"Well," George said, sticking a cigarette in his teeth and lighting it. "I can keep trying."

"Are you even how?" Curt said.

"George called me every few days all summer long," Bill said. "I only returned one of the messages."

"Harsh!" Curt said, but he smiled.

What Curt didn't know, and what Bill would never tell him, was that in every one of George's messages on Bill's answering machine, twenty-some of them, George had apologized for nearly getting them all killed. When Bill finally did answer the phone, he and George talked for two and a half hours, and George spoke to Bill about suicide and how it had felt to experience his mom's attempts. Bill explained what being on the other end was like. It was the best conversation they'd ever had, and Bill always answered the phone after that.

Curt didn't need to know about their conversation. That was between him and George.

"It's good to see you, man," Bill said.

"It's especially good to see you since you brought back all my cassettes," George said. "You brought them, right?"

"In the Mustang. You'll get them. But here's what you need right now." Bill pulled the Niobe High School Select Artists 1976 mix tape from his pocket and handed it over.

"Yup," George said. "This hits the spot." He slid it into his shirt pocket with his cigarette pack.

The audience applauded as the song ended. Sheriff Junior Zoellner tapped the microphone, setting off a screech of feedback.

"Hello? Is this thing on?"

Applause, cheers, and whistling answered him. Curt hollered out, "Free Bird!"

Laughter rolled through the assemblage nearby.

"Where's Travis Mussberger?" Junior tented his hand over his eyes. "Ah, there he is. Would you come on up here? And bring Toni up with you, will you?"

George, Curt, and Bill traded grins.

Bill watched as Travis and his fiancée emerged from the throng and mounted the steps. Travis used a cane and limped a little, but the doctor had assured everyone it wouldn't be permanent. The doctor also said he'd never seen anyone work that hard at rehab and physical therapy before.

Enthusiastic applause and cheers erupted all around them.

"And the crowd goes wild," Curt said.

Once Toni and Travis joined Junior in the center of the stage, Junior said, "For those of you who might not know, Travis and Toni will be getting married at the Lutheran Church tomorrow evening—"

Travis leaned toward the microphone and said, "And you're all invited!" as he waved a hand over the masses like a rock star.

More cheers, and Curt stuck his fingers in his mouth and let out a shrill whistle.

When everyone quieted, Junior continued. "You all know that we very nearly lost Travis, who's one of our leading citizens, in early June. So before the band's last couple songs, we'd like to take this opportunity to honor him."

A deputy crossed the stage and handed a palm-sized case to Junior. "In recognition of meritorious and courageous public service in the saving of three lives, we hereby award you this medal of valor from the Niobe City Council and the Niobe County Sheriff's Department."

Travis's neck, ears, and scalp glowed hot pink, and his face was split into a wide grin.

Junior opened the case, and the medal fell to the ground.

"Oh, shit," George said into his hand, and stifled a laugh.

Junior glared at the deputy, who threw his hands up in a not-my-fault gesture. Junior picked up the medal, which was attached to a red, white, and blue ribbon. He dusted it off and put it around Travis's neck then shook his hand. Toni snapped their picture, and the herd clapped and cheered again.

"And now," Junior said, "the Niobe County Brass Band has worked up a tribute song for Travis."

The band swung into "Semper Fidelis."

Bill locked eyes with Curt then looked up to the sky, willing the tears to stay put where they belonged, but it was pointless. Over the course of the last ten weeks, he'd turned into a crier.

Six weeks ago, Bill had received a cashier's check in the mail, no return address, for $65,000. Although Curt wouldn't own up to it, Bill knew that's where it had come from, and he paid off his creditors. He, like Curt and George, had been granted immunity from prosecution in exchange for testimony against Richie and had gained a measure of notoriety, complete with media interviews and TV appearances. Pete said he could use all this attention to speak about how he hit bottom and sought addiction treatment, but Bill knew he needed a lot more than just two months' worth of sobriety before he started acting like some authority on the subject.

The Marine Corps March came to an end, and Sousa's "The Kansas Wildcats March" took its place.

"No," George protested, and began counter-singing the KU alma mater, "The Crimson and the Blue."

"Will you pipe down?" Curt said. "Show some respect."

"For K-State?" George said. "Never."

They watched as Travis and Toni came down off the stage and were surrounded by friends and admirers.

"Hey," George said. "Let's take a quick stroll down memory lane before we head to the reunion."

"Sure," Bill said.

"Lead the way," Curt said to George.

They walked away from the bandstand and into the park through the deep green grass and clover. Beyond the swings and teeter-totters, they were surrounded by the long shadows of the oaks, elms, and silver maples that had stood sentry here since long before any of them were born.

"So George," Bill said. "What did you decide? Did you tell your folks about the twins?"

George shook his head. "I couldn't do it. They've been through enough. Let them believe what they want to believe." George took a puff of his cigarette. "But I'm glad that I know. Does that sound crazy?"

"No question," Bill said.

"Crazier than hell," Curt said. "And what's the story with your snot-nosed cousin?"

"He's back in Topeka at Washburn," George said. "I'm going to try to spend more time with him."

Bill knocked himself in the head with the heel of his hand. "I'm sorry. I thought you said you were going to—"

"I know, I know," George said. "But I didn't realize how messed up he is. Boy's got some serious issues. He needs… maybe I can, I don't know, be his friend or whatever."

Bill caught Curt's eye and they smiled at each other.

"Not that I've forgiven the little shit, or anything…"

Bill wanted to tell George he needed to put it behind him, because holding on to grudges and slights and resentments could make you sick. He'd learned this in treatment and twice-weekly therapy. And once Liz saw that Bill was serious, she joined him for marriage counseling.

He had taken to carrying around the lost bullet from the attempted suicide in his pocket as a reminder. He'd come to understand in therapy that he'd been saved from death in more ways than one, and his friends, old and new, were a huge part of that. He also came to understand the depth of his own need for forgiveness working his twelve Narcotics Anonymous steps, so he'd never threaten to withhold forgiveness from anyone ever again, no matter what they did or didn't do. Because they were all just bozos on this bus.

Whenever Bill started to feel superior, he'd reach into his

pocket and squeeze that bullet.

And remember.

CHAPTER FORTY-SEVEN

George

"So I was thinking." George glanced back at the bandstand.

"That's always dangerous," Bill said.

"That TV station wants to do interviews with the four of us at the reunion, right?"

"KAKE-TV Wichita," Bill said in a deep announcer's voice.

"Yeah," Curt said. "I don't know about you guys, but I'm not exactly stoked to give another interview. If I have to tell that story one more time, I'm going to lose my shit."

"Any time we've done group interviews like that," George said, "Travis kind of gets lost in the crowd, you know? We all kind of talk over him. What if we give him this one, all to himself? Let's let him be the damned *hero*. Let's wait until after ten to go to the reunion."

Bill gave him a playful shove. "Aah, you just want to go so you can tell everybody you're going to law school."

"So?" Even as the word left George's mouth, he realized he

didn't care if his old classmates knew or not. Not much, anyway. It wasn't about that.

Cicadas droned in the trees. The three of them wandered to the far side of the park at the edge of the city pool parking lot in silence.

This was George's fourth road trip back to Niobe since the unholy events of late May, preferring to hang out with Curt and Travis to spending empty hours in Lawrence when he wasn't working. And now that he and Bill had reconnected, George planned to see him at least once a quarter, starting Labor Day weekend in Hays following his first week of classes at KU Law.

George had thought a lot over the summer about what Curt had said that horrible night in the trailer, which had become a beacon in George's mind, a combination of charm, mantra, and prayer. The events of the spring had released him from stasis in ways he never could have imagined. He had to laugh at the cliché: facing death had made him want to live.

As he gazed at the playground from across the grass, he recalled the moment he'd found out his brothers had died, on the last day of eighth grade. He, Curt, Bill, and Travis were hanging out here in the park, and "Me and My Arrow" by Nilsson was playing on Bill's transistor radio. Grandpop drove up, parked his old Pontiac Chieftain by the bandstand, and walked quickly across the grass.

And in that moment, George had somehow known his brothers were dead.

As his three friends gathered around him, Grandpop

explained the details and that George would spend the night at his grandparents' house.

Stunned and in shock, George hadn't cried then. He told Grandpop he wanted to stay in the park, had had the feeling that if he didn't, something else central to his existence would be lost. Grandpop had tried to argue, but Curt said, "We'll take care of him, Mr. B."

George remembered now the quality of that feeling from fifteen years ago, the heaviness and dread that eventually solidified into the sense that disaster was a vigilant hawk on a light pole just waiting to strike. But Curt's words that night in the trailer had shooed that hawk away somehow.

The new life, the better life, begins today.

He now followed Bill and Curt to the other side of the pool and reached into his shirt pocket for a cigarette but pulled out the 1976 Select Artists cassette case instead. He studied the image of the four of them then held the case out.

Curt took it from him and examined the photo. He pivoted so he was facing away from the pool and held up the case.

"This is right where that picture was taken," Curt said. "This very spot. If G-Ho was here, we could re-create it." He handed the case back to George and they walked to the chain link fence surrounding the swimming pool.

George watched the water ripple in the dying light, reflecting the green and brown of the trees, the blue and white of the sky and clouds.

"Do we even want to go at all?" Curt said. "Maybe the best

thing to do is let G-Ho have the whole reunion to himself. He'll be the total star of the show."

There would be other reunions, but Travis might never have this kind of shining night again.

George hooked his fingers in the chain link. "You know what? It's G-Ho's night. Fuck the reunion."

A lone car George didn't recognize entered the parking lot and stopped twenty feet from them. The doors opened Travis and Toni hopped out.

"Where the hell did you all go?" Travis said, his scalp and ears an indignant pink. "I told Toni, I said, those jerks are gonna go do something without me."

Everybody started talking at once, explaining they were trying to do something nice for him for a change.

Toni stood grinning, a camera around her neck. Curt threw an arm around her shoulders, his face lighting up. "This is like a sign from God! We can do the picture now!"

"No, we can't," Bill said. "It's a long way from sunrise, and I got rid of the Pinto years ago."

Looking into the pool's deep end, George pictured the blissful expression on Travis's face the one time he jumped the fence with them, the night of graduation, ten long years ago. "Maybe we can't take that picture, but we can do the next best thing."

George planted his foot in the chain link and began the climb, then looked down over his shoulder at Travis. "Oh. You can't—and you probably don't even want—"

Travis tossed his cane away and leapt onto the fence. The other two followed, and suddenly they were eighteen-year-olds again, jostling each other, racing to beat the others over the top.

George hit the concrete surrounding the pool, then Travis, then Curt, and finally Bill, all panting and laughing. The sound of Toni's camera shutter clicking away echoed across the pool.

The four of them kicked their shoes off.

"This one's for you, G-Ho," George said.

And they jumped into the cool, cool water.

ALSO BY LS HAWKER

The Drowning Game
Body and Bone
End of the Road

ACKNOWLEDGEMENTS

As usual, so many people to thank.

Elizabeth Copps of MCA, who believed in this novel and came up with the perfect title.

The incomparable editor Chelsey Emmelhainz.

Tireless beta readers Amanda Deich, Maura Jortner, Andy Hawker, Chloe Hawker, Eugene Scott, and most especially, Claire L. Fishback, who cared for and fed *The Throwaways* as if it was her own beloved Lab-Pit mix Belle.

The Byerly family, Bob, Deirdre, Joel, Drew, and Tara, who have read so many versions of this novel they've begun to believe it's a personal memory.

Stacey Davis, who volunteered for the hazardous job of Character in an LS Hawker thriller.

The original Highlands Ranch Fiction Writers, who first encouraged me to turn a short story into this novel: Drue Deberry, Tom McGeary, Holly Lazzeri, Diane McCracken, Judy Gooden, Naomi Helterbran, and Terri Spesock.

The golden age of the Highlands Ranch Fiction Writers (Because Magic): Lynn Bisesi, Deirdre Byerly, Claire L. Fishback, Marc Graham, Nicole Greene, Mike Haspil, Laura Main, Vicki Pierce, and Chris Scena.

Sue Benbow, the Facebook fan who suggested "*Miracles*" by Jefferson Starship for the barn scene.

My family:
Chloe, who will make her own mark in the publishing world before long.
Layla, my pillar of fire.
My husband and muse, Andy, without whom my dream-come-true life would not be possible.

ABOUT THE AUTHOR

LS Hawker is the author of the thrillers *The Drowning Game*, *Body And Bone*, and *End Of The Road*, published by HarperCollins Witness Impulse. *The Drowning Game* is a USA Today bestseller and finalist in the ITW Thriller Awards Best First Novel category.

Hawker grew up in suburban Denver, indulging her worrisome obsession with true-crime books, and writing stories about anthropomorphic fruit and juvenile delinquents. She wrote her first novel at 14.

Armed with a B.S. in journalism from the University of Kansas, she had a radio show called "*People Are So Stupid*," edited a trade magazine, and produced fitness videos for moms to do with their babies and toddlers, but never lost her passion for fiction writing

Her extensive media background includes everything from public affairs director at a Denver radio station to grammar podcaster to website designer.

She's got a hilarious, supportive husband, two brilliant daughters, and a massive music collection. She lives in Colorado but considers Kansas her spiritual homeland.

Visit LSHawker.com to view her book trailers, listen to her podcast with daughter Chloe, *The Lively Grind Cafe*, and read about her adventures as a cocktail waitress, traveling Kmart portrait photographer, and witness to basement exorcisms.